The Kindness of Dr Avicenna

Moreton is the representative in Rome for a London insurance broker who deals at Lloyds of London. He is the narrator, aged fifty-two, married to a girl in her twenties.

Moreton's troubles begin with the appearance of Dr Avicenna. *Some instinct of self-preservation should have warned me against Dr Avicenna from the start ... how many times since have I cursed myself for getting so easily, so light-heartedly involved with him?*

Avicenna's proposal is for a gigantic insurance policy on a dissolute Italian prince, to include a clause insuring the prince against a kidnap ransom. Moreton can see at once that almost everything is wrong with this, but events in his private life, plus harassment from London, lead him to recommend the policy.

The subsequent events are marvellously exciting, intricate and funny. To add to the delights of this book the author offers a love/hate view of Italy and certain aspects of Italian life that is often illuminating and sometimes profound.

John Pearson is very well known as a contemporary biographer, *The Profession of Violence* won the Edgar Allan Poe Special Award, but this is his first crime novel since his first book, *Gone to Timbuctoo* was awarded the Author's Club prize for the year's most promising first novel in the early sixties. It is entrancing to read, and rare to meet such a rounded and splendid rogue as Dr Avicenna.

THE KINDNESS OF DOCTOR AVICENNA

JOHN PEARSON

Macmillan

ISBN 0 333 33118 4

First published 1981 by
MACMILLAN LONDON LIMITED
London and Basingstoke
Associated companies in Auckland, Dallas, Delhi,
Dublin, Hong Kong, Johannesburg, Lagos, Manzini,
Melbourne, Nairobi, New York, Singapore, Tokyo.
Nairobi, New York, Singapore, Tokyo,
Washington and Zaria

Typeset in Great Britain by
MB GRAPHIC SERVICES LIMITED
Bovingdon, Hertfordshire

Printed in Great Britain by
THE ANCHOR PRESS LIMITED
Tiptree, Essex

Bound in Great Britain by
WM. BRENDON AND SON LIMITED
Tiptree, Essex

For Mark and Rachel

PART ONE

1

Some instinct of self-preservation should have warned me against Dr Avicenna from the start; a feeble enough excuse I know, but he was hardly the sort of man I take on trust, and how many times since have I cursed myself for getting so easily, so light-heartedly involved with him?

He simply breezed into the office one wet April afternoon, shaking his big umbrella over everyone and looking every inch the bounder that he was in his grey-and-white-checked suit and snakeskin shoes.

'At last! We meet!' He laughed, though what there was to laugh at I had no idea. He was a big man with a pitted yellow face, protruberant brown eyes, a shaggy, walrus-style moustache heavily flecked with grey. With his mouthful of gold teeth and that compulsive laugh of his, he rather reminded me of a Mexican bandit in an old B movie – perhaps a bandit leader even, the one who wears the big sombrero and the bandolier and is still laughing at the gringos as they gun him down in the final reel.

He had no introduction, no appointment, and I had recently become extremely careful over whom I saw in person. I should have kicked him out at once, of course, and later I questioned the security people on how he had managed to get past the two guards in the outer office.

'He told them he was your brother, *Signor Direttore*.'

'Don't be ridiculous.'

'He knew all about the *Signor Direttore*, and produced a letter from the *Signora*, your wife, saying you had asked to see him.'

I asked to see the letter, but of course they hadn't kept it, and by then the damage had been done.

I make it all sound more dramatic than it was, for I am using hindsight: at the time I was, I must admit, somewhat tickled by this outrageous character.

'You will have heard of me, of course,' he said.

I shook my head.

'Avicenna. *Dottore* Avicenna. Commercial consultant. At your service, Sir.'

He offered me a big, hard, suntanned hand, garnished, so to speak, with an enormous gold and emerald ring on the middle finger. An impressive grip and more of that contagious laughter.

'I must be honest with you, *Signore*. Some of my colleagues did advise against seeing you. Is understandable. They think an American company would suit us better. Some people think that everything American is best. I have to tell them firmly that when it is a matter of insurance, England still rules the bloody waves. Who heard of an American insurance outfit one can rely on when the chips are down? You have a phrase, I think. A1 at Lloyds.'

I nodded, feeling slightly flattered, but without the faintest notion what he wanted. I tried to ask him, but he cut me short.

'That's what I tell them all. A1. Unbeatable. The very best like your Rolls Royce motor-car. And I convince them. In the end they all see the point. If I may say so, *Dottore* Avicenna did a top-hole selling job on your behalf.'

He settled himself in the easy chair opposite my desk and crossed his legs. He was wearing very elegant mauve silk socks.

'Extremely kind of you, *Dottore*, but —'

'Don't mention it. My pleasure to be doing business with a British gentleman from Lloyds of London. I am a great admirer of your Royal Family, so this is both an honour and a pleasure for me I admit.'

As if this settled everything, he paused and belched politely, then reached out for the silver cigarette box on my desk. I can

10

recall no other visitor ever doing this, but he calmly took a cigarette, and as he lit it – with what appeared to be a genuine solid-gold Dunhill lighter – spelled out the inscription on the lid. I was still somewhat sentimental over my cigarette box, having received it just before I came to Rome.

'Henry Moreton. Captain 1974–5–6. From his many friends at the Beckenham Golf Club.'

He read the words out slowly, so that they sounded strangely unfamiliar, and Beckenham was far away, the inscription serving as a brief obituary to some happier self buried in my past. The house and the little garden in Tregunter Avenue, long since sold, the 8.27 to the City every weekday morning, and those 'many friends' to drink with at the club at the weekend. Ah me!

'A most fortunate coincidence!' said Avicenna as he finished.

'Please?'

'That you are a golfer. So is my client. It will form a valuable point of contact between you both, which in turn could lead to other things. You will benefit, dear Signor Moreton. My friend is on the committee of the Borghese Club. Is most chic. You have played there?'

'No.'

'I will arrange it, personally. Later no difficulty arranging full membership for you. My client gets on well with English-men, and has many influential friends in the City of London. He is said to have English blood himself. And, between the two of us, he invariably acts on my advice where people are concerned.'

He started chuckling, and raised his hands.

'You see, Signor Moreton? Already there are things that we can do for one another. Good basis for a friendship. I knew from the moment that I see you that we get on well together.'

I found myself chuckling as well.

'But, Dr Avicenna, you really must explain this business

11

you are proposing. Why don't we start at the beginning?'

He shrugged his shoulders, and looked faintly bored.

'The beginning? But of course. What really matters is that you and I are in agreement. We understand each other, yes?'

'Apparently.'

'Good. My business here is very simple. My client – I say client, Signor Moreton, but you understand is actually a friend – he is a most important man in Italy. He is extremely, but extremely rich, with properties and companies in many places.'

A sudden note of reverence was softening his voice.

'For several years I have been honoured with his trust and friendship, but only recently I discover he is uninsured. With friends it is difficult to say such things, but if anything should happen it would be disaster. Finally I tell him this and he agrees.'

'Quite right. Extremely wise of you. And what sort of sum had you in mind to insure him for?'

'A minimum of ten million US dollars.'

'A lot of money.'

'Too much for you? The Americans will take it on without the batting of an eyelid. That's for sure.'

'No, it's not necessarily too much. It would all depend on various important factors. Your client's health —'

'Is excellent.'

'The nature and extent of his resources.'

'Are immense.'

'And if I knew his name I could of course be more precise.'

'That will come later, now that I know that *in principio* we are agreed. There is one further matter, Signor Moreton, which I will ask of you. If you insure my client for this sort of sum through Lloyds of London, I gather it is also possible to have a clause to cover him against a *rapimento*.'

'*Rapimento?*'

'Kidnap, Signor Moreton. A kidnap clause, I think you call

it in your country. As you know, Italian insurance companies are not permitted to provide this, but I am told that in certain circumstances Lloyds include a clause which will guarantee the money for a ransom up to an agreed sum in the unlikely event of a kidnapping.'

'Your friend is worried on that score?'

'Goodness gracious, no! He is a rock. Nothing worries him. And he is sensible, you understand. He takes precautions now as all rich people do. I feel pity for anyone who tries to kidnap him. But while we insure him against personal accident, it seems prudent to insure for this as well. Is possible?'

'Quite possible, but again we would need to know the circumstances of your friend – his way of life, the nature of his personal security, his routine in Italy and abroad.'

'Of course, of course. No problem. You will know everything about him. As I say, no one will kidnap *him*, but you understand that I am a perfectionist. When I take on a subject I tie up all loose ends. I think you are the same.'

He rose, laughed, took another cigarette, and held out his hand.

'So, Signor Moreton, we are in accord. I will convey your informations to my client, and you will soon be hearing from us both again.'

2

As Dr Avicenna had discovered, I represented a firm of Lloyds insurance brokers, and since I had been in Italy had actually arranged several life-insurance policies which included a discreet kidnap clause of the sort he evidently had in mind. Such clauses were an attraction to rich Italians sufficiently important or neurotic to imagine themselves potential kidnap victims, and their numbers had been growing.

The actuarial risk on such clauses were fairly minimal. I had worked them out some months before and found that an Italian in the very highest income bracket was seven times more likely to find himself involved in a car crash than a kidnap. But actuarial risks aren't everything, and kidnap is the sort of situation every rich man dreads – for himself and his dependants, and particularly in sunny Italy. As a crime it remains a national speciality, perfected by the Mafia, but also practised by Sardinians, the Red Brigades, and any enterprising criminal who thinks he can get away with it. The publicity is usually considerable, the victim's plight unenviable, and the dislocation in the family immense

For these reasons there has always been a strong potential market here for the insurance companies, but as the good doctor evidently knew, the Italians were forbidden to exploit it on the grounds that such insurance, once it spread, would make things much too easy for the kidnappers. And probably quite right. The whole point of a kidnap clause is to guarantee that ransom money is available on demand, and one can see how quickly this could be abused.

But as always, the very rich suit themselves and although kidnap clauses are illegal with Italian companies, there is nothing to prevent Italians with sufficient wealth seeking cover of this sort abroad. It is an expensive privilege – but extremely profitable to the insurers – and a few London underwriters had been growing very fat by specialising in this sort of business on big insurance policies for their top Italian clients. This was what Avicenna evidently had in mind for the mysterious figure he had mentioned and we would simply have to see if it was possible.

I rather doubted that it would be: not unnaturally the London underwriters are extremely choosy over all such business, and although they usually accepted my advice, I needed to be careful over anyone I recommended. Something told me it was most unlikely any friend of Dr Avicenna would be the sort of person who would qualify.

Not that I spent much time debating this, for we were busy and there were more important claims on my attention. In the insurance business, and particularly in Italy, April really is the cruellest month; people are careless and elated with the end of winter and catastrophes invariably ensue. At the beginning of the month a Lear jet with some appalling female movie star aboard had crashed while coming into land at Fiumicino – no survivors; a few days later a spaghetti factory outside Brescia had gone up in smoke – damages of several million dollars being claimed; and this was followed by an awe-inspiring pile-up on the *autostrada* near Cassino – final death-toll still not certain, but half a dozen harmless Italians had been *Carbonizzati*, as the Italian press had tenderly described their fate, and the claims had already started rolling in.

Given my current attitude to Italy, I was inclined to feel that the victims had probably got what was coming to them anyway but, feelings apart, I was professionally involved in each of these costly tragedies, since my company had originally placed the business on the aircraft, the spaghetti works, and one of the burned out motor-cars.

Some coincidence, one says! In reply I answer that one soon

16

becomes accustomed to coincidences in my business. They form part of its essential fascination and in a sense one lives off them as well. For what else does anyone insure against? What is death but a coincidence? For that matter, think of the odds that one would offer against ever being born, let alone reaching one's maturity unscathed. We are coincidences, all of us, but I digress.

The actual risks on the policies involved in all this recent trouble had been passed on to the London reinsurance market, so that the losses would be spread across a range of underwriters, who would pay up as they always did. But in the office we had been having all the donkey-work of sorting out preliminary settlement of claims, attempting to assess liability, and making some sense of the inflated estimates of sorrowing dependents.

I found this slightly worrying work. Normally I deal impersonally with such transactions, but lately I had been all too well aware of certain losses Lloyds had been incurring on its Italian business. The work was also time-consuming. Since the air-crash I had been spending too much time on the wrong end of telephones and hadn't been getting home much before nine at night. My wife had been more than understanding – as she always was – but I had had enough.

The weather hadn't helped much either. Spring it may have been, in theory, but since February it had been raining every day. Rome enjoys – if that's the word for it – an annual rainfall slightly heavier than Manchester: this is a fact that's never mentioned in those glossy books on the Eternal City, but water had become a part of our Italian life, streaming and dripping down from roofs and overburdened gutters, swirling along the Tiber in a murky torrent, and turning *Bella Roma* into a place of soggy gloom and irritable despair.

Just to complete the happy picture, my teeth had been troubling me as well – or to be strictly accurate, my gums. One of old nature's nasty little tricks for the unwary as the years

17

advance. I had been quietly investing in my teeth for years by going to a most expensive London dentist and had smugly counted on reaching old age still chewing happily with a mouthful of my own white teeth. Now, aged fifty-two, I had to face the fact that this would not be so: a sad admission of decrepitude for any man to have to face, and for me with a young and very pretty wife it was doubly degrading. Her teeth were perfect, mine were coming loose as my gums receded, and my dentist was explaining there was little he could do. Sooner or later they would have to go, but I was putting off the dreaded day when the glass of Steradent appeared beside my bed.

All that gold apart, Dr Avicenna's teeth, I noticed, had seemed very good. So had his gums, as far as I could see. Damn and blast the man with all that bogus nonsense, wasting my valuable time! Ten million dollars and a kidnap clause! But just to be on the safe side – and with so much money being mentioned – I knew I had to check him out, and rang the buzzer on my desk to summon my private and intolerable secretary, Signorina Getatelli.

She was overworked, like all of us, a statuesque young woman with the bosom, temperament and presence of a romantic operatic *prima donna*. She had fine eyes and a pronounced moustache. Like everybody in the office, except Cirri, my good-looking office manager, I was rather frightened of her.

'Eh?' she exclaimed as she whirled in through the door. (There is no true equivalent in English for the Roman 'eh?'. As used by the Signorina Getatelli, it implied fury and contempt and how could I have the male effrontery to bother her at such a time?) I handed her a memorandum upon which I had scribbled Avicenna's name.

'Please find out for me everything you can about this gentleman – address, dependents and the company he works for. Some sort of commercial consultancy, I think. It'll be in the book. And ask Colombo what he knows about him.'

Colombo was the inquiry agent we always used, and I knew the Signorina hated him.

'It will have to wait until tomorrow. And anyhow Colombo won't be in his office now. He never is these days.'

'Just do your best. It's somewhat urgent.'

'Boh!' she replied – another of her untranslatable expletions – and flounced away.

Personal relationships have never been my forte, but as with my teeth, I hate to be reminded of the fact: and as usual I found refuge in my work. At least, I attempted to, but for some reason this proved difficult today. Avicenna had disrupted my routine.

I attempted telephoning London, but the lines were permanently engaged, so I turned to the preliminary report on the Fiumicino crash. One of my rear left molars had begun to ache, and the gum seemed swollen and inflamed – the beginning of what my dear old London dentist termed a 'flare-up of infection'. I was using the patent mouthwash he had recommended when the Signorina made another of her operatic entrances.

'He does not exist, this friend of yours. There is no Avicenna in the Rome *Elenco Telefónico*, nor does his name appear in the Italian Directory of Directors. No one has heard of him.'

I swallowed the mouthwash.

'What did Colombo say about him?'

'As I said, he is not in his office. There is no one there. You should find another man for your inquiries.'

'That is for me to say, Signorina Getatelli. Signor Colombo is my friend, and a very good private detective. I will discuss this with him when I lunch with him tomorrow. Thank you for your trouble.'

That made her pause, but all she said was, 'Moh!', before exiting abruptly, leaving a waft of warm young woman in the room. My mind turned once again to Dr Avicenna.

19

There was something very odd about him but I couldn't say exactly what it was; certainly it was strange he wasn't in the telephone directory. Hadn't there been a famous Avicenna, a medieval surgeon and one of the founding fathers of modern medecine? Could it be this character's real name as well? Suddenly I had my doubts. The man was patently a fraud, although for the life of me I couldn't make out what that elaborate performance in my office had been in aid of. Why the mystery about his unnamed client, and why all that nonsense about joining the Borghese Club? He must have known quite well that we would consider his friend purely on his merits, and make elaborate inquiries before recommending anyone on a kidnap clause for the sort of money he had mentioned.

The Italian mind never ceases to surprise me, with its witless passion for devious arrangement. Someone once told me that Italians can be very like the Japanese – deals within complicated deals, a compulsion to place everyone in sight under obligation for a service rendered. Perhaps this was Avicenna's game, and he was hoping for a favour or a fee for all his trouble. Or perhaps he was just a little touched. Those eyes were very strange, and I had found his presence quite disturbing, now that I thought about it. If he had the nerve to contact me again, I would know what to do. I attempted to dismiss him from my mind, and turned to the accident report from Fiumicino.

Accident reports fascinate me – both privately and professionally – for time after time they demonstrate what I have come to call the Moreton Theory of Disaster. This has been a hobby-horse of mine for years.

One of the first things I discovered in the insurance business is the mysterious nature of a genuine disaster. I had to trace the causes of catastrophes – fires, deaths, industrial explosions – and the more I studied them, the more I found these causes so involved, so improbable and interlinked, that no mathematical theory of chance could possibly explain them. Coincidence was one thing – a series of coincidences another: and it was this uncanny stringing of coincidences together that intrigued me. This always seemed to happen when disaster struck. No ordinary logic could explain it and I began to see disaster as a sort of malady which strikes at a particular time for reasons of its own. There were times when people – and organisations and probably whole societies, who knows? – became prone to its infection.

Why? This intrigued me, and I began to think in terms of some sort of virus which began the malady, making it develop step by step, just like an ordinary illness which would reach its crisis of destruction, and then pass, leaving its ravages behind it. I am simplifying, but in its essence this is the Moreton Theory. What is difficult, of course, is to isolate the virus and explain the different forms that it can take, as well as the reasons why groups or individuals become vulnerable. This is the real problem, and as a rule one can only guess the answer.

The Fiumicino crash appeared a case in point, and I would have liked more time to apply the Moreton Theory to it properly. On the face of it it looked as if the unfortunate pilot had been suffering disaster sickness for quite some time on the morning of the accident. He was a solid, unemotional man with fifteen years' airline experience behind him, but there was evidence that he was suffering fatigue and some sort of mental stress which dulled his judgement; a small thing on its own with a pilot of his undoubted skill, but that morning there had been a muddle over ground control, and a threatened strike which caused chaos as the plane was coming in to land.

These two factors still would not have caused the crash – a pilot of his length of service had obviously coped with worse things in his time – but because of the strike threat, the flight path was changed an hour before and he was not informed. There was a service vehicle on the runway he was using.

By now the odds were mounting up although logically the

pilot should have seen the lorry and avoided it. But the disaster virus really was at work that day, for the author of the crash report – clearly a conscientious character – had discovered an undoubted fault in the aircraft's altimeter, making the plane come in to land some fifteen metres lower than it should have done. A small discrepancy, but now it was enough. The service vehicle was straight ahead. The pilot who, on form, might just have squeezed the aircraft past, failed to respond, and the chain was complete. Disaster was inevitable. The plane hit the three-ton truck, and the Moreton Theory of Disaster seemed to have proved itself again.

I took longer reading the report than I intended, and although I still had several hours' work to plough through, I suddenly couldn't face it. This was unlike me, since I am not a temperamental man and attribute much of my success to this.

I glanced at my watch. 6.30. The staff in the outer office would have left by now, the night security men would soon be taking over. I took our office security seriously, particularly in the last few months since various threats had come from ultra-left-wing groups against foreign companies in Rome. Nothing had happened – yet. But Colombo had warned me that we could be vulnerable, and I wasn't taking chances. Needless to say, I did not believe in them.

I must have sat for quite some time brooding on the crash and staring at the blank cement wall of the courtyard opposite my window. When we moved here I expressly chose an office without a view to distract me, but now I found myself regretting this. I would have liked the reassurance of the world outside. And then I realised that after a succession of grey, miserable evenings, rich evening sunlight was lighting up that unprepossessing wall. Above the roof there was actually a patch of blue as background for the television aerials. Spring had suddenly arrived, and there and then I made up my mind.

London could wait until tomorrow morning and I would give myself the simple treat of walking home across the city and taking my wife to a restaurant for dinner. After these last few boring weeks I felt that both of us deserved an evening out.

I acted quickly now before I had a chance to change my mind, put a call through to the garage, cancelling the car that normally took me home, double-locked my desk, switched my private telephone over to the answering service, and seconds later found myself in the street below, a touch surprised that truancy was quite that simple.

The ancient cobbles of the street had dried already: washed, revived and temperate, the evening city even smelled of spring, the Roman spring, quite different from the year's awakening in any other city in the world, a magical disturbing time of excesses and release when the ancient city buried underneath the asphalt shell of modern Rome seeps to the surface, so that I felt a sort of ghostly haunting as I continued down the lovely-sounding but unlovely street of the Four Fountains towards Trinita dei Monte, swinging my umbrella.

By the time I reached the hippy-strewn Spanish steps, the sun had gone, sunk into its accustomed slot behind St Peter's but the sky was clear, the stars emerging, and the city down below me seemed to quiver in a lilac-coloured jelly as the night came on. I started to descend the steps, picking my way judiciously between the recumbent young and the banked azaleas placed here, presumably with tourists in mind, by the Rome municipality, when someone called my name.

'Signor More-ton. We meet again. I told you that we would.' Laughter followed, echoing across the evening air, and it was this I recognised at once; otherwise I doubt I would have known the figure standing by the balustrade for Avicenna. The terrible checked suit had gone. As if to welcome in the change of weather he was now in a smart cream linen jacket, what looked like an Old Etonian tie, two-tone co-respondent shoes, and a wide-brimmed borsalino. He was leaning on a cane

23

and smoking a cigar.

'A wonderful coincidence!' he said. 'Here we stand talking about you and you appear like the jack in the bottle. May I present to you His Highness, the Prince of Santo Stefano?'

He gave a funny little bow, like a compere introducing some illustrious star on stage, and I found myself facing a tall, disconcertingly good-looking man in what was probably his early forties. I say 'probably' because he was one whose age was difficult to guess beneath the gloss of cosmopolitan good living which seemed to cover him from balding cranium to Guccied toe. He was suntanned and immensely charming, turning on a smile of instant welcome, offering a firm dry handshake, and honouring me with a faint inclining of his head. His smile persisted – like the smiles one sees on the faces of the beautiful and rich in the pages of the fashion magazines – but I noticed that the Prince's eyes were very dark and sharp, half hidden by the thickest pair of eyebrows I had ever seen.

He was immaculately, sleekly dressed, in a dark-blue light-weight suit with a faint metallic sheen. He smelled of some expensive male scent, and the heavy gold-chain bracelet he was wearing puzzled me. For dangling from it, like a charm, was a miniature gold spoon. (Later I was told that such spoons have their uses in the sniffing of cocaine.)

I was distrustful of him but he couldn't help responding to the charm. Avicenna was beside himself with reverence.

'Highness, this is Signor Moreton, the gentleman I mentioned. He is a friend of mine and has agreed to help insure you through Lloyds of London.'

3

I escaped as soon as possible from that strange couple – but not before the Prince had elaborately invited me to visit him during the next few days.

'I will arrange it, Signor Moreton,' Avicenna said, as if he arranged most things where his client was concerned. With this we had shaken hands once more, and the Prince had ambled off among the tourists, head bowed, hands clasped behind him like the Duke of Edinburgh, with Avicenna trailing in his wake like an anxious ADC.

Somehow this accidental meeting managed to upset my peace of mind. I dislike chance encounters in the street: random happenings of any kind disturb me, and I completed my walk home only to discover one more serious still. I had mislaid my latch-key – something I'd never done before – and suddenly found myself stuck in the deserted street, pressing the buzzer by my own firmly shut front door, and trying to get an answer from the electric 'Speakerphone' controlling it.

'Darling! Hullo, hullo there! I say, *darling*!'

There is something demeaning about trying to call one's wife over this sort of mini-microphone. Anger and panic seized me, and for a moment I thought I was locked out for good. The house was like a fortress, standing on its own in a street near the summit of the Janiculum hill – grim stone walls, iron grilles on all the lower windows, and with the latest kidnap scare, no one in any of the other apartments in the house would open up to me.

Where *was* my wife? What could have happened to her? I was home early, but she had always made so much of being in to greet me from the office: it was the high point of the day for both of us. Possibly the beastly 'Speakerphone' had broken.

Darkness was falling and although the rain had gone, it was chilly in the street. Could I have lost my key? I put my finger on the buzzer yet again and kept it there.

'Darling! Damn you, darling! For God's sake are you *there*?'

Still no answer, and I felt an uncharacteristic impulse to start kicking at the door – a pointless gesture as I knew quite well: it was enormous and extremely solid, constructed to repel assassins from the time of the renaissance, and would have bruised my foot – when the electric apparatus which controlled the lock buzzed back at me like an infuriated bee. I pushed. The solid door swung open. At the same time a voice came from the Speakerphone – not my wife's, but the bullfrog croak of Luisa, the hopefully-styled housekeeper cook who dominated our domestic life in Rome.

Luisa was a witch: of that there was not the faintest doubt. She looked like one and smelled like one. Boss-eyed, bewhiskered and malevolent, she haunted the apartment, and plagued us with her temper and complaints. But we could not get rid of her. Under the latest labour laws of the Italian state, we would have been required to pay a considerable fortune in dimissal pay had we sent her packing. Worse still, who knew what might have happened had we risked ejecting her? She had belonged to the apartment when we took it on, and potent Roman maledictions would undoubtedly have followed with God knew what results. It wasn't worth the risk.

'No,' her disembodied voice announced, the *Signora* had not returned, and she regretted that the lift was broken, *guasto*, jammed, *kaput*.

'So what am I supposed to do?'

There was a click and the 'Speakerphone' went dead. It was a silly question for I knew the answer – stairs – all ninety-four of them. I'd counted them each time the lift broke down, and knew them intimately. One night, I told myself, they'd finish me with one great massive heart attack as I went puffing up to the apartment on the inexorable sixth floor.

26

'So rare to find an apartment on the edge of historic Rome combining such advantages,' the hag of a house-agent (Roedean educated, long deserted by successful US author-husband, and currently making all ends meet in Roman real-estate) had assured us when she originally showed us round.

'Such as?' I inquired.

The hag had smiled collusively towards my wife.

'Such as the view from the Janiculum, the garden on the penthouse roof, the perfect taste with which the house has been restored – all this with gas-fired central-heating for the winter, *and* two bathrooms and a modern lift,' she answered.

Not for the first time as I stumbled up those unremitting stairs, I cursed her and her modern Roman lift. The stairs were old and worn and badly lit and smelled of damp and cold and cat – not just the occasional animal caught short, but genera-tion on far-off generation of rank old tomcats, who had been peeing here for centuries so that the very stone was impregna-ted with their presence like a great Stilton cheese with port.

On each of the six floors was a landing, each with a set of doors which opened onto our unknown neighbours' flats below us: distinctly grand doors on the first floor, but dimin-ishing in splendour as one climbed, so that ours was an undistinguished door, once used by housemaids, hangers-on, the lowest of the low, in the days before the house was made a condominium and the dread word 'penthouse' was invented. By the time I reached it, all concern about Avicenna and the Prince had quite evaporated. Winded and slightly dizzy now, all I could think of was a drink. That and the upsetting absence of my wife.

Luisa opened the door to me, and then went scuttling off towards the kitchen, croaking as she went.

'The *Signora*?' I shouted after her. 'Did she leave a message?'

For reply there came the angry rattling of saucepans. I repeated my question.

'No. No message.'

This was most unlike my wife and I felt suddenly uneasy, as one might about a child who had failed to return from school: the flat seemed empty, incomplete without her, and I consoled myself with gin and the evening papers.

The curtains in the sitting-room were still pulled back. Normally they were drawn by the time I returned, but now with the big picture-windows bare to the night, the room felt vulnerable, uncomfortable. Even so I left the curtains as they were. Drawing them was not my job, and I was not to be deprived of my little gesture when my wife arrived. Thoroughly aggrieved by now, I turned the lights down, and lowered myself, drink in hand, into my big armchair, from where I could glare across the valley of the Tiber.

As my eyes adjusted to the dark, the view came into focus – first the jewelled string of lights along the river, then the surrounding buildings with their ghostly towers, domes, indistinct façades partially lit up and jostling each other in the dusk. Closer, on the left, were the dark pines of the Janiculum, crowned with bronze Garibaldi on his horse, and the crazy lighthouse, gift of the Italian community in Argentina, flashing the Italian colours out across the city; far to the right the distant mountains and a gold moon rising. It was absurdly beautiful, of course, but unconsoling.

What was it someone wrote? 'In Italy the eye is feasted but the heart goes hungry.' Now, why should I remember that? Swearing to myself, I rose, turned up the lights, and pulled the wretched curtains after all. Then, with another solid drink, I settled to the evening papers.

This was more like it – the *real* Italy: the Rome Express derailed by terrorists outside Bologna – pictures of gutted carriages, seven killed; the son of a construction millionaire kidnapped in Rome a few streets away from us; fresh violence at the University. A smell of burning wafted through the room, but it was only our Luisa sacrificing supper to the erratic gods

28

f Roman cookery.

The sudden ringing of the telephone made me jump. It had o be my wife – or had something happened to her?

'Hullo!' I shouted. (I refuse to adopt the word Italians use vhen answering the telephone – '*pronto*!', 'ready,' which ounds as if one's just about to mount a horse.)

'Hullo, yes?'

No reply.

'Who is it? Moreton here.'

Still no reply. It was not my wife, nor, thank God, someone rom a hospital or the British Embassy as I had half expected. But there was someone on the line: I could hear breathing – nost unpleasant – and a background murmur like the sound of a distant party in full swing. There was a further pause, then a man's voice asked,

'Signora Moreton, please.'

'She is not available. Who wants her?'

'No matter. My apologies. I will contact her tomorrow.'

'Who's speaking?'

There was no reply and the telephone went dead.

Normally I would not have given such a call a second hought, but suddenly too much was happening which I failed o understand. Besides, I felt I half recognised the voice but could not place it.

'Is the *Signore* ready yet to eat?'

Luisa was standing in the doorway and must certainly have heard my conversation. Supper was waiting on the table in the dining room.

'Of course I'm not. I'll wait for the *Signora*,'

She gave no reaction but stood where she was, dumpy body in its old grey dress, and watching me with those small black-currant eyes of hers. I was certain she knew something and was quietly enjoying the whole situation.

'You've no idea where the *signora* is? She said nothing about where she might be going?'

29

Luisa shrugged then glanced at the table in the dining-room beyond. There was a faint smile on her skinny lips and following her glance I noticed an envelope beside my place. It was addressed to me – my christian name in my wife's neat writing. I need not have opened it: some instinct already told me what was in it. I could hear her voice in the words even as I read them.

Darling,

I'm so sorry to be doing this to you, but there is absolutely no alternative for me. I'm leaving you – for good. There is somebody I love, and I just *must* be with him. Don't try to contact me – my mind is quite made up. Elly darling, I'm so sorry – truly sorry – to be doing this to you, but you'll be better off without me. Take care of your dear old self, and know that in my way I'll always love you.

Diana

And that was all.

(I should explain that 'Elly' was the pet name she had always used for me. It was short for 'Elephant' I'm afraid. In the circumstances I wished she hadn't used it, but it was somehow typical of her.)

4

There are two great moments in a woman's life, some fat cynic once remarked: the first when she gets the man she loves, the second when she leaves him. For men it's different, and this was the second time I'd found myself the victim.

I felt no pain at first – nor, I gather, does an amputee – and I have noticed that when this sort of sad event occurs, men divide into two distinct groupings: some blame their wives and some themselves. The second forms the gloomier category, but I am afraid that it was mine.

'What have I done?' I asked myself.

I could think of no specific answer. I might have asked Luisa, but she had prudently disappeared.

Strangely I still felt hungry and might easily have started eating had it not seemed inappropriate to dine alone at such a solemn moment. (More to the point, perhaps, the food was cold by now and quite disgusting.) So I began to wander round the flat. As a second-time deserted husband, I should have known better, for it was when I saw her clothes still hanging in their cupboard, the Iris Murdoch novel she had been reading still lying open on the settee, her makeup bottles neatly lined up on her dressing-table, that I began to realise my loss and how much I depended on my wife.

Pain began slowly tingling through my senses, and suddenly I all but panicked, for without Diana the flat was uninhabitable, Rome a wilderness, my whole life at an end.

I tried to tell myself I was exaggerating and that with time and alcohol and random consolations I could adjust to her departure and begin my life anew, just as I did when Marion deserted me. But I was that much older now, and men grow soft with middle-age. Loneliness was suddenly a great grey

31

ocean all around me. I would inevitably drown in its depressing waters.

I briefly contemplated suicide which was consoling in its way – sleeping pills, a quick dive from the balcony, even a razor in the bath, the messier the better. Nonsense, I told myself – vulgar self-pity. You wouldn't have the nerve, and anyhow the only point of doing it would be to make her feel remorse, and that was patently ridiculous. It wouldn't work – and even if it did, even if my self-inflicted death reduced her to a state of sobbing guilt and misery I'd not be there to reap the benefit.

All that I wanted was to get her back, and I could think of nothing else.

Had this been London, I would have telephoned some wretched friend or other and inflicted myself on him till long past bedtime, telling him my woes, begging his advice, and feeling that much better for his drink and sympathy. But I was an exile. There was no one I could call, and the flat was hideously silent, save for the intermittent murmur of the nightime traffic and a door that kept on banging in a flat below me.

I drank a lot more gin and went on sitting, mesmerised by the glittering city in the valley, source of my troubles, guessing that my wife was in it somewhere with her unknown lover. The moon had turned to silver in a cloudless sky. Finally I fell asleep where I was sitting, and was awakened by the telephone. I must have turned the lights out without realising it, for the room was faintly lit by moonlight, and I suppose that I was fairly drunk as I went stumbling across the room to take the call, certain it must be my wife.

'Darling!' I mumbled.

Someone chuckled.

'Signor Moreton. There must be some mistake. Such tenderness!'

'Avicenna! What on earth do you want? I was asleep.'

'And expecting someone else to call. Really, Signor Moreton, really. A married man like you. My apologies for disappointing you. But I have good news and thought that you would like to hear it. Yes?'

'It's very late.'

'But not too late for what I have to tell you. Signor Moreton, you are a lucky man to meet the Prince this evening. I had not given you his name earlier because from the beginning one thing worries me. How do I introduce my good friend Signor Moreton to His Highness? Frankly he can be difficult with people. As an aristocrat it is in the blood. If he dislike a person that is that. Is over. Finished. Nothing more to say.'

'So?'

'Signor Moreton, the Prince loves you. Is remarkable. I have known nothing like it in the years that I have known him. What is it you British say? You are his perfect cup of tea. After we part this evening, he remark to me – "That Signor Moreton, now there is a man I trust. Go ahead with him. Settle matters. With such a man I rest content." Now how do you react to that, Signor Moreton?'

'Most gratified, I'm sure. But as I said this afternoon, one simply cannot rush insurance of this sort. There are various formalities and the decision always rests with London. Most kind of you to ring, Dr Avicenna. We can continue our discussions in the next few days. And now good night to you.'

'Ah, Signor Moreton, you are tired. I hear it in your voice, but there is just one further thing before I go. Here in Rome you are the boss, and your friends in London rely on your advice. You will strongly recommend the Prince to them as soon as possible. Is very urgent now for all of us.'

'Perhaps for you, Dr Avicenna, not for me.'

'For you too, Signor Moreton. Possibly more urgent than you realise. And now, good night. Sleep well. I trust you understand the reasons for my call.'

To tell the truth, I didn't, but I had more pressing things than Avicenna on my mind, and thought of them instead until I drifted off to sleep again.

Early next morning I awoke from a nightmare that my wife had left me – and when I found myself still fully dressed, with a bad hangover in the empty flat, I realised she had. There was no sign of Luisa, so I pulled myself together like a ship-wreck victim on a lonely shore, shaved, changed my shirt and underwear, and filled myself with strong black coffee.

It was a flawless April morning, with the wistaria along the balcony coming into bloom, and like the engine of a very battered motor-car, my brain and senses shuddered into life. Whom could I telephone about Diana? Her various friends? Careful, I told myself. Do nothing rash. No point in starting gossip yet until you know for certain that she is off for good. Left to her own devices she will probably return, so act as normally as possible and see what happens.

Sage advice. I did my best to follow it, rinsed out the coffee-pot, brushed my shoes, and when, at 8.30 sharp, my driver, Oliviero, called for me, I was quite grateful for the prospect of escaping to the office, knowing my wife could ring me there should she wish to get in touch.

My eyes were dazzled by the unaccustomed sunlight – the first that we had had for weeks – and as the big green Rover hummed through the morning traffic, I tried to force myself to concentrate on the world outside, a useful therapy I've always found in time of crisis. By the river, plane trees were breaking into leaf, and further on the Goldwyn-Mayer monument to Victor Emmanuel the First was gleaming like an iceberg in the early sun. Outside the Pantheon there were women selling flowers, and motor-coaches crammed with German tourists, ready and eager for the long day's slog around the ruins. I normally enjoy the sight of Germans suffering for culture, but this morning all I could think of was Diana.

I should have had the sense to know that something of this sort was bound to happen in the end. She was a romantic, age an insuperable betrayer. When we married I had been forty-eight, she just twenty-two, but she had looked considerably younger even then. I endured a lot of ribbing in the office on the subject at the time as was to be expected – jokes about the child-bride and whether she packed her gym-slip for the honeymoon. I took no notice. Envy, I told myself. We had been very much in love, and I thought I could afford to smile.

Besides, in so many other ways it had appeared a most suitable match. Her family were Lloyds people, and I had known her father several years before he died: old Arthur Goodwin, I can see him now – a cantankerous old snob, but very shrewd and one of the most successful brokers in the business. His son Hugo took the firm over at his death and hired me. It was through Hugo I had met Diana.

My previous marriage ended two years earlier when Marion, my first wife, suddenly departed with an Air Force officer. (This came as quite a shock. She is still with him, stuck in some RAF married quarter in the North of England, and bitterly regretting it from all I hear.)

That was when I sold the little house in Beckenham, resigned from the Golf Club, and for a few months joined the happy bachelors' circuit in the great metropolis: this could have gone on for years, for in a way it rather suited me. There seemed no shortage of unhappy women willing to donate their all for a decent dinner and a spot of sympathy, but unhappy women weren't what I wanted, not at all. I needed youth and happiness, and fell in love with Hugo Goodwin's sister from moment I clapped eyes on her. After we married and the chance of taking over the syndicate's Rome office suddenly came up, we took it in a flash.

Diana had holidayed in Italy the year before and loved it, and I knew Italy quite well myself, having served there in the

35

army soon after the war ended. Now, years later, I was returning with a young bride and the chance to build up our Italian business with a five per cent commission on the profits. Quite an opportunity. I thought myself a very lucky man.

And so in a way I was – although nothing had worked out quite as I expected. To my surprise I found that I was soon the one who was missing England: Italy had changed, and so had I. My wife, on the other hand, adored the city from the start, was thrilled with the apartment, and soon had a circle of devoted friends I barely knew. She also had a knack with languages, and within six months was chattering Italian with a fluency I envied.

Only one thing had really troubled us – our lack of children. Diana was particularly concerned; she had had a bad miscarriage just the year before, and I had done everything I could to cosset her and make her take things easy since.

So much for my efforts! What could have happened to us both? I suppose the twin mineshafts of our marriage had diverged – until I read her letter I had not realised how much – and now I had really no idea in which direction hers had tunnelled. Would I ever? I told myself I really didn't care as long as she returned to me.

We reached the office slightly ahead of time, quite a feat this in the Roman traffic, and I congratulated Oliviero on his driving. He was a most agreeable young man, and seemed genuinely delighted with my pointless compliment. He smiled, revealing perfect, milk-white teeth. He was tall, with a commanding Roman profile, powerful black hair, a resounding voice, and all he did in life was drive the office Rover. The thought struck me, could *he* be her lover? Unlikely – but she knew him, and he was an extremely beautiful young man. Rome was full of beautiful young men, one thing I disliked about the place to tell the truth.

Come, come! Enough of such ridiculous suspicions! Young Oliviero was my chauffeur, and my wife, like her old father, was something of a snob. I slapped him on his rocklike shoulder.

'Usual time tonight, unless I telephone to tell you otherwise.'

'Same time, *Signor*. You can count on me.'

I was sure I could. He was in love with our new Rover to the exclusion of all fleshly lusts: as the car purred away he was smiling as only a poor Italian boy can smile behind the wheel of an expensive motor-car, and I took the lift up to the floor we occupied. In the reception area one of the day security men had just taken over, a surly looking fellow in a stained grey uniform, a pistol dangling from his belt.

Suddenly I loved the office, and felt a sort of sanity returning to me there, for it embodied order, reason and efficiency, those precious northern virtues I immutably believed in. Those ranks of desks, those pale grey walls, the telephones, computers, duplicators, filing-cabinets, would not betray me. Even the smell of the confounded place – air-conditioning and body odour with an underlying hint of fitted carpet and erasing fluid – seemed welcoming and wonderfully familiar.

My first question to Signorina Getatelli was whether my wife had telephoned. She raised her eyebrows. But of course she hadn't. Then London was on the line.

'Mr Hugo for you, Mr Moreton,' carolled some bell-voiced, far-off secretary and I groaned. London was an hour behind us, and I knew from grim experience that my brother-in-law was never in his office at this time of morning unless something was savagely amiss.

'Hugo, my dear old chap! Whatever are you doing at this God-foresaken hour?'

'What d'you think? Sitting on my arse in this empty bloody office trying to save the sinking ship. The rats appear to have departed. Alright for you in sunny Italy, but it's been raining here for bloody days on end and everything is up the spout. Profits non-existent and claims through the flaming roof.

37

Particularly from your end of the business, Buster, if I may make so bold.'

'That's what insurance is all about, old boy. Win some, lose some.'

'Lose too bloody much as far as you're concerned old scout – and I'm not joking.'

'I never thought you were.'

'Now, now, my friend. Manners! And none of the old acid with me, *if* you please. It does not become you. All I'm doing is offering a spot of brotherly advice. I'm not breaking any confidences if I tell you that not all that many people hereabouts have all that much patience with Italian business any more. A burned out spaghetti factory and a cool two million claim forms! Can you blame them?'

'The reports sound pretty genuine.'

'Do they now? *Sound* genuine? Have you seen the place yourself?'

'Not yet.'

'Possibly you should. Should anything untoward transpire over this cheery little claim, the underwriters here will have your dear old guts for garters. Just warning you, old scout.'

Hearty laughter followed. (Hugo and Dr Avicenna would have got on well together.) And as I sat there, having to endure his so-called humour, I could picture Hugo all too clearly in the office in St Mary Axe – small pallid eyes, large, partly-smoked cigar, blancmange-like belly wobbling against the over-burdened buttons of his Harvie and Hudson shirt. He always laughed at other people's troubles and I dutifully laughed back.

'Well may you laugh, my friend, but our livelihood's at stake.'

Not strictly true, alas! Mine could be, Hugo's wasn't.

'There is a lot of promising high-yield business in the pipe-line,' I replied. Hugo's sort of clichés are contagious.

'Delighted to hear it. We can certainly do with it. Talking of which, my friend, I practically forgot. Hot tip, straight from the gee-gee's mouth. I was lunching yesterday with this character from the Stock Exchange. Something-or-other Witherspoon. Rich of course. Italian wife. Extremely big wheel. Know him?' 'Should I?'

'Probably. Tells me some very juicy business as of now is going for the asking with one of the biggest families in Italy. Immensely, but immensely rich. And reputable for once. Blue chip security, he says. Just the sort of business we need. What did he say the name was? Sure I made a note of it.'

'Well done, Hugo!'

'Here it is. The blighter's actually a Prince. I told you it was something big. Prince of Saint Steveno. Heard of him old boy?'

'Yes, Hugo. Yes I have.'

'So the ball's firmly in your court from now on, eh? Follow up fast. See what you can make of it, and let me know at once how you get on.'

'Most certainly I will.'

'And how's my lovely sister?'

'Blooming.'

'I'll just bet she is. You're a lucky man, you know, but make sure she behaves herself. And don't forget about that other business. Prince Steveno's the name. Bye old boy!'

'Bye Hugo. We'll be in touch.'

As always, Hugo had managed to upset me, but for once the irritant was welcome since it stopped me brooding on my wife. He was quite right about the state of business, which if anything was even worse than he suspected. We were losing money: something fairly drastic needed to be done or I would find myself without a job, for Hugo wasn't sentimental. What we required was an injection of reliable, highly profitable business – easy enough to say, but hard to find with Italy col-

39

lapsing in the world recession.

On the face of it a prestige policy like the Prince's could be useful. Provided the security was right, the risks were minimal and the premiums considerable. More important still was the advertisement value of this sort of business, for in Italy the very rich are something of a village where news and gossip travel swiftly. One influential client like the Prince could lead to others, each paying heavily for the protection we could offer them through Lloyds.

Normally I would have had no hesitation now in setting up the deal as soon as possible, with Hugo urging it from London. Only one thing made me hesitate. Avicenna. Why so eager yet so mysterious about it all? And why that thinly veiled threat the night before?

It was probably no more than Avicenna's character, but just to be on the safe side I told my secretary to try Colombo once again, asking him to do a rapid run-down on the Prince, so he would have something positive to tell me when we met for lunch.

I was kept busy for the remainder of the morning, and when I left the office there was still no news about my wife.

5

'Ah, Signor Conte, there you are! I was getting worried that perhaps you have been kidnapped!'

I was a mere ten minutes late and Colombo, punctual as ever, was sitting at his customary table near the door of his favourite restaurant in Trastevere. He spoke in the throaty whisper which he evidently thought his chosen role in life demanded, making us the instant object of attention of everybody in the place. My ennoblement, I should explain, is one of Colombo's more tiresome so-called jokes against the bourgeoisie – like his insistence that we always had to meet in this crammed, extortionately expensive Communist restaurant on the wrong side of the river.

'No such luck. I'd not be worth the ransom money. Who'd kidnap me?'

'No one in his senses from the way you're looking, Signor Conte. What's the matter? Work or women?'

'Both.'

'That's bad, the two of them together. Anything I can do?'

'I'm not sure.'

'Not sure?'

He gave a knowing smile, and placed his index finger in a gesture of peasant cunning by his nose. It was a very splendid nose, a Roman nose, only more so, supple, high-bridged, a nose of dignity and great intelligence.

'Why not tell me what is on your mind? You have known Colombo long enough to trust him, and he has some experience of women. Too much experience.'

He laughed and lit a yellow-papered cigarette.

'I don't think experience comes into it,' I said. 'The more experience I have the worse things seem to be.'

'That is often true. But you are English, I am an Italian. The English are a very silly race where women are concerned. They take them far too seriously I think.'

I wasn't arguing that one with Colombo, feeling as I did.

'Let's just stick to work – for the moment at any rate. You received my message about Santo Stefano?'

'Ah, His Highness! You prefer to talk about somebody like that rather than women. Signor Conte, I despair of you!'

He pulled a face that made him look like the late Vittorio de Sica in one of his more outrageous Neapolitan roles. He was shorter and fatter than De Sica, but had a perfect actor's face and he once boasted that he had been all set for a great career in films with Dino de Laurentiis, when he lost his left leg in the circus where he used to work. Since then he had pursued a multiple career – one-legged sword-swallower and escapologist, one-legged clown, even for a period one-legged stunt-man at *Cinecitta*, before settling to his rightful métier as a one-legged private-eye.

Strangely his lost leg proved no disadvantage here – rather the reverse. He was highly mobile and his one leg was something of a trade-mark with his clients. It was also said to make him irresistible to women of a certain type. With prosperity he had bought himself a silent, modern artificial leg, and I am certain that he always overdid the limp with me, if only to remind me of the battles he had waged against society.

Despite much opposition from people like my secretary who insisted I was courting trouble employing an avowed and blatant communist on company affairs, I had used his services a lot, and never been disappointed. He was expensive but reliable – one of the very few private eyes who were – and his background and beliefs gave him an unrivalled knowledge of the seamier side of Rome. Besides, I genuinely liked and trusted him, and he amused me. The fact that he also treated me as a fairly amiable old idiot was, I felt, neither here nor there.

42

As usual, we had trouble ordering, for the waiters were overworked and the restaurant crowded, though not, as one might have imagined from the decor, with Rome's horny-handed sons of toil. Beneath the big framed photographs of Lenin, Mao Tse Tung and Ho Chi Minh, sat prosperous accountants, well-fed lawyers, rising journalists. I suppose they were fashionably left-wing, but I'm also sure the nearest any of them came to the struggles of the proletariat was their battle with the menu, which conveyed a revolutionary ardour all its own. There was *Rigatoni Democratichi* (macaroni), *Zuppa Gramsci* (vegetable soup), *Vitello Karl Marx* (veal cooked with mushrooms), and the speciality of the day was *Pollo Berlinguer* (roast chicken). Names apart, the dishes tasted like the food in every other restaurant in the city, where the food is rapidly becoming the most boring in the world. I ordered Signor Gramsci's soup and Herr Karl Marx's veal. Colombo, brave man and stalwart Roman that he was, had the tripe *Rosa Luxembourg*.

'So what have you discovered?'

'About this *cretino* of a Prince? Your idiot of a secretary didn't seem to know what sort of information you required. How can you work with such a stupid bitch? She is your mistress?'

'You know quite well I haven't got a mistress.'

'Then why keep her? She has no manners and is very ugly. Possibly you are a masochist, Signor Conte.'

'Quite possibly, but it's Santo Stefano I want to know about.'

Colombo rolled his eyes and took another swig of the particularly filthy red wine the restaurant got away with.

'Why the interest? Business or social reasons?'

'Business, of course.'

'Thank God for that! I was getting worried that you and your wife were getting mixed up with our so-called aristocracy. I wouldn't recommend it. Not with this one anyhow.'

'Why? What's wrong with him?'

43

'You honestly don't know about him, Signor Conte? Don't you ever read, my friend? Until quite recently one couldn't open any of our grotesque scandal magazines without seeing some reference to the wretched man – usually disastrous. If he wasn't smashing up a Maserati he'd be brawling on some rich idiot's yacht. The man's a total mess. Most of the very rich in Italy are a mess these days, but he's worse than most.'

'You wouldn't be a little prejudiced?'

'Me, prejudiced? Now you insult me, Signor Conte! How can I be prejudiced when I am a rationalist and a Marxist? I have no prejudices. None. But it's a simple fact that men like the Prince are the scum of history, and the historic process will soon sweep them all away for good. He is quite unimportant.'

He wiped his empty plate and licked his lips.

'You should eat tripe, you know, Signor Conte. Good for the blood and for the virility. At your age you must have to think about such things. Perhaps it is the answer to your troubles.'

'Do you mind?'

'Just trying to be helpful. No, I would say that people like the Prince do have their uses – if only for the bad publicity they give our crooked social system. But recently the rich have been growing more discreet, and pulling up the drawbridge as the proletariat advance. Also I hear that Santo Stefano has only just come out of a rich man's sanatorium in Switzerland being cured of drugs and alcohol. That's probably why there's not been much about him in the press for several months, but he can't have changed. His sort don't.'

I remembered the tall man with the persistent smile I'd met with Avicenna.

'He didn't seem particularly depraved when I met him. I thought him rather charming.'

'People like him are always charming. They can afford it. Charm is the weapon of the rich, but it has no meaning – nor have they. No role in life, no function. Tell me now, what does a man like Santo Stefano really consist of? His title. An old one, I admit, but so what? He didn't earn the bloody thing and has done nothing to enhance it. Then there's his money and his property. He didn't earn them either and has done his best to squander them. What more do you need to know?'

'The usual things. To start with, how rich is he?'

'Enormously. At any rate in theory. With the very rich, as you should know, it's always hard to tell how much they can actually lay hands on at a given moment, but the Santo Stefanos are certainly among the biggest landowners in Italy. They have huge estates throughout the South, and the present Prince's father was a cunning bastard. Not like his son at all. Very smart with money. He diversified his holdings before the war, putting a lot of money into property in Rome and in the North when it was going cheap. Also into industry, like the patriotic fascist that he was – Fiat, Montedison, Ansaldo. I'll need a little time to find out the details, if you need them, particularly of what's gone abroad, but there's a family holding company of which your friend is one of the principal beneficiaries. The paid up capital must run into many billion lire, and I know that considerable sums are also invested with the banks in Rome and Sicily.'

'So, financially at least, a personal insurance of ten million dollars on the Prince's life would be quite realistic?'

'In what sense realistic?'

'In terms of his resources.'

'But of course. He must be worth much more than that. But why should he bother to insure himself for such a sum? His only sexual interests these days are in boys so there are no wives or children to consider. On his death the title and inheritance will pass to his cousin, Alessandro, the present Count Roccopaldi, and they've been at daggers drawn for years. So why the need to insure himself on such a scale? It doesn't make much sense.'

'I think you miss the point. It's not the life insurance aspect that concerns the Prince, but kidnap cover that he's really

45

after. He wants it included in the policy, and as you know it can be done but only for the very rich. Kidnap cover isn't cheap, and Lloyds are careful over anybody they accept. That's why I'm consulting you.'

Colombo lit another of his filthy cigarettes and frowned.

'Offhand I'd say avoid it, but of course I'll make inquiries. I ask myself why somebody like Santo Stefano should suddenly get the wind up over being kidnapped.'

'Isn't everybody worried about it now?'

'To a point. But I'd have thought he'd have already made his own arrangements. His sort generally do. He'd be very very careful where he goes and what he does these days and certainly have a private bodyguard. He probably pays protection money too.'

'Protection money? Who'd protect him?'

'Signor Conte, don't be naïve. In Italy, kidnapping is big business and it's highly organised. The cases that you read of in the papers are the mistakes – political extremists, as in the wretched Moro case, or criminal outsiders chancing their luck. The real money's made by the smart boys behind the scenes who guarantee immunity. It has been going on for years.'

'You mean the Mafia?'

'Who knows? In Italy there are many Mafias. It is a way of thinking and we all indulge in it. All I am saying is that this Prince of yours ought not to need to insure himself like this. He rouses my suspicions. Tell me, did he come to you himself?'

'No, his agent did. A man called Avicenna. Dr Avicenna. Ever heard of him?'

Colombo scratched his ear and frowned again.

'Avicenna. Avicenna. Strange name. Sicilian?'

'How would I know?'

'Don't like the sound of him. The Prince's agent, eh? Perhaps I'd better see what I can learn about him too, while I'm about it. And now, Signor Conte, we have talked enough about these unimportant people. Tell me about yourself and why you look so bloody miserable.'

6

By now I should have recognised the definite onset of the disaster syndrome, with all the symptoms of Moreton's Theory of Disaster, but curiously I didn't, probably because Colombo calmed me down by assuring me that he would find my wife for me and everything would be all right. Since this was what I wished to hear, I tended to believe it, and left the restaurant in far more optimistic mood than I had entered. Then the toothache really started.

It had been worrying me for several days, a nagging little pain that would not go away, but by the time I found myself a taxi it was as if my jaw were suddenly exploding. The journey to the office took a while and by then I was quite dizzy with the pain, the left side of my face swelling like a small balloon, and even my secretary seemed concerned.

'Perhaps you should see your dentist, *Signor Direttore*?'

'Please telephone at once for an appointment for me.'

'You are in great pain?'

I nodded.

'Men are not good at bearing pain. They are not like women.'

'Nonsense!' I shouted. 'Telephone at once!'

Minutes later I was in another taxi, groaning softly with each jolt as we crossed the city to the Via Stradivarius where Professore Cocchi, Dental Surgeon Emeritus of the Universities of Rome and Sydney, had his surgery. On such small objects as a rear left molar can life's calamities depend.

The professor was a dapper, homely little man with silvery hair, moustache and frames to his spectacles. He spoke English with an accent part Australian, part Italian, and his great claim to fame was that he had once extracted all the teeth from Pope

John XXIII – teeth being, apparently, one area where Papal Infallibility fails to apply – and fitting His Holiness with snappers. He was a gentle, sympathetic man, but once he had X-rayed my jaw he did not beat about the bush.

'Sport, and are you in trouble? See that dark area around the root?'

I glanced at the transparency of my jaw's tortured cavities, feeling distinctly sick.

'Abscess?' I ventured.

'And how! A beaut!'

'Can you save it?'

'A tooth like that? You must be joking. Only one thing for it.'

'Extraction?'

'Too right! Won't hurt. You're better off without it.'

I hate losing anything and the tooth had served me, man and boy, for close on forty years. I thought of the meals it had helped me to enjoy.

'Must I?'

The professor nodded.

He was deft and wonderfully discreet, like a conjuror careful to conceal the way he does his tricks. A painless jab of local anaesthetic, then a pause as it began to work.

'Open just a little wider. Lovely!'

There was a flash of dental pliers, followed by a wrench and something cracking in my jaw. And then I must have fainted.

When I came to, a telephone was ringing and from very far away I heard Professor Cocchi saying, 'One moment please. I'll see if he can speak with you.'

He rocked me gently by the shoulder.

'Moreton. Signor Moreton. That's the ticket. It's your wife. Something urgent. Can you take the call?'

I nodded dopily and groped for the receiver.

50

'Yes, yes? Who is it?' I was still baffled, even when I heard her voice. She sounded suitably concerned – and very anxious over something.

'It's me. Diana. Elly, darling! Are you all right. You sound most odd.'

'I'm at the dentist. Abscess on my tooth. I think I fainted.'

'Poor lamb! Now listen darling.'

Her voice had suddenly grown tense.

'I've got to see you. Right away. It's desperately important.'

'Where?'

'In your office, silly. I'm there now. How else d'you think I discovered where you were? Miss Getatelli's being absolutely marvellous. Darling, I have to talk to you at once.'

'Where?'

'Elly, pull yourself together. Here of course! I'll be waiting for you. Hurry!'

'Very well.'

'Darling, aren't you pleased to hear me?'

'Of course – but I'm still feeling rather odd. I'll get a taxi straight away.'

'Elly, do you love me?'

'I'll always love you.'

'Hurry, then!'

I did my best, but the Via Stradivarius is not the easiest place in Rome to find a taxi, and when at last I did, the rush hour had begun. My head had cleared and as we buffeted our way amid that sea of traffic, I kept asking what Diana wanted. Could she be ready to return already? It was what I longed for, but why had she turned up at the office, and why the urgency to see me? Why couldn't she have chosen any other moment?

It was the most laborious taxi-journey of my life – streets had erupted suddenly with road-works, traffic-lights were permanently against us and the taxi shuddered as if about to die at any

51

moment. The driver, a gross silent fellow, kept on farting, and the stink was overpowering, along with the fumes from all that constipated traffic. Constipation – the great curse of modern cities! Rome was seizing up, my jaw was aching, and by the time I reached the office, I was in that state of chronic panic Rome inflicts on those who fight against her.

'Well?' I shouted when I saw my secretary. 'Well, where is she?'

I must have made an interesting sight – grey-faced, hair disordered, blood (though I didn't realise this until much later) congealing on my chin and shirt.

'Who?' replied la Getatelli, eyeing me demurely.

'My wife, of course.'

I could smell her scent. (*Cabochard* by Gres. I always bought it for her.) But of herself there was no sign.

'Ah, I am afraid that the *Signora* could not wait. You took so long returning from the dentist, *Signor Direttore*. Your tooth – I trust it is no longer hurting?'

'When did she leave?'

'A quarter of an hour ago. She asked me to give you her apologies, and said she would telephone you later.'

'When?'

'She did not say. She seemed upset that you did not arrive.'

'Couldn't you have told her about the traffic?'

'I did my best, but a gentleman called for her, and he was most insistent that she had to leave.'

'A gentleman? What sort of bloody gentleman?'

My secretary gave a faint, a very faint, but quite unmistakable, tiny smile of triumph.

'A young gentleman.'

'Describe him to me.'

'How, *Signor Direttore*?'

'Was he tall or short? Well-dressed? Ugly or good-looking?'

My agony had started.

'Very good-looking, since you ask. Taller than you. Well-

52

dressed and very charming but extremely firm with her. He was in a hurry, otherwise I'm sure she would have waited.'

And so my jealousy began. Until then, with the memory of Marion behind me, I had had the sense to keep it carefully at bay by consciously refusing to consider the presence of my wife's lover. This had not been difficult, since I had had no evidence of who or what he was, and jealousy, for me at any rate, requires a solid base on which to fester. But now I had this, thanks to Signorina Getatelli, I was at its mercy.

Jealousy must surely be the worst of all emotions, for apart from the degradation it involves, it can make those afflicted by it quite unscrupulous, and change their personality. My wife's adultery with this good-looking stranger was suddenly the only thing that mattered in my life. I had to know about it – like some old voyeur observing the affair. I also had to get her back. There was no question about this now, no argument. I simply could not live without her.

Luckily, as always, there was work to do and it kept me occupied, dampening my feelings and I gradually calmed down. Come six o'clock and I was happy with the illusion of being in control again, and in a sense I was. My jaw no longer throbbed, my brain was functioning, and I was even looking forward to an evening drink and wondering quite sensibly with whom to share it.

But jealousy was quietly at work, making me ring Colombo first to ask if he had any news about her. He sounded pleased to hear me, and I was surprised to see my hand was shaking.

'Ah, Signor Conte. You have saved me a call. I have some news for you.'

In contrast with his conversation face to face, he bellowed down the telephone; my eardrum winced, my stomach lurched.

'Well done, Colombo! You've been quick. Where is she? Who's she with?'

'You wife? Easy on now, Signor Conte! I'm not clairvoyant and I can't work miracles. You must be just a little patient. But I have found out considerably more about the two gentlemen we discussed at lunch.'

Colombo was always wary of mentioning anyone by name over the telephone knowing, so he said, how easily and often it was tapped.

'Really?'

'You don't sound very interested. Perhaps you have already decided not to have anything to do with them. I think it would be extremly wise.'

'Why?'

'Because, in the first place, Signor Conte, the distinguished gentleman is by no means as flush for money as I thought originally. There have been major disagreements with his family and for a long time he has been gambling and losing heavily. In fact I learn that he is seriously in debt, and several major banks here and in America have turned him down for further loans.'

'You're sure of this?'

'Totally. My sources tell me that he has been getting desperate for money during the last few months and has even pledged his stake in the holding company I mentioned to the hilt. I have also been finding things out about that Sicilian friend of his. You are still there, Signor Conte?'

'Yes, Colombo. I'm still here. Go on.'

'You sound strange. Are you unwell?'

'I had to have a tooth out this afternoon after we parted, and my mouth's still tender.'

'How stupid of you, Signor Conte. You should have mentioned it at lunch, then I could have sent you to my dentist. He is a genius and would have saved the tooth. Still, what's done is done. I was telling you about this character who came to see you. I was right about him. He is Sicilian – not a person I would recommend at all. He is what I think you call a conman, although he has also been many things as well. He was once a pimp in Naples, then some sort of gangster in the United States, and I am told he has also done time for forgery in Canada. He returned to Italy eighteen months ago, and since then has become very much involved with the gentleman we mentioned, trying to raise large sums of money on the strength of his distinguished name, for what that's worth. He's also been attempting to insure his life for very hefty sums, and you're not the first he's approached about it. I know of two companies at least in Switzerland who've turned him down. Not a person to do business with, I think.'

'I'd not have thought so.'

'You don't sound particularly convinced, Signor Conte.'

'Oh, but I am. After what you told me during lunch, I'd more or less decided to steer clear. This settles it. I'm truly grateful. Oh, and Colombo.'

'Signor Conte?'

'You'll do your best about the other business, won't you? Spare no expense. It's desperately important to me now.'

'I have given you my word. I shall be handling it personally.'

7

But nothing happened. I spent that evening on my own in the apartment waiting for Colombo or my wife to ring, but the telephone stayed silent. I had such faith in Colombo, and Diana had sounded so relaxed and loving on the telephone that I managed to stay fairly calm. Clearly she wanted to return to me and would have done so had I only managed to get back in time to meet her. Her lover may have made her change her mind – for a while. But if she was having doubts about him after a mere night together, they were bound to grow, and she would soon be back. No one would stop my wife from doing what she wanted in the end.

But by next morning I was feeling more uneasy over what had happened to her and rang Colombo soon after entering the office. He sounded liverish and irritated by my concern.

'No news yet, I'm afraid. It's far too early.'

'But you promised to do everything you could to find her.'

'And I will. I've not been standing still.'

'But she can't have disappeared without a trace.'

'Why not? Rome's a big place. Women do it every day.'

'Italian women do, but my wife's foreign. She attracts attention. She has expensive tastes, a lot of friends, and we know she's not in hiding. Only yesterday she came to the office of her own free will to see me. Now she's gone again.'

I heard Colombo sigh. One man's agony, another man's boredom – especially at 9.30 in the morning.

'Signor Conte, you are old enough to know that women change their minds. It is what gives them interest value.'

'She could be in danger. She promised she would ring.'

'She is not in danger. She is in love. Be patient, and I promise I will let you know the instant I have any news of her.'

And that was that.

Five minutes later Avicenna rang. After what Colombo had discovered I would normally have contacted him at once, given him a straight refusal and have done with it. But with my other problems, I had forgotten all about him. At first I even failed to recognise his voice.

'Signor Moreton. Your old friend here. I am feeling very well and how are you?'

'Who's speaking?'

'I catch you by surprise. You are forgetting Dottore Avicenna, but he does not forget Signor Moreton. Nor does His Highness. It is at his suggestion that I telephone you now. His Highness is wondering when we can meet to finish our discussions and to sign the papers.'

'There's no question of signing anything, I'm afraid.'

'No question? Signor Moreton, I do not understand. It was agreed between us. We shook our hands. What is it they say? When an Englishman give his word it is his bond.'

'I didn't give my word. I warned you quite specifically that everything depended on the decision of the London underwriters, and that they have stringent rules about kidnap policies. Italian business isn't popular these days. I am afraid the answer's no.'

A pause. When Avicenna did reply his voice was lowered in tones of solemn shock.

'This is terrible, Signor Moreton. Quite terrible. It is an insult to His Highness. You have considered that?'

'No insult intended, Dr Avicenna, and I must emphasise that this is not my decision. It is a matter of business – nothing else. If there has been any misunderstanding, I am truly sorry and I would be grateful if you would tell the Prince as much.'

'I would like you to meet the Prince yourself to say all this in person. It would be polite, and there are certain things I know he would still wish to discuss with you.'

'I fear there is nothing further to discuss, Dr Avicenna. No disrespect intended to the Prince, but I fear a meeting now would be a waste of time – for him, and for all of us.'

This produced another pause, then Avicenna said,

'Signor Moreton, I am destroyed. I will convey all this to His Highness, and you will be hearing from me later.'

In fact it was Hugo I heard from, later that morning – a blustering and very irritated Hugo, petulant that I had let him down by not arranging matters with the Prince at once. Avicenna or the Prince himself had evidently been in touch with London.

'Witherspoon is particularly put out. You could have had the decency at least to tell me what was going on. He rang me half an hour ago. The Prince is a close friend of his wife's family – I told you she's Italian – and you know quite well that Witherspoon's a member of my club.'

I didn't, but it all made sense.

'Sorry, Hugo, but in Italy it takes a little longer to assess a case like this than in London, and one can't be too careful. From what you were saying of the current feeling in the London market over Italian business, I think it prudent to play safe on this one.'

'Play safe? Don't be ridiculous.'

'I have my reasons. They are quite compelling.'

'Reasons? What sort of reasons?'

'Rather a lot of shady business has been going on around the Prince. And I don't like what I've learned about his personal adviser – a man called Avicenna. He's a crook.'

'Old boy, are you all right? We're talking about one of the richest men in Italy, a Prince, and a close friend of Witherspoon's wife. The family have known him for years. Besides, what would I say to Witherspoon?'

I nearly told him – but restrained myself.

'Hugo, I'm just advising caution – and I don't need to tell you of all people how to make excuses in the cause of business.'

'And I shouldn't have to tell you how to do your job. This is an important client and there's a lot at stake – not just in Italy. I suggest you reassess the situation. Treat it as top priority, and if these so-called reasons still apply, I want them down in writing. Then at least, old boy, I'll know exactly where I stand.'

Hugo rang off. I should have been outraged, but honestly I didn't really care. Normally I would have argued back and finally convinced him that there could be no question of the policy – Witherspoon or no Witherspoon – but I had more important things to think about. To be fair to myself, I did begin a memorandum, setting out in detail all I had learned about the Prince and Avicenna, but it proved impossible to concentrate, and the whole affair seemed so unreal and totally far-fetched that I rapidly gave up, and telephoned Colombo for the second time that morning. And for the second time I got his answering machine. I had already left a highly coloured message, begging for news and saying what I thought of him, so there was nothing further I could do – except telephone the headquarters of the *Carabinieri* to report my wife missing. And just before lunchtime, this was what I did.

It was Signorina Getatelli who reminded me about my long-standing lunch-date – otherwise I'm sure that in the state I was in I would have totally forgotten. It was with the Anglo-Italian Business Circle, founded in the palmy far-off days of Italy's 'economic miracle', and now continuing, somewhat lamely, as an excuse for British businessmen in Rome to commiserate upon the fate of Europe and the Common Market with their

talian counterparts over an excessive luncheon in a large
hotel.

For some strange reason, this is the sort of thing that businessmen enjoy. Normally I did myself, and even in the state I
was in, I was quite grateful for a good excuse to leave the office,
meet some compatriots, and dwell on the plight of Italy rather
than my own. As they say, it 'took my mind off things', and we
were really quite a jolly bunch as we traded anecdotes of doom
over prawn cocktails in the *Excelsior Hotel.* I was sitting next
to Ripley, 'Bunjy' Ripley, an enthusiastic, know-all little man
– keen yachtsman, *paterfamilias,* and addictive giver of barbecue parties in the back garden of his house on the Via Salaria –
who was something important with British Petroleum in Italy,
and believed in 'oil' as other men believe in Christian Science.
He spent the whole of the prawn cocktail expounding the
hazards the oil crisis in the Middle East was posing to demo-
cracy in Italy.

'It's hanging by a thread. Their whole goddammed economy
is hanging by a thread.'

'Isn't it always? It doesn't seem to make much difference.'

'That's what they all say. But the thread's weaker now.
When it snaps – and take my word for it, it will – then things
will really start to hum. Modern Italy is built on oil, and when
the oil dries up and your Italian citizen can't take his Fiat on
the autostrada any more, look out for trouble.'

General conversation followed about right- or left- wing
power bids, the army stepping in, a total breakdown of society,
and Ripley made it clear to one and all that whatever
happened, he and his family had their plans worked out: emer-
gency supplies of petrol in the cellar to get them to the coast,
fuel and two weeks' stores aboard the yacht, 'and we'll be
sailing back to the old UK as the West collapses.'

He seemed to be relishing the prospect.

'But why should England fare any better than the rest of
Europe?' somebody inquired.

'Of course it will. Oil again, our North Sea oil. The good Lord's on our side. Here in Italy we're living on one bloody great volcano. When it goes up it's going to be each man for himself.'

I nodded. The idea had much to recommend it, and Ripley seemed pleased by my assent.

'Glad that you see it my way, Henry. Take my advice and make evacuation plans as well. Oh, and by the way, I'm sorry about the house.'

'Really? Which house?'

'Our place at Toriella. As Gladys told your wife, we've let it through to mid-July to these Americans. He's a professor from New Jersey. Had we only known you wanted it, of course we'd have let you have it. Much preferred to have had you two there than an American with a load of kids, but you know how dangerous it is to leave a house unoccupied these days. Bloody Communists be squatting in it before you can say knife, and then where are you? Might just as well say goodbye to it. I tell you, everything's collapsing – law, order, the old Italy we used to love, gone for good. If I had my way —'

'When did she ask?'

'Who?'

'My wife. When did she ask if she could have the house?'

'Last night, of course. Rang Gladys just before dinner. Said you suggested it to get away from Rome for a week or two. Can't say I blame you. As I say, if only we'd known earlier.'

Toriella was a pretty little seaside place an hour or so by road to the north of Rome: sand dunes, pine trees set along the shore, secluded bungalows for summer foreigners and well-to-do Italians, and not much else. My wife and I had spent a week or two there just the year before and thoroughly enjoyed ourselves. But that had been July, the beginning of the season. Now it would be more or less deserted – apart from the professor from New Jersey and his swarming children. Just the place to disappear to with a lover if you wanted to avoid your husband. And my wife had made her call *after* her attempt to contact me.

I found myself starting to shake, though whether from jealous rage or nerves or sheer frustration I have no idea.

'Feeling alright?' asked Ripley.

It was embarrassing. Nothing like this had ever happened to me before.

'Actually not. Think I'd better go.'

'Probably this gastric 'flu. Lot of it about. Gladys and the children had it. Not going to be sick, old boy?'

'I'll be all right.'

I staggered to my feet.

'Like me to come with you?'

'No, really. Need some air. Be fine. Thanks Bunjy.'

'Don't thank me. Better see your doctor. And once again, sorry about the house. You must come up and stay with us this summer.'

Once I was in the street, the shaking stopped, and I found myself a taxi. Had there been anyone at home except Luisa, I would have written off the day and probably retired to bed; but the flat was a place of desolation now without my wife. My only refuge was the office, and there might be news of some sort waiting for me there. One never knew.

In fact I had a visitor already, a short, trim, bearded figure in a pale khaki uniform, who rose at my appearance, jerked to attention, and offered a brisk military nod of greeting.

'Moreton? Colonello Rossi, Corps of the Carabinieri, at your service.'

We shook hands – also very briskly. He had a nut-brown face – what one could see of it above his all-consuming beard – and quick dark eyes like those of a small bird of prey. I asked him to sit down, and felt a little more secure myself with my desk between us. He had a high-pitched, strangely penetrating voice, which I found instantly disturbing.

'I hear you have a problem, Signor Moreton. This morning you telephone to my headquarters to report the disappearance of your wife.'

He made this sound a sort of accusation. As I nodded, I was already starting to regret my call.

'I never imagined you would be so quick, nor did I expect an officer of your distinguished rank, Colonello. I'm sure it's nothing serious. I was probably panicking unnecessarily, but you know how it is. One's wife . . .' I tried to laugh, but knew it sounded unconvincing.

'First things first, Colonello, may I offer you a drink? Whisky, a little cognac, some Martini?'

In my experience, Italian policemen never refuse the offer of a drink on duty, but the Colonello was the one exception.

'Thank you, no. According to your report, Signor, your wife left home the day before yesterday. Correct?'

Again I nodded.

'And you have no idea where she might have gone?'

'I'd not have rung you if I had.'

'Nor why she went?'

He was beginning to annoy me now. I shrugged my shoulders.

'I've really no idea.'

'No arguments? No hint beforehand of what was on her mind.'

I shook my head.

'Signor Moreton, that is very strange and most unusual. No woman leaves a comfortable home without a reason – unless she has been forced. There was no evidence of violence in your apartment after she went?'

'None.'

'Then she must have had a reason for leaving of her own

64

ccord. Signor Moreton, I must ask you this. Was yours a
appy marriage?'

'For me, extremely.'

'And for her?'

I realised that he was watching me intently now.

'I thought so. How can one be sure?'

'Signor Moreton, how old are you?'

I told him.

'And your wife?'

'Ah!' he replied, and paused to suck his teeth.

'Again, forgive me asking this, but did she have a lover?'

'Now, Colonello!'

'Did she? It is important that we have the truth.'

'Possibly. I don't know for sure.'

Another pause as he consulted his notebook. Then he produced a photograph, which he laid before me on the desk.

'Was this him?'

The photograph was what is termed, I think, a 'mug-shot', a
full-faced, flashlight picture taken of a prisoner by the police.
It showed a dark-eyed, dark-haired, thin-faced man of twenty-
five or so. Mug shots are never flattering, but the face was
extremely handsome, in an unpleasant sort of way.

'Colonello, I have never seen this man before. But then I've
not the least idea of the identity of her lover – if she has a lover,
which I'm not convinced she has. Why show me a picture of
this character? He seems to be a criminal.'

'A terrorist, Signor Moreton. He calls himself Aldo Petinacci. Ever heard the name?'

'Never. And what possible connection has he with my wife?'

'Aldo Petinacci was arrested last November after a raid on a
bank in Reggio Calabria in which a guard was killed. We think
he fired the shot.'

He paused and lit a Nazionali, inhaling deeply.

'During the interrogation several of his accomplices made
full confessions, admitting to membership of a group of terror-

ists who call themselves the MPM – the Movimento per Pac Mondiale. This was our first actual contact with the group although we had heard mention of them before. The confession named Petinacci as one of the leaders.'

'What did he say?'

'Absolutely nothing. Refused to speak. And before we could make him change his mind, he escaped. A bad mistake which shouldn't have happened, Signor Moreton. Since then he has moved to Rome and has led new members of his group in further raids. Extremely daring raids. Generally for money but also against NATO installations in our country. Signor Petinacci and his MPM have started causing us serious concern.'

'But Colonello, what has this to do with my wife, or me?'

'Simply this, Signor Moreton. Not long ago we discovered Petinacci's whereabouts in Rome. A tip-off about the apartment he is using, and we have been keeping the place under close surveillance. We did not arrest him straight away because you understand that in a case like this it is not the leader of a cell we want, but all its members too. Several times we have seen him with a woman. We believe she is your wife.'

'My wife? Believe to be? For God's sake, Colonello, was she or wasn't she?'

'Signor Moreton, I appreciate the pain this must be causing and I am trying to be as tactful as I can. Yes, it was your wife. We followed her on numerous occasions after she left this man and naturally we checked. There is no room for doubt. I'm sorry.'

'So why bother me with your questions if you know where she is?'

He sighed, and carefully stubbed out the cigarette.

'That is the problem, Signor Moreton. We no longer do. The day your wife went missing, Petinacci left the apartment and has not returned. Perhaps he had discovered we knew he was there. He is very sharp, you understand, very slippery. It would seem highly probable that he is with your wife.'

He stared at me in silence, and I knew what he was up to now, and why he had called on me so quickly. Who better to betray this Petinacci character than the jealous husband of his mistress? But even then I felt the need for caution. I wasn't doing anything until I knew exactly how involved my wife really was with him. I wanted her back – not caught up in a full-scale trial with a dangerous terrorist.

The colonel must have read my thoughts.

'Signor Moreton, why not trust me? I am a married man myself, and I have no quarrel with your wife. But believe me, she is in a situation of some danger with this man. He is violent. We know that he is armed and will stop at nothing to avoid arrest – nor will his followers. It would be tragic if she was hurt because of them, don't you agree, Signor Moreton?'

'But this is ridiculous, Colonello! Terrorists, my wife – I've never heard such nonsense in my life.'

The colonel shook his head and eyed me sadly.

'Not nonsense, Signor Moreton. I wish it was. And if you have any feeling for your wife it is your responsibility to help us find her now before anything serious occurs. Help us, and I guarantee to do my best to see that she is safe, and keep her out of any trial that follows.'

'But how can I help you?'

'Keep in touch with me.'

He produced a small card from his notecase.

'My home telephone number, and the number to the direct line to my office at headquarters, so you can reach me at any time of day or night. Should anything happen, or anything occur to you, ring me immediately. Please keep the photograph.'

He rose and clicked his heels. I had not realised quite how short he was.

'Above all, Signor Moreton, trust me. If you don't and anything should happen to your wife, you'd always have it on your conscience.'

needed time to think things over and collect my wits, for the idea of Diana, of all people, mixed up with a common terrorist – even a good-looking one like this Petinacci character – was difficult to take. She had no interest in politics as far as I knew, certainly not in violent ultra left-wing politics as practised by the MPM. The very thought was laughable. Still less could I see her pigging it with a gang of unwashed, half-baked student desperados, for she had always loved life's luxuries – jewellery, expensive cars, comfortable surroundings, and above all, clothes. (Her monthly dress-allowance was regularly over-spent).

Since I had learned about her lover, I had been picturing him as the man my secretary described after his visit to the office – stylish and smart and rich enough to offer her the sort of jet-setting social life I knew that she would like. I could not believe that I was wrong. The colonel was obviously making some ridiculous mistake and it was just as well that I had kept my head, and said nothing of the visit to my office or her call to Gladys Ripley. Think of the extra complications had I involved my wife in a man-hunt for a dangerous terrorist.

Just the same, I had to make sure that the colonel was talking through that smart peaked cap of his, so I summoned Signorina Getatelli. I knew she was obviously agog to learn why a high-ranking officer of the Carabinieri had been paying me a visit, but I did nothing to enlighten her at first. Instead I gave her half an hour's dictation – with all my troubles I had got seriously behind with routine correspondence – and it was not until we finished that I casually mentioned what was on my mind.

'Oh, Signorina, by the way. The gentleman who called here

for the Signor the other day. You saw him clearly?'

'Naturally. He was here several minutes, and he spoke to me.'

'He was well-dressed, you say? A well-to-do young man.'

'I have already told you so. A beautiful dark grey suit. Extremely tasteful and one could see at once it was expensive. Also the shirt and tie.'

'So this couldn't have been him?'

I handed her the photograph. She stared at it and frowned as if I was trying to involve her in some joke she didn't understand.

'Of course it is. But why is he dressed in such a manner? The picture doesn't flatter him at all. He was actually much better-looking.'

In my work, when faced with the dramas that afflicted others, I was always admirably decisive and clear-headed, but now that I had one of my own, all power of decision seemed to have deserted me. How could a wanted terrorist also be her wealthy lover? And if he really was, should I trust the colonel, tell him everything I knew, and count on his discretion when he found her? I hesitated. The Carabinieri had been getting very trigger-happy in their dealings lately with armed terrorists, and I had visions of a final shoot-out, and my wife wounded, even killed, because of something I had told the colonel. Even if he captured her unharmed, there was bound to be publicity which could be fatal to us both.

Somehow it must be possible to sort this ghastly muddle out, if only I could see her, find out what she really wanted, and talk a little sense to her. If only she would ring!

I tried Colombo yet again, but still he had nothing to report, and he was quite apologetic.

'I am sorry, Signor Conte. She has vanished. None of my usual contacts have reported any news of her, and there is little we can do but wait. I gather a gentleman in uniform has seen you in your office. He called on me as well. This is becoming a most serious affair, and we must all be very careful, you included, Signor Conte.'

'Thanks for the advice,' I shouted. 'Of course it's serious. That's what I've been saying all along, and you promised you would help.'

'I've done my best.'

'Thank you very much. It happens to be *my* wife – and *your* bloody country.'

'Signor Conte!'

'Don't Signor Conte me! I'm sick of it.'

I slammed down the receiver. All the worries and frustrations of the last few days were suddenly erupting now, as they sometimes do in Italy. I had seen it happen to Italians, wretches *in extremis* gripped with useless fury at the way this dreadful country treats them. Now it was afflicting me, and I was on the edge of losing all control and throwing things around the office, when the telephone began to ring. It had to be Diana.

It was a particularly bad line, and at first I could hear nothing but a high-pitched crackling. Then a woman's voice said,

'Signor Moreton? Just a moment. I have a call for you.'

I waited several minutes, then from what sounded very far away someone spoke. It was not my wife, but I recognised the voice at once. It was the man who telephoned the night she left.

'Moreton?'

'Yes? Who is it?'

'You have been very stupid, Mr Moreton. You have been talking to the Carabinieri. That is no way to make your wife return to you.'

'Where is she?'

'Safe and sound. Somewhere where your friend, Colonello

71

Rossi will never find her. She is very happy.'

'Listen, I must speak to her.'

'Why?'

'Because I love her. There are important things I have to say to her. I must know what is going on.'

'Then please be sensible, and not another word to the authorities. Someone will contact you. Do as he says, and everything will work out perfectly – for you and for your wife.'

'And if I don't?'

'If you don't, Mr Moreton, I would not care to be in your shoes, that's a fact.'

With that the conversation ended and I sat for several minutes feeling stunned and having not the least idea what on earth to do. I had always heard that a sense of impotence and isolation is the worst part of the ordeal that any kidnap victim's relative must face and I could understand it now. But was she kidnapped? She had left home of her own free will and if what Colonel Rossi said was true, she was in love with Petinacci. So why this threat about her safety and the clumsy offer to return her if I did as I was told? And who had made it? Was it Petinacci? It seemed unlikely. Far more probable was that it was some other member of the MPM who knew what was going on and was trying to exploit the situation. Hard to see how he thought that he could get away with it, but my wife clearly gave an impression of some affluence. So did I, and a demand for money would be certain to arrive.

At first this worried me of course, but the more I thought about it, the more it seemed to offer grounds for hope. I had no capital to speak of, but Hugo was extremely rich, and if it turned out that Diana was being held against her will, I could count on Lloyds' resources to back the settlement of the ransom. I would get practical support from London and if I

72

played things right, my wife would be grateful and happy to return to me. Everything depended now on who was behind the offer and how serious he was. I realised I had to be discreet, so when Colonel Rossi telephoned me later, asking if anything had happened, I told him nothing. He had no further news himself, but promised to inform me the moment that he had.

More than ever now, I was at the mercy of the beastly telephone, waiting for that unknown voice to call again but although I spent the whole evening in the flat the telephone stayed silent. Just before going off to bed the thought occurred to me that possibly he would use some other method to make contact. I had no notion of how these things were done, but had read of Italian terrorists leaving their messages in garbage cans. I checked – but the garbage can outside the front door of the flat was empty. Next morning it was empty still. No one had rung me in the night, and there was nothing for me in the morning mail. The caller was evidently in no hurry, and I began to get the feeling that he was playing games with me.

So what? There was nothing I could do, except cancel a luncheon date I had, ask Signorina Getatelli to fetch me coffee and a sandwich, and continue my weary vigil by the telephone.

I had just finished my unappetising little snack – sliced white and plastic ham: we are all Americans these days – when the Signorina buzzed me to announce a visitor. Dr Avicenna!

'Tell him I'm out,' I shouted.

But it made no difference. Already I could hear his deep infuriating laughter from the outer office, and a moment later he was in the doorway, waving my secretary away, raising his hands to greet me, and filling my office with the overpowering reek of after-shave.

'Ah, Signor Moreton. I promise to arrive and here I am. It is a great delight to see you and for a friend like you, nothing is too much trouble. I come to take you now to meet His Highness who is waiting to receive you. What do you say to that?'

Resplendent in dove-grey suit, pink foulard tie, and wearing those ghastly snakeskin shoes which I had seen before, he positively gleamed with goodwill and brilliantine.

'Dr Avicenna, you are extremely kind. So is His Highness. But I have told you we have nothing further to discuss.'

I might have made the joke of the year, for Avicenna had to hold his sides with laughter.

'Nothing to discuss? Signor Moreton, what a thing you say! We are involved together, you and I, and it is for your sake that I am here to see you now. I have heard something of your troubles. Why not trust me, eh? I think there is something I can do to help.'

'What troubles, Avicenna?'

He was suddenly no longer laughing.

'Signor Moreton, you have been suffering. I can see it in the face. You are worrying about your wife. I understand, indeed I understand, but —'

'What about my wife?'

'Dear Signor Moreton, all the troubles women cause us! Sometimes I think the good God had it in for us when he invented them. Surely he could have used his ingenuity to devise some other means of reproduction?'

'Avicenna. Stop this bloody nonsense. What do you know about my wife? Where is she?'

'Gently, Signor Moreton. Take it easy. As I tell you I am here to help you, and if you trust me, everything will work out perfectly. Just do as I suggest. Away from the office we can talk more freely, and you will enjoy seeing the Palazzo Santo Stefano. Come!'

He was smiling blandly and there seemed no further point in arguing. The voice on the telephone had promised that someone would contact me. Someone had.

9

As I left the office with Dr Avicenna I was very much aware of what Colombo had told me of his earlier career: behind the blustering façade there was patently a ruthless operator who would stick at nothing. Blackmailer, extortionist and pimp – it all made sense. I could understand him now. The underworld of Roman crime is a complicated jungle where crime and terrorism mingle. Someone like Avicenna would have contacts with the MPM and do their business for them – for a price. He might even mastermind their operations. Anything was possible. All I could do was play along with him, keep my wits about me, and rely on him to settle things as efficiently as possible.

As we left the building he took me by the arm.

'Signor Moreton, you are highly honoured. His Highness insists on sending his personal automobile to meet you. He does not do that for any ordinary Dick or Harry I assure you.'

He pointed past the line of tightly parked cars by the pavement. In the space normally reserved for the city buses stood an ancient black and gold lancia, more like a carriage than a motor-car, with a distinguished-looking white-haired chauffeur dressed in livery behind the wheel. Avicenna opened the door for me, and bowed me in.

The interior of the car reminded me of a box in some very old provincial opera house – upholstery in dark red plush, a whiff of mothballs, and a small silver vase, empty and in need of cleaning, fixed to the glass partition just behind the driver. Avicenna rapped against the glass and the stately vehicle started on its way.

I had never ridden in a car like this before, sitting so high and grandly over the ordinary traffic and peering through the big square windows which were set at such a height that human beings on the pavement scarcely intruded on the view, leaving one free to watch the sights of Rome that glided past in lonely splendour – the strange upper storeys of the Coliseum, the taller pillars of the Forum swathed in scaffolding, the angel of death, black wings outspread, above the Castel Sant' Angelo.

Avicenna was clearly in the best of spirits and slapped me on the knee.

'So, Signor Moreton, this has been a trying time for you, I understand, but all will now be sensibly arranged, and your troubles will be left behind you.'

'Where is she, Avicenna?'

He shrugged and scratched his ear, as if my question had embarrassed him.

'She is safe, Signor Moreton. I promise you that she is safe.'

'Listen, you bastard. How much are you demanding? Stop all this bloody nonsense and tell me what you want.'

He appeared genuinely shocked at this.

'Signor Moreton, you are not polite. I am not a bastard, I try to treat you like an English gentleman, and we will carry on our conversation only when you speak with proper digntiy.'

With this he snorted gently, wiped his forehead with a pink and white silk handkerchief, and stared out of the window for the remainder of the journey.

We had crossed the river now and were soon trundling through a warren of small streets, the old chauffeur needing all his skill to keep that unwieldy vehicle from grazing the protruding porticoes and walls of the houses we were passing. It was a sunless maze, a crumbling medieval slum, with the eaves of ancient tenements all but meeting high above us, and I had soon lost any sense of direction as we jolted on, the odour of antique sewers now competing with the mothballs and Dr Avicenna's brilliantine.

We halted in a small piazza I had never seen before: there

76

was a wine shop on the corner, a dead fountain, and a long high wall, plastered with old election posters. At the far end of the wall was an entrance flanked with two stone pillars surmounted by an illegible coat of arms. A pair of great double gates were firmly shut, but the chauffeur hooted twice and they swung open. Then with much grinding of protesting gears, the car climbed slowly up a long stone ramp that led to an inner courtyard. The gates were closed behind us, the car shook like a terrier as the engine shuddered to a halt, and with the chauffeur holding back the door, the two of us descended.

Avicenna had recovered his composure and was smiling rather proudly as he pointed to the high façade before us.

'The Palazzo Santo Stefano, Signor Moreton! One of the most ancient palaces in Rome, and few people know of its existence. None of the guide-books mention it, and the Prince does not encourage visitors.'

Water was splashing from a dolphin fountain, and lilac and wistaria were in bloom, scenting the air and making the place a secret garden in the centre of the city. The palace was impressive with its high carved pillars and its echoing arcades, but despite its grandeur it seemed a melancholy spot which had seen better days: the windows above were barred and shuttered and the air exuded sadness and neglect.

Suddenly the peace was shattered by frantic barking and an enormous dog came bounding out at us.

'Hitler! Good boy, Hitler! Heel!' shouted Avicenna.

The brute was the size of a Shetland pony with grey and black matted hair and wolflike fangs. I am not good with dogs. Indeed, unlike my wife, I loathe them, and they invariably reciprocate. Hitler did, and was at the point of leaping for my throat when Avicenna grabbed his metal studded collar.

'Easy, Hitler! Signor Moreton is a friend.'

Hitler growled with disappointment and subsided, waiting for a fresh excuse to make his presence felt. Avicenna patted his enormous head.

77

'A fine dog, don't you agree, Signor Moreton? A neapolitan wolf-hound, one of the oldest breeds we have. Nero trained them for the arena, and His Highness breeds them on his estates in Sicily. Hitler is his private guard-dog: he has had him from a puppy.'

'Why does he call him Hitler?'

'That is the Prince's little joke.'

Someone whistled and the brute was on his feet, trotting obediently towards a doorway at the far angle of the court, where a man in a dark blue suit was standing. He was very large, like Hitler, six foot three or four at least, with enormous shoulders and a close-cropped head. Avicenna waved at him and he nodded back but did not speak.

'That is Pulcione.'

Avicenna had dropped his voice.

'*Pulcione* is Italian for 'Big Flea' and that is the name he used as a professional all-in wrestler. He was very good, the champion of Italy for three years running, but he was obliged to retire when he unfortunately killed a man. In the ring, you understand. It created problems. Now he is the Prince's body-guard, and he goes everywhere with him. His real name is Zanobetti, but the Prince always refers to him as his big flea.'

'Another of the Prince's jokes?'

'Exactly, Signor Moreton. As I tell you, His Highness has a very English sense of humour. I am glad that you can now see for yourself how closely he is guarded. Come, His Highness waits for us. We must ascend to meet him.'

Squaring his shoulders, Avicenna marched past Pulcione, and led me through an elaborately carved doorway and into an enormous painted hall. It was in semi-darkness and smelled of age and damp. At the far end I could see a staircase wide enough to take a coach and four: it was set with ascending marble busts, but the stairs were uncarpeted, the chandelier above was in its dustbag, and the painted walls were peeling. At the top of the stairs the windows had been opened, and

78

Avicenna led me through double doors and into the room beyond.

This was another vast apartment, even bigger than the hall below, and must have dated from the middle ages: black and white marble floor, a high-beamed, painted ceiling, frescoes all around the walls. Avicenna gripped my arm.

'Your Highness! Signor Moreton!'

The Prince was by the great fireplace, dressed in a dark blue tee-shirt and black checked golfing trousers, and holding what looked like a five iron in his hands. He had an admirable golfer's stance – head down and shoulders properly relaxed – and seemed to be practising his swing. Then I saw a golf ball teed neatly on the carpet and realised that the long windows at the far end of the *salone* were wide open, giving an untrammelled line of fire to what must be the Tiber far below.

He balanced himself nicely. With his height he had an enviable figure for a golfer, and his swing was excellent. In his position I would certainly have fluffed the shot, causing untold damage to the pictures, the spectators or the chandeliers, but he drove off in style, with head still down and copybook follow-through. The ball went whistling like a bullet out through the windows, and I saw it plummet into the middle of the river. The Prince looked rather pleased, as well he might.

'Ah, Mr Moreton. Do excuse me. Quite unforgiveable, I know. "Manners!" as my old English nanny used to say. But this new club has just arrived from Lillywhites and I really had to try it out. You know how it is.'

He offered me his hand.

'Avicenna tells me you are a golfer. Have a go yourself.'

'Extremely kind, Prince, but I'm somewhat out of practice.'

'Absolutely sure? No trouble.'

The prince's big bald head gleamed, and there was quite a twinkle in the eyes as he smiled an effusive welcome.

'Now, Mr Moreton, really you *must* forgive me, but it's been that sort of day. We need a drink.'

79

All that I wanted was to discuss my wife with Avicenna and settle everything as soon as possible but the Prince's presence made this difficult. Did the Prince know what was going on? This was difficult to credit, but one never knew. He sat on a sofa and motioned to me graciously to do the same. I saw that the Flea had made a silent entrance, followed by Hitler, who padded up to the Prince, nuzzling his crotch and wagging his heavy ropelike tail. His master patted him then pushed him aside, and nodded to the Flea. The dog subsided, slavering and the enormous man, more like a butler than an all-in wrestler now, moved to a massive gilt and marble table by the fireplace, and uncorked a bottle of champagne.

'There now,' said the Prince, smiling at me, glass in hand. 'That's more like it. Your health, Mr Moreton. Most kind of you to visit me like this, a busy man like you. I had hoped we could meet properly before, but so much has been going on. You know how it is.'

I didn't, but I nodded, sipping my champagne.

'What dreadful times these are for Italy! Violence, strikes, everything collapsing. It is my own country, and I trust I am a patriot, but you know, Mr Moreton, I am very near despair. Do you see any hope for us?'

'Not a great deal, but times will change. It's practically as bad in England.'

'No, Mr Moreton, it is not so bad. I am speaking to you frankly now: if I had just myself to consider, I would now sell up and find myself a small place in your Cotswold hills. Some hunting and a little shooting. I have some dear friends near Stroud in Wiltshire. You know Wiltshire? It is my dream to live there, and my friends have found the ideal house for me, but alas I cannot go there. I am condemned by this.'

He raised his hands wearily as if to show the burden of the great room around us. He sighed.

'Someone must protect it for the future. What else can one do? Nor is this all. There is our land in Sicily and in the North.

It is a trust which I cannot betray, particularly at a time like this. I see you understand. Some more champagne?'

He nodded to the Flea, who silently refilled my glass.

'Which is why we decided finally to approach you to insure His Highness,' butted in Avicenna. 'His Highness and I have talked about it many times, and we appreciate that he is particularly at risk. As you can see we take precautions, but there have been threats which are not agreeable and there is always danger.'

The Prince gave a further sigh of sad agreement.

'How true! Indeed, how very true! As you must realise, I am still young enough, like you, to wish to live an active life. Were I content to retire here from the world and live like a monk, we would not need to trouble you. Signor Moreton, I am not a monk.

He shook his head gloomily, as if this were one further source of sorrow.

'I have to ask myself that if the worst occurred – as it so often does – and I were kidnapped, Mr Moreton, how could the ransom money possibly be found? It might be necessary to sell this place, and that would be unthinkable. Unthinkable. But I have friends in England who assure me that once one is insured through Lloyds against the possibility of kidnap, one can set one's mind at rest. Everything is taken care of from that moment on. Should something dreadful happen, the insurers employ experts who handle all negotiations with the kidnappers, settle the details of the ransom, and make sure that one returns without too much delay. That is the important thing – that one returns. Oh, one does not relish the idea of mistakes occurring in that sort of situation. Oh, indeed not. Dreadful, dreadful!'

He laughed nervously, and his hands fluttered at the thought.

'I must tell you that I have – or rather had – a friend this happened to last year. Poor man, he was kidnapped here in

81

Rome. Yes, here in his very own *palazzo*, taken from his bed at gunpoint. Just imagine! The shock, the suffering, the terrible indignity. He was a dear friend, a most sensitive, kind, loving human being, and although his family sent the ransom money, things went wrong. Ah me, dreadfully, dreadfully wrong. There were misunderstandings and the idiotic Carabinieri butted in as well, which was not clever. No, not at all. They found the body three months later at the bottom of a lake in Northern Italy, along with several other of the gang's mistakes. Mr Moreton, I do not wish to end up at the bottom of a lake as somebody's mistake. Oh, dear me, no! So you must help us, Mr Moreton.'

He made it all sound most convincing but I remembered Colombo's warnings about the Prince's reputation – not to mention Avicenna's. Besides it was Avicenna that I had to speak to now about my wife, so I tried to make my refusal as final and as definite as possible, and shook my head.

'I am extremely sorry, but I have already told Dr Avicenna that the way the market stands at present, it is impossible to offer you the sort of policy you want. Perhaps an American company . . .'

The Prince looked hurt.

'But, Mr Moreton, I do not trust Americans in such matters. I would not feel safe. And why is it impossible? This talk of yours about the market. I do not understand.'

'I'm sorry, but it isn't my decision. Very few London underwriters take on business of this sort, and those who do have been getting very difficult over Italian business.'

He had drawn himself up and was watching me intently now. His voice was suddenly quite sharp as he replied,

'Are you sure that it is not you who is getting difficult, Signor Moreton? I have been in touch with certain friends in London and they assure me there should be no problem, once you have given your assent.'

'That's not how these things are done, Your Highness.'

'Then how are they done? Pray explain why someone of my rank and financial standing is turned down like this. Frankly I find it mildly insulting, to say the least.'

His voice had risen and to my surprise I could see that he was quivering with fury. It was probably an act which he was used to putting on with social inferiors who offended him, but it was quite alarming. Certainly there was no question now of telling him the truth – especially as I still had to talk to Avicenna on his own before I left.

'Prince, I assure you no insult is intended, but I can only repeat what I have already said. And now if you'll excuse me . . .'

I spoke my piece as firmly as I could and began to rise, although I hadn't finished my champagne. The Prince said nothing, but Hitler growled and I was suddenly aware of the Flea's mountainous presence just behind me. Then Avicenna leaned back in his chair and started laughing.

'Really, Signor Moreton, really! This is no way to treat your friends. Come now. Please to sit down. Some more to drink, and we can calmly sort out this misunderstanding with the goodwill of gentlemen. Please!'

His gold teeth gleamed and his whole presence seemed to exude goodwill and cheerful common sense. The Prince was pointedly showing his displeasure by ignoring me; instead he was scratching Hitler's belly with his foot, making the great brute yawn with pleasure, but Avicenna turned to him and said,

'We must not be too hard on Signor Moreton, for I am sure that what he says is true and he has been under great strain during these last few days. We must make allowances for his personal difficulties. That is why I make this meeting. So that we can come to a good arrangement which will suit everybody so we can all be happy.'

The Prince gave no reply, but shrugged his shoulders. Even then I did not have the sense to realise what was coming as

Avicenna went on smiling like the pimp he was and spread his hands before him like a deck of cards.

'Signor Moreton, now we talk turkey as the Americans say – the truth between the three of us. Yes?'

'What sort of truth?'

'There are certain things I know. Do not ask me how I know them for I shall not tell you, but about your wife . . .'

I understood then.

'Avicenna, don't think you can blackmail me.'

'No more insults, Signor Moreton. Let us just stay very calm. Is best. I believe that you still love your wife and wish her to return.'

Something about the way he said this maddened me and I lost control, lunging forward in an attempt to punch that oily smile off his face: it was a futile gesture, for long before I reached him, the Flea's great hand was on my shoulder pushing me back into my seat. Neither Avicenna nor the Prince appeared to notice.

'Where is she, Avicenna?'

'As I have told you, Signor Moreton, there are certain things I cannot say, but I ask of you the truth. You want her back?'

'Of course, but —'

'No buts, please. They are a waste of breath, and why waste the breath when everything is now extremely simple. You desire your wife. We ask that His Highness is properly insured against kidnap as soon as possible. Now it would seem we have the basis of a deal.'

10

I had always thought that I was incorruptible, not from any overriding sense of virtue or morality, but because integrity, like tidiness or punctuality or the way I dressed, was an essential part of my profession. Had it been something more than this, I should have known how to act, and would undoubtedly have refused Avicenna's offer there and then. Even on the worldliest of levels, I should have had the sense to know that it never does to compromise with crooks, unless you are one yourself (for the simple reason that they know the game better than you do, and will always beat you at it).

But I am not a worldly man, nor am I a crook, and during these last few days I had become infected with anxiety, frustration, self-doubt and desperate jealousy – all symptoms of the Moreton Personal Disaster Syndrome. I was literally 'not myself' and wide open to a man like Avicenna, as he must have realised.

He played his part adroitly. So for that matter, did the Prince. The Prince maintained his front of aloof displeasure, and Avicenna did almost all the talking, parrying my questions about Petinacci and the MPM and giving not the slightest hint of how he thought that he could influence a gang of terrorists. Nor would he tell me much about my wife, except that she wished to return to me and that this would be tackfully arranged in return for my cooperation. He was well informed about what had been happening in London, for he seemed to know that my report to Hugo was all that really stood between the Prince and the policy he wanted.

'It is so very simple for you, Signor Moreton. Let me arrange things with your wife. So nothing till she is safely back with you. We will trust you. Then when you have her back and are a happy man again, forget all this stupid opposition to His Highness with your London office. What have you to lose?'

I found it hard to tell him.

'Dear Signor Moreton, I think that you begin to understand that this is not as you originally thought. Those words you used about me, and those unfortunate suspicions. We are just friends who help each other. A kindness here, a kindness in return, and isn't that what makes the world go round?'

'I need time to think about it.'

'Of course, dear Signor Moreton. But of course. But not too much time. You will let me know tomorrow your decision?'

'By midday.'

'Excellent! And now some more champagne?'

I refused, of course, and made my departure with what dignity I could muster. The Prince gave the frostiest of nods but did not offer me his hand – nor his car back to the office – and once I was clear of the Palazzo I found myself a taxi.

It was a perfect sunny afternoon: Rome appeared slumbrous, lush, almost tropical with summer coming, and once out of the orbit of the Prince and Avicenna, I began to realise how sinister their proposition really was and how impossible it was to trust them. Their behaviour more than confirmed Colombo's warnings: they were a pair of crooks and the odds were that they were planning some sort of insurance fraud once the policy was settled. It wouldn't be the first time it had been tried in Italy, and why else take so much trouble winning my assent? It was all patently a trick, and totally in character: Avicenna must have somehow heard about Diana's departure, put two and two together, and was simply using it to bluff me into the deal he wanted.

I was not that stupid, and by the time the taxi reached the office I had made up my mind to have done with Avicenna and the Prince for good, and settle everything myself. In my new decisive mood I had Oliviero drive me to the headquarters of the Carabinieri by the river, where I asked for Colonello Rossi.

I was received at once, and the little man seemed pleased to see me. I told him everything I knew – except about the Prince and Avicenna's offer – but he gave me the impression that the whole case had turned into one more routine inquiry. He seemed efficient and confident that he would find her,

'But these things take time, Signor, and this Petinacci is even smarter than we thought. He has money and I've an idea that someone influential is protecting him. So we must wait. Eventually he'll have to make a move. The MPM will call for action somewhere and when this happens we'll be more than ready for them.'

'And what about my wife?'

'I have told you that my men have the strictest orders to ensure no harm befalls her.'

'And in the meantime?'

'Wait, Signor. Be patient. We know exactly what we are doing and I give my word that everything will be all right.'

How many times had Italians said that to me before some hideous catastrophe? But I did my best to hide my disquiet, and back in the office telephoned Colombo.

'Ah, Signor Conte, it is a very interesting case. I have known nothing like it, particularly as she was free to come and go when she called at your office. I have tried everything and questioned all my contacts. There is still no trace.'

'D'you think he's killed her?' I asked bleakly.

'Who, this Petinacci character? Most unlikely, I would say. It would not be his style at all. He is a wide boy and an adventurer rather than a real terrorist. People who know him tell me the hard-core terrorists of the Left have always distrusted him and his movement. There is a rumour that he's only in it for the money. He wouldn't be the first who was, and he certainly cleaned up from his bank raids in the South before they caught him. No one knows exactly how much he managed to hang onto, but he has always lived extremely well, and my guess would be that he and your wife are living very

87

comfortably in the sort of place where no one would expect to
find a wanted left-wing terrorist at all.'

'Such as?'

'Who knows? Some smart hotel on the Italian Lakes. Or
even Venice.'

'She couldn't stand the place.'

'Switzerland then. Geneva's full of wealthy criminals. Nobody bothers them provided they behave themselves – and pay
their bills on time. That of course is when the crunch will
come. In my experience, it always does. Boredom and lack of
money are bound to bring her back, if you still want her.'

'Of course I will.'

'Then Signor Conte, do absolutely nothing. Wait. Be
patient. When it's over you'll have the privilege of picking up
the pieces.'

'Don't be so bloody cynical,' I muttered and rang off. And
all that night I waited patiently for somebody to ring, but nothing happened.

To my credit I still made no attempt to contact Avicenna.
Next day midday came and though I was tempted to pick up
the telephone I resisted – staunchly. I had made my decision
and was sticking to it. Stick to it I did, for the rest of the afternoon, and when Avicenna rang me I hung up on him. I was
tempted to try Colombo yet again, but knew there was no
point, and left the office at 7.30, dined, horribly, at home, and
tried to settle to a book.

At ten o'clock the telephone again. And again it was
Avicenna. But this time I answered – cautiously, as one might
when dealing with a shady medium, promising contact with a
loved one in another world.

'Well, Dr Avicenna?'

'Signor Moreton, I am getting worried for you. We agreed
that we would talk at midday and I hear nothing from you. I

have the feeling you are trying to avoid me. It would not be sensible, when I know that I can help you. I have news for you.'

'News? What sort of news?'

'It is not something I would wish to tell you over the telephone. It is better that we meet. You know Giacosa's Café in Piazza del Popolo? In twenty minutes I shall be there, and will offer you a drink. Then we can talk. I think you will be wise to come.'

How could I possibly resist? I had been begging everyone for news and had been fobbed off. I might have rung Colombo for advice, but I already knew what he would tell me. Besides, there wasn't time. As Avicenna must have known, I had to hurry if I was to meet him.

It was a warm spring night and the Piazza del Popolo was crowded. Most Roman bars are dreadful places, furtive and unwelcoming, with nowhere one can sit and drink in peace, but at Giacosa's the tables were outside on the pavement, and the view is one of the liveliest in Rome – the big circular piazza like the arena of a circus, traffic hurtling around the Egyptian obelisk in its navel, and on the far side an illuminated fountain, statuary, a small road that zig-zags up to the Pincian Gardens, capped with stone pines at the summit of the pretty hill where it is said they buried Nero: extremely picturesque, romantic and designed, as one might have known, not by an Italian but by a Frenchman for Napoleon.

Avicenna was sitting at a table on his own, smoking a large cigar. Was it my imagination, or was he looking slightly sleazy? The eyes were bloodshot, the linen jacket needed pressing, and there was silvery stubble on the big bald surface of his chin.

'So, Signor Moreton! You condescend to speak with me.'

He didn't offer me his hand – not that I would have shaken it if he had – but this disturbed me.

'What did you expect?' I said.

'Ah, Signor Moreton. I, Dr Avicenna, offer you my friendship. We discuss business. I introduce you to His Highness and
you offend him. Then you ask me what do I expect.'

He shook his head gloomily. I was uncertain whether to sit
down or leave, but a waiter was hovering, so I took a chair and
asked what he was drinking.

'Whisky, thank you very much. A double whisky. As I am
saying, I am in two minds whether to continue trying to be of
help to you. Our life it is too short to bother with those who
fail to respect one. Signor Moreton, I am being frank with you.'

'Why telephone and ask to see me then?'

He leaned towards me so that when he spoke I felt his spittle
on my face.

'Please understand that it is not Dr Avicenna's nature to
brush off a friend, even when he treats him badly. Even then, I
attempt to offer him my benefit of the doubt.'

The drinks arrived.

'You told me you have news about my wife.'

He nodded, then all but drained his glass in a single noisy
gulp, after which he belched.

'First there are things that I must say.'

'For God's sake, Avicenna, don't try playing games with
me.'

'Games, Signor Moreton? It is not I who play the games.
Despite what you were warned, you visit the Colonello at the
headquarters of the Carabinieri yesterday afternoon. You
make things very difficult with such behaviour. Everything is
nearly buggered up. The work I have to reassure my friends
that they can trust you after this!'

'But of course I go to the police. My wife —'

'No more, Signor Moreton!' he interrupted, wagging an
admonitory finger underneath my nose. If·I will help you now
no further contact with that man. Your word on it?'

I nodded wearily.

'And you also give your promise as an Englishman that His Highness will receive the kidnap insurance he desires once your wife is safely back with you?'

'If she returns, I'll recommend it.'

'Strongly recommend it. You will strongly recommend it, Signor Moreton.'

'I'll do my best. I can't do more.'

He frowned and pondered this.

'Very well. I trust you. I hope I do not make some big mistake.'

Silence fell between us, and as I gazed across the bustling piazza, pigeons came fluttering up above us, dazzled by the light against the night blue of the sky. Something about the panic beating of their wings, seemed to forebode disaster, and I had a final urge to tell Avicenna I had changed my mind, and see no more of him.

'I saw her yesterday,' he said, as if knowing what was in my mind.

'Where on earth?'

'As if I could tell you. Be sensible. Too many people are involved.'

'How is she?'

'Well enough. And ready to return to you.'

'Then why doesn't she?'

He shrugged his shoulders.

'Signor Moreton, you are being just a little bit naïve. There is much to be arranged and precautions to be taken. Lives could be at risk.'

'Whose lives?'

'No more questions, for I cannot answer them. Tomorrow evening someone will contact you in your apartment. He will require a code word so you will know that he is someone you can trust. Perhaps you would suggest a word yourself.'

I looked around and saw the blind of the café with its large blue letters.

'How about Giacosi?'

'Excellent. Tomorrow night Giacosi will be in touch with you. And just one final warning, Signor Moreton. Not a word of this to anyone. If certain people found out you had talked . . .'

His gold fillings glinted as he drew a finger across his throat and grinned. Then he patted his chest and rose and I saw him as the gangster that he really was.

'You talked of games. These people are not playing games – and nor am I. Good night to you.'

11

So I had given in and Avicenna had his way but suddenly it didn't seem to matter. I felt no pangs of conscience, not even a faint premonition of disgrace and slept contentedly; after those days of worry and uncertainty there was a wonderful relief in having settled things – or so I thought.

The next day dawned, another day of bland good weather and it was then that I began to have my doubts. My wife had disappeared, the incident was over, and life was going on exactly as it always did in Italy. How could Avicenna bring her back?

By the time I reached the office, I was hoping that some miracle would still occur, and that Diana would suddenly come back to me of her own free will, or that Colonello Rossi would call to tell me that his men had found her. But this was not a time of miracles. Nothing happened, and I did not believe it ever would.

That night Luisa cooked my solitary supper. Since my wife's disappearance, I had actually grown quite fond of her. At least she was there. She asked no questions, and her evil temper could always be relied on, which was something. I ate mechanically, drank a little, then tried watching television. Avicenna had promised he would contact me but hadn't told me how. All I could do was wait.

There was a game of football, something I am not remotely interested in, but instead of switching to another channel, I forced myself to watch the tiny figures and the changing patterns they were making on the screen. Who was playing I had not the least idea, but I became interested to see how one side built up its attack, trying to force a goal and failing every time. It had a sort of mindless fascination and at a deeper level it seemed a sort of metaphor of life: I was quite excited when a goal was scored just before the final whistle.

Then came a gangster movie, American of course, but dubbed into Italian – rather badly: murder and mayhem in what was presumably downtown Chicago with bomb attacks, beatings up and much shooting from fast cars. As if there wasn't quite enough of this in Italy! I was beginning to doze off when I was roused by the urgent ringing of the telephone over the rattle of machine guns from the screen.

'Yes? Hullo, yes?'

No reply, apart from the peep-peep-peep of a callbox telephone and the call went dead. Ten minutes later the same thing happened. Then, shortly after midnight, there was another call, and this time someone spoke. The voice was muffled but I think I recognised it as my previous anonymous caller.

'Moreton?'

'Yes.'

'Giacosi here. Come downstairs straight away, and wait in the street outside your apartment. Someone will meet you.'

'Who?'

'No questions. Straight away, Signor Moreton. There is no time to lose.'

For once I didn't pause to worry about what I was letting myself in for as I grabbed my coat, slammed the front door behind me, and headed for the lift. This time it was working, and I reached the street in record time, but there was no one there, and I waited, feeling vulnerable and rather cold. Rome was out of sight below, but I could hear the night-time murmur of its distant traffic; then a screech-owl started, like a cry for help from somewhere in the pine-trees on the hill. The street was still as empty as the wrong side of the moon and I must have waited several minutes, imagining all manner of disas-

94

ters, when I saw car lights approaching up the hill. They belonged to an old grey Fiat, with an exhaust that needed fixing; reaching me, it braked abruptly. I had never seen the young man at the wheel before, but the rear door opened, and Avicenna's big grey face peered out at me.

'Signor Moreton! Good night to you! I trust we do not keep you waiting. Hurry! We have quite a journey now before us.'

This time he offered me his hand, and I took it without thinking, then piled in beside him. Inevitably the wretched fellow started laughing.

'Long past your bedtime, eh, Signor Moreton? Ah, women! What we do for them! At our age too. It is too much I think.'

'Where is she?'

'She is fine. We go to fetch her. No problems now.'

'For God's sake, Avicenna. No more of your bloody nonsense!'

'Bloody nonsense? Signor Moreton, again you are not polite. But again I forgive you, since you are still my friend. I forgive you everything.'

The car was roaring on its way, the silent driver gunning the old engine as we sped towards the outskirts of the city, through the long shadows cast by a waning moon, past a silent goods yard, over traffic lights permanently set at amber for the night, and on through interminable empty streets of factories and workers' flats. It could have been a city of the dead.

Then scrappy countryside began, and we seemed to be heading West – towards the coast. Avicenna lit a cigarette.

'I am sorry that I have to bring you with me here like this. It is profoundly boring for us both, but things were not as simple as I hoped.'

'But she *is* all right?'

'She is waiting for you, but she insists on seeing you in person before she will return. But I must tell you, Signor Moreton – you forget all this. Tonight, whatever happens, you have seen nobody and this journey has not taken place. You get the Signora back and that is that. Agreed?'

'Why?'

'Listen to me, Signor Moreton. I am not laughing with you any more. I and His Highness make a deal with you and we will keep it. But after tonight, whatever happens, you will say nothing about how your wife came back to you.'

'If I do?'

'If you do, Signor Moreton, things will be very difficult for you – and worse still for your wife. She knows this herself and she also knows exactly what to say to your friend Colonello Rossi when he questions her, as of course he will. All explanations you will leave to her. Agreed?'

'If you say so.'

'Excellent. And now Signor Moreton, I am afraid that I must blindfold you.'

'You must what?'

'Blindfold, Signor Moreton. That is what they call it. Cover up the eyes. As much for your sake as for anybody else's. If you have no idea where you are going now, there is nothing you can give away.'

I refused at first, but Avicenna wasn't arguing. Instead he simply told the driver to draw in by the roadside, and we waited in the dark beside a stretch of God-forsaken countryside for nearly twenty minutes. Neither Avicenna nor the driver would reply to anything I said.

'OK.' I muttered finally, 'you win. She had better be there.'

'She will be and I am relieved you understand,' said Avicenna.

He had a black silk scarf smelling of cheap scent. He tied it tightly round my eyes, and I heard him ordering the driver to continue.

I have no idea how far or where we drove. Several times I felt the car turning and it must have been a good half hour before

96

we started to slow down. We seemed to be passing over cobbles now. Then came another turning and we halted.

'Excellent,' said Avicenna. 'We are arrived. Gently, Signor Moreton. I will help you to descend. You are in safe hands. Have no fear.'

I felt the cold air as the car door opened, and Avicenna gripped my arm to guide me out. There was some sort of paving underfoot; I tripped, and but for Avicenna would have fallen.

'Slowly, Signor Moreton. Slowly. Not much further. There. Now to sit down.'

He was still holding me, and as I put my hand down I felt the surface of some sort of rough stone bench. I sat and felt considerably safer.

'Now, Signor Moreton. Listen carefully. Stay here and keep your blindfold in its place. We must leave you, but somebody will come to take you to her. You must not see him, Signor Moreton. If you do, everything is lost. And remember everything I said. We will be in touch later.'

I tried to plead with him to stay, but he patted my shoulder reassuringly and was gone. A moment later I heard the car start up, and I was totally alone.

I must have sat there several minutes in the dark. Despite Avicenna's words of reassurance, I was scared – especially when I heard footsteps come towards me. I heard them pause quite close to me and was tempted to cry out, but managed to restrain myself. Was it some member of the MPM or a hanger-on of Avicenna's? Whoever it was muttered something, then I heard his steps receding.

That was the moment when I felt most vulnerable: I would have given almost anything for the sound of Avicenna's stupid voice but knew I had to stay exactly where I was. I had endured so much that there was no question now of spoiling my wife's return by panicking. But someone else was coming towards me now – or rather something else. It was hard to tell exactly what it was, but it sounded like some sort of animal, roaring and trampling through dry brushwood. It moved slowly and there was a strange splashing noise as well.

It was that that terrified me, and I sat there petrified, waiting for the brute to go away. But it came closer still, and suddenly I'd had enough. My wife's return, and Avicenna's warnings no longer mattered now that I felt my life was actually at stake. I paused a moment longer, still gripping the edge of the stone bench – then tore the blindfold from my eyes.

The animal had all but reached me now. It was orange-coloured and I had seen it many times before – the big municipal sweeping machine that washes and sweeps the street below the apartment three times a week. I even recognised the driver – a surly, red-faced fellow who eyed me very strangely, as well he might. Dawn was breaking and I was standing in the street where I lived, outside my own apartment.

12

One's self-respect is often more compelling than one thinks, for my relief at finding I was still alive changed rapidly to indignation at the way I had been made a fool of. At that moment I forgot entirely about my wife and I was very angry. For here I was at fifty-two – English and honourable, and with a certain reputation in insurance circles – the victim of a tasteless and idiotic practical joke. The Prince was obviously behind it with his 'English sense of humour': it was presumably his way of scoring off me for refusing him his wretched policy.

Silly idiot! And as for Avicenna! Just wait until I found him! If it was meant to be a joke I failed to see the funny side of it, for my head ached and I was hideously tired. All I could think of was some suitable revenge.

The municipal sweeper was grinding and splashing on its way and I dodged an early car and crossed the street. My watch said five o'clock. No one was up yet, but the lift, thank God, was working, and I had my keys. Inside the flat there was the grey cold light of very early morning. Perhaps it was still worth trying to snatch two or three hours' sleep. I took off my shoes and, swearing to myself, opened the bedroom door. To my surprise the shutters had been pulled.

'Elly darling!' said a sleepy voice. 'I'm back.'

I tried to ask her where she had been and when she had returned, but instead of answering she snuggled close beside me in the bed. I think I made some token show of husbandly annoyance and aloofness, but there was little point: I was so tired and relieved to have her back that I put an arm around her, kissed her on the neck, and sank gratefully back into the warm matrix of our marriage. There would be time for questions later.

I must have been exhausted, for when I woke the shutters were pulled back, sunlight suffused the room, and Diana was already up and dressed. She had brought me breakfast on a tray – something she hadn't done since I was ill in bed with 'flu two years earlier. She was wearing a pale pink dress I'd never seen before and with her hair done up and her makeup perfectly in place, she seemed as self-possessed and quietly unflustered as if she had just returned from a shopping trip to London.

She placed the tray on the bed and offered me her cheek to kiss: as I brushed my lips against her firm young flesh it was like kissing a complacent stranger. But I was the one who seemed put out by this and somehow in the wrong. She could have been welcoming back an erring husband as she smiled at me (as if to make it clear that in spite of everything, she forgave me), spread a clean napkin for me on the sheet, and poured the coffee.

No one could make such delicious breakfast coffee as my wife.

'Well?' I said.

'Well?' she replied and went on smiling. She had never looked prettier – small, flower-like face, with clear blue eyes and an expression of carefree innocence as she stared at me and started laughing.

'Elly, darling! Don't look so worried. It's only me. Your wife. I'm back. For good if you still want me.'

'Of course I want you, but —'

'Drink your coffee then, you old silly. Nothing else really matters, darling. I have been stupid, but it's over. I promise you it's over.'

'Is it?'

'But of course it is. Why else do you think I'm here? I knew I had made a hideous mistake the day I left.'

'Why didn't you come back earlier? We were looking for you everywhere.'

'I tried to, but I couldn't.'

'Why couldn't you? Wasn't there some way you could have let me know that you were still alive? I've been off my head with worry.'

She was sipping her coffee – holding the cup in both her hands – and stared solemnly across at me.

'Are you sure you want me back?'

I nodded.

'Then no more questions, Elly dear, for I won't answer them. I've said it's over and I gave my word to say nothing of what happened while I was away, as much for your sake as for mine. If you go on asking me, I'll have to leave you.'

Silence followed. Her small face was set in an expression of determination I had rarely seen before, and as she sipped her coffee she was watching me intently. I met her eyes, then looked away. All that really mattered was that she was back. All I could think of was how much I desired her.

'Well?'

I moved the tray off the bed.

'Finish your coffee!'

'Why?'

Instead of telling her, I took the cup from her hands and kissed her slowly on the lips.

'No more questions, Elly?'

'No more questions.'

I could not remember the last time I actually undressed her, and she had to help me with the zipper of her dress.

'Clumsy darling Elly!'

I thought of her lover and imagined he had been more adroit. But I did my best.

It was the telephone, of course – prime douser of desire – that brought us back to earth. Luckily we had accomplished all that really mattered in two happy minutes. My wife would have let it go on ringing, but I am as remorselessly conditioned to the beastly instrument as one of Pavlov's white rats to its dinner bell.

'Yes?' I answered, still in a daze of post-coital refulgence.

'So you are happy, Signor Moreton? Everything is well? I trust that you forgive my little joke with you last night, but it was necessary. You could not be there to witness her return. She is well?'

'Avicenna, I could murder you!'

'Murder, Signor Moreton? Come now. Come. Where is your sense of humour? Me, I am still laughing at it, and I told His Highness. He is laughing too. I think you are now a very happy man.'

'Of course I am.'

'And in the midst of all your happiness, you won't forget our agreement, will you, Signor Moreton? It would be very good if you could deal with it today.'

I had told Oliviero not to collect me for the office until I let him know when I was ready. Now it was far too late to ring him, so I decided to make the most of it, and celebrate my wife's return by walking to the office: it would give me a chance to think about the future and savour life a little after the nightmare of the last few days.

Rome is a two-faced city – either hideous beyond belief or the loveliest city known to man. Today it had its best face forward, with May on its way, and the air still fresh and clear before the heavy heat of summer. The sunlight made a rainbow in the spray from the fountain at the bottom of the hill: the river, normally so murky, actually sparkled; barrows were stacked high with fresh spring vegetables, and even the traffic bowled for once quite merrily along the Tiber. My wife was back and Rome appeared to promise everything I could desire. I knew the promise was deceptive, but this didn't worry me at all.

I reached the Corso. It was full of shoppers but I actually enjoyed the sight of those big expensive shops with all the goods they offered there to make someone happy – furniture, fur coats, tennis rackets, shoes, cigars. I felt a sudden urge to buy something for my wife to welcome her return, and inevitably a jeweller's shop caught my attention, a stately, big, old-fashioned shop, with the name 'Steinmetz' in florid gold italic over the window, and a display of just the sort of objects that I knew she loved, set in the window on small velvet-covered stands like holy relics to be worshipped by the faithful: a shell-shaped gold powder compact, a platinum and diamond ring, solid gold lighters, earrings, necklaces – badges of wealth for those who could afford them.

Two people, clearly tourists, were staring in the window – a tall man with thick grey hair, a leathery good-looking face and one of those Black Watch tartan jackets loved by middle-aged Americans: he was at least as old as me, but his companion was a kittenish young woman with a lot of spun-gold hair and baby-doll blue eyes.

'But why not, honey?' I heard him saying in his plaintive Texan. 'Gold is a prime investment.'

'Lover, you promised me a diamond.'

'An' my girl's sure that's what she really wants?'

She was. I caught his eye and smiled, one sugar-daddy-oh to another, but he looked away, and it was this that finally decided me. I would show how a mature man bought a present for a younger woman, and a moment later I was in the shop.

I had to spend a little time deciding what to buy my wife in exchange for the lover she had lost. A ring? Tasteless. Necklace? She had several which she rarely wore. Finally I chose a bracelet, a highly polished chunk of gold which I knew that she would love. I paid by cheque, and as the girl assistant was wrapping up the box – elaborately, as Italian jewellers do – I caught sight of myself in the big gilt mirror set behind the counter, and was agreeably surprised. I really didn't look my age that morning, simply a solid figure of a man in a well-cut, dark grey, English double-breasted – hair a trifle thin perhaps and some grey on the tips of the moustache, but no evidence at all of the strains and troubles of the previous few days.

The girl handed me the box and smiled – not so much at me, I'm sure, as at the thought of her commission – and I noticed that two buttons of her blouse were carefully undone, giving a brief glance of a well-developed breast, a shaded nipple. I remembered my wife's breasts then, happy thought, and was only sorry when I left the shop that the Texan and his child-bride had gone. In the mood I was in, I would have thanked them both and wished them well.

Decisiveness – there is nothing like it for restoring a sense of order to one's life, and this was now my principal objective. After the chaos and disorder of the last few days, I was firmly in command again, and by the time I reached the office, I had my programme neatly and efficiently mapped out.

First I would pay my debt to Avicenna, straight away before I had time for second thoughts, and so have done with him and his shady friend the Prince for ever. This was what everybody seemed to want and I was long past worrying about the ethics of it all. If I was giving in to blackmail from a pair of crooks, so what? Who wasn't crooked in this frightful country? As for their contacts with the terrorists of the MPM, Petinacci included, these were entirely their own affair. With Diana safely back with me, I simply did not wish to know.

She was all that mattered to me now: if nothing else, the little episode had taught me that. Yes, she had been stupid, but I partly blamed myself, and I blamed Italy – particularly Italy – for I could understand exactly how the trouble had begun. I had been far too keen to cosset her after her miscarriage. I should have had the sense to realise that she was not a child – nor an invalid – and she had obviously been bored, pampered and left alone too much in the apartment. Rome is a very sexy city. What did I expect?

It was all too easy now to picture how she had first met the smooth young Petinacci. She could have been having coffee, quite innocently, even at somewhere like Giacosi's, with one of her women friends. A handsome, rather flashy young man sitting at a nearby table. A smile, a note entrusted to a waiter, followed by an invitation out to lunch. She would have wondered whether she should accept – and then accepted – and everything would have followed in the time-honoured Roman manner. Further invitations, protestations, hurried meetings, and the inevitable surrender.

Petinacci would have known from long experience how to play her carefully along, until that disastrous afternoon when she decided she must bolt with him. No thought for the future, only the romantic moment mattered, and like most victims of young men like Petinacci, there would be time to repent at leisure. It was a commonplace enough affair, particularly in Italy, and the more I thought about it now the more I realised our time in Rome was over. We had stayed too long, and the sooner we were back in England now, the better.

I was entitled to apply for a home posting, and once we were safely back in London, all this nonsense would be over and utterly forgotten. She would have her friends, her family, her favourite shops, the flat in Chelsea we had talked about so often in the past. The very thought of London was exciting here in Rome; the city of an autumn evening, pubs with proper English beer, kippers and sausages and trips to the country at weekends. How had I lived without such things for quite so long? I climbed the Spanish Steps and realised a new and better life was just about to start – for both of us.

*

105

I had no trouble getting through to Hugo to give him the go-ahead about the Prince's policy. This reassured me: fate was clearly on my side, and Hugo sounded wonderfully relieved – the wretched Witherspoon must have been on at him again at White's – and promised to telex me the underwriters' terms by lunchtime.

'Can't tell you how delighted I am that it's all worked out, old boy. You were absolutely right, of course, to take your time and check everything thoroughly. Very professional of you. You're satisfied?'

'As much as one ever can be, Hugo. You know I've never gone a bomb on kidnap policies as such, but if we really want the business, I see no reason for refusing him. Besides I'm reliably informed that the latest trends in kidnap here are to go for the foreigners and *nouveaux riches*. Big boys like the Prince have grown too difficult to catch.'

'You don't say? Fascinating. *Entre nous* this could lead on to quite a lot of goodies here through Witherspoon, and it won't do your end of the business any harm either, take it from me. That's why I pressed it. Anyhow, old scout, well done!'

'And how's my sister?'

'Since you mention her, Hugo, I am getting just a little worried about her. I've an idea she's been missing England more than I realised of late. The women do, you know. Shops, friends, a settled life. It'll have been three years this autumn. Time to up sticks and head for Blighty if it's all the same to you.'

'Dear old boy, that's quite a facer. Do you have to? Couldn't persuade you both to stay another year?'

''Fraid not Hugo. You know your sister.'

'Absolutely! Tricky though to find someone of your calibre old boy at just this point of time to take your place. No great urgency I trust?'

'No great urgency – but as soon as you can dig up a replacement. More for her sake, you understand, than mine.'

106

'Point taken. I will cogitate, and be in contact. As for that other business, once again, well done!'

The chief reason for the continuing success of Lloyds' Insurance Market – despite massive and aggressive foreign competition – is its flexibility. To outsiders this strange institution in the City always seems somewhat casual and old-fashioned in the way it operates – too many well-heeled idiots like Hugo, messengers decked out in tail-coats and fancy waistcoats, and the strange charade of acting as if Mr Lloyd's eighteenth-century coffee house still acts as the insurance centre of the world.

But curiously it works – and rather well: for somewhere, tucked away behind the bullshit and the chinless wonders are some very smart characters indeed, and long before lunchtime I had a definite acceptance of the Prince's insurance on the telex, along with all the special details I had asked for. Everything was tailor-made – the premiums, details of beneficiaries, and the all-important kidnap clause which provided cover up to ten million dollars to be called on for ransom payment in the event of sequestration of the Prince's person.

This was dependent on a number of standard conditions, most of which he observed already – proper security, a full-time bodyguard and the insurers asked to be kept informed of the Prince's movements in advance. They also insisted – normal practice in this sort of business – on their right to employ agents of their own choosing to conduct ransom negotiations with any kidnapper in the event of the forcible disappearance of the person insured.

This was what the Prince had mentioned earlier to me as one of the main attractions of the deal; the comforting assurance that in any kidnap situation the victim would not have to sit and wait for the dubious assistance of the local police, whose main aim might be less to free him than to nail the criminals. These two objectives can be diametrically opposed – and often are, particularly in Italy, hence those unfortunate 'mistakes' the Prince had been so exercised about. Firms in this line of business usually by-pass the police, and during the last few years have built up a discreet but most effective task force of so-called kidnap experts – ex SAS security experts, and Scotland Yard detectives – who have developed their own techniques for handling what they call a 'kidnap situation'. This has become part of the expensive package that the client pays for with his policy.

Unlike the police, these men have no scruples about bargaining directly with kidnappers as if it were any ordinary business deal. And unlike the victim's family, they are not likely to be blackmailed by emotion or stand for any nonsense. They know the going rate for ransom, work fast, and keep their word, so that the kidnappers always know that in dealing with them there is no danger of betrayal to the law.

The ethics of it all are somewhat dubious (hence the strict secrecy with which these agents work) but it has certainly become effective. The insurers claim that out of sixty or so kidnap cases their agents have dealt with in the last three years, many victims have been freed unharmed in every case but one the exception being a rich industrialist in Spain shot in error by the police when his captors already had released him.

I explained all this as best I could to Avicenna after I spelled out the details of the policy. I had rung him the instant I received the telex, and he was in my office twenty minutes later. He was certainly not one to waste time collecting his pound of flesh, but when I had finished my explanations, and we had shaken hands on the deal, he treated me like some long-lost, slightly dim-witted but doted-on member of his family. It was an inspired performance, his best to date; as he clasped my hands in his, I could swear that there were tears in those enormous ox-like eyes of his.

'Signor Moreton, it is my turn to thank you – from the

bottom of my heart. Now I can breathe once more, knowing that His Highness is protected by the best insurance in the world and so is safe whatever happens. I think you have no idea the worry I have been through lately for I feel responsible for him. I tell you the truth now, Signor Moreton, that I love the Prince. No, do not laugh. I do not mean like that. But he has done more for me than you could ever understand.'

'You have been very fortunate.'

'Ah, I can see you don't believe me. Once more you are saying to yourself that Avicenna, he is not sincere, but you misjudge him. You have been hearing things about me, haven't you, Signor Moreton?'

I shook my head wearily.

'Signor Moreton, in my life I have done things of which an Englishman like you would not approve. At times I have had to survive. But to my friends I have always been sincere, and I have kept my sense of honour in my heart. His Highness is the same, and so we respect each other. Now it is the same for you. When first I saw you in this office you remember that I offered you my friendship?'

I nodded.

'It is now stronger in my heart than ever. If there is anything you want of me you have but to ask.'

He paused to light a cigarette – one of his own for once – and looked across at me with a strangely rueful look.

'I am sorry if at times it has seemed as if I tried to force you over this question of insurance, but it was necessary, and you can now see that all has turned out for the best. The Prince is safe and you are reunited with your wife. This makes me very happy, for I am a sentimental man. Again you smile. Oh, I have had much experience of women – common harlots, women of the rich, even some movie stars in the United States. It would be easy for me to become cynical about the female gender, but I do not. I love all women, and I comprehend your feelings for your wife. She is so young and very beautiful.

Having spoken with her I am certain that she loves you.'

'I know she does, and now perhaps —'

'Now, not to shrug aside my good advice, for again I am speaking from the heart. Perhaps as an Italian I understand these things better than an Englishman like you. Have no bitterness or jealousy for what is past. She has been stupid but women are stupid creatures and it is up to older men like us to guide them and be firm with them as with a child. This lover that she had.'

'Petinacci?'

'So, you know his name. Not to concern yourself about him. Just forget him. He will disappear.'

'They won't catch him?'

'Who, that stupid policeman that you know? No chance at all. He is very smart, this man.'

He shook his head and lit another cigarette, inhaling deeply now before continuing.

'Signor Moreton, listen carefully, for nothing must go wrong now through stupidity. Your Colonello Rossi will have to know your wife is returned to you, so you will tell him. Say she returned to you last night and nothing more. Nothing about the Prince or this Petinacci or the journey that we made last night. She came back to you and that is all you know.'

'The Colonel's bound to question her.'

'That is for her to deal with, and she will. She knows what to say. Just do exactly as I tell you, and I promise everything will turn out right.'

And then he started laughing, leaning back, his arms out-spread, his gold teeth gleaming.

'Signor Moreton, cheer yourself up! You worry too much. The world is fine and we are both alive. Enjoy it! I, Dr Avicenna, will teach you to enjoy it. It was a lucky day for you when we met, a lucky day for both of us. From now on, you are my brother. What do you say to that? We shake the hand upon it, yes?'

I felt sheepish as I proffered him my hand, but he grasped it and shook it energetically.

'Tell me now what you wish. In what way can I be of assistance to my brother? Is there some kindness I can do for you?'

He seemed so eager for my welfare that my reply seemed positively churlish.

'We will soon be going back to England. My time in Rome is over and with my wife back —'

'You return to England? That is an enormous pity. There are such things we might have done. You go there soon?'

'In the autumn.'

'Ah! Possibly it is wise. I have never been in England, but His Highness comes there often. Perhaps I come with him, and will visit you in London, and you can show me your Big Ben and the Palazzo Buckingham. Or do you wish to see the back of me?'

'But of course not. As soon as I know my new address I'll let you have it.'

'No kidding? You remember me?'

'Always.'

'That is good. Friendship is the most important thing we have. Now in return, what can I do for you to show I am sincere?'

'I think you've done enough.'

He shook his head and frowned, and then his face lit up.

'I know. Fool that I am, I should have thought of it before. His Highness owns a *castello* in the hills in Umbria, between Arezzo and the sea. You know that countryside? No? It is most beautiful I think in all of Italy. Tranquillity with nature all around you. And the castle, it is lovely. Like something in a fairy-tale. Beauty and the beast – a magic castle.'

'Really?'

'The Prince goes there for the shooting in the autumn, but that is all. He has a couple who guard it for him, and you will love them. You will take your wife there, Signor Moreton, for a little holiday. You both deserve it, and I will arrange it.'

'Now Avicenna, in the circumstances I hardly think —'

'Signor Moreton, you are my brother now and so will do exactly as I say. His Highness will insist. It is the most romantic place on earth. Springtime, no tourists, the gardens coming into bloom.'

He gave his appalling grin and winked.

'I tell you that I understand about women. Take it from me that everything will turn out shipshape if you do exactly as Dr Avicenna tells you to.'

PART TWO

13

That summer was the happiest I spent in Italy, one of those rare golden periods of life when everything goes right – perfect weather, personal well-being, tranquillity at home. The Prince's insurance now went through without a hitch and everyone seemed happy, my wife and I included; for the Prince was particularly insistent that we spent ten days as his guests at his castle, and it turned out to be a second honeymoon. The castle was quite lovely, miles from anywhere, in the hills above a tiny village called Mariella and we lived *en prince*, waited on hand and foot by old Anna, the Santo Stefano's housekeeper and her husband Adriano. They seemed delighted to have a couple to look after. Anna's food was the best I ever ate in Italy and Diana had never seemed more tenderly in tune with all my moods. (As I had guessed she was delighted with the bracelet I had bought her, and from the night I gave it her, I resolved to treat her brief affair with Petinacci as if it had never happened.)

I never did discover quite how she squared the Colonel, but she did: we heard no more from him after one fairly lengthy interview, and the disaster virus, which had plagued me in the spring, seemed to have spent itself at last. I felt like somebody reprieved.

I even felt grateful now to Avicenna: thanks to him my wife was safely back with me, order was restored, and even my business had picked up, for as he prophesied, the Prince's kidnap policy had led to others and the doldrums of the beginning of the financial year finally receded.

Hugo of course was cock-a-hoop; apart from my success the Witherspoon connection had brought in even richer pickings than he had hoped for, and there is nothing like financial gain for spreading private happiness. We had suddenly become the closest friends.

'Are you absolutely sure about returning, dear old boy?' he asked me several times. 'Not that I don't want you back, but you're reaping the rewards of all the hard work you put in at the beginning. Pity to be leaving just as it's really coming good.'

There was some sense in what he said – for once – and I was tempted. But something told me it was wise to get back to England before anything went wrong again, and Diana was also anxious to return. She had been thrilled when I suggested it, and at times had seemed to talk of little else. The arrangements had gone inexorably ahead. It had been settled that, come late September, I would take over all the European business in the London office – quite a plum job this with a satisfactory salary to match – and in the meantime my successor, Deryck Robinson, had arrived in Rome to learn the ropes, a genial young man, pink-faced, bespectacled, apparently enthusiastic. I rather wondered what effect Italy would have on him.

Then, in the middle of July, came the best news of all – my wife's pregnancy. Apart from her miscarriage, we had had several false alarms before, but this time her gynaecologist, Dr Panzini, confirmed that everything would be all right. We were both overjoyed.

Only one setback marred these golden months – my teeth. They were a constant problem, and Professor Cocchi told me the only answer now was dentures. I resisted, but a second opinion confirmed his diagnosis, and the grisly business started. I won't go into details, but it was painful and unpleasant, and although Diana was wonderfully supportive, I had no wish to inflict myself overmuch on her during this unattractive process. Besides, she was suffering morning sickness now; the heat of Rome was troubling her, so I encouraged her to accept the Ripleys' offer of a few weeks at Toriella. She

116

got on well with Gladys Ripley and would have the sea, the sand, and that oil-rich little family to jolly her along.

'But I hate leaving you, Elly dear,' she said. 'I feel you need me.'

'That's not the point. We've someone else to think of now. Besides, I can drive up at weekends.'

This was hardly something I looked forward to, but there were certain sacrifices I was prepared to make in the cause of our new-found happiness: they even included barbecues and Bunjy Ripley's conversation. So it was settled, and as July ended, I found myself alone with Robinson for company. Professor Cocchi got to work.

Since returning from the castle, I had heard nothing from the Prince – although of course I wrote to thank him – nor from Avicenna. The invitation to play golf at the Borghese Club never did arrive – to my infinite relief. Summer in Rome is far too hot for strenuous exercise, and now I wanted to forget them both. I felt they knew too much about my private life for comfort, while in my heart of hearts I also knew that there was something fishy in that whole uncomfortable deal with the Prince. It had to lead to trouble in the end and I knew I should never have agreed to it, however strong the pressures at the time. But all that was over now, thank God, and it is strange how rapidly the human mind can tuck away the traumas of its recent past. In April I had been contemplating suicide: now I had difficulty recalling what the fuss had been about.

This was why my meeting with Colombo came as such a painful shock. Since the Prince's policy went through, we had not spoken to each other: this in itself was not unusual, months often passed without our meeting, so when I spotted him eating in the restaurant where I was lunching with Robinson, I naturally waved, then went across to have a word with him. He was with a female I had never seen before, a busty big mouthed redhead, in a magenta-coloured dress, very much his type. She smiled at me, but he was stony-faced. There was not handshake, no introduction to his girlfriend, and I was firmly 'Signor Moreton' now.

Yes, he was in perfect health. And busy? But of course. He puffed his cigarette and an embarrassed silence followed as I stood there wondering how I had managed to offend him.

'So, Signor Moreton, your wife returned safely after all. I hope that you are happy.'

'Very, thank you.'

'And your rich crooked friend got the insurance he was after. Did he pay you well, or was there some very special favour that he did you?'

'What the hell d'you mean?'

'You know quite well what I mean. Normally you'd not have touched that bastard with a bargepole.'

'What I do in my business is my own affair, and you'd better mind your manners.'

'Manners, Signor Moreton! You lecture me on manners? I am an ignorant Italian, and you an English gentleman, but at least I am not a bloody crook.'

I suppose I would have hit him then, but for the merciful presence of the redhead, who clearly understanding not one word of English and who smiled happily throughout this muttered conversation.

'I'll deal with you later,' I replied. 'I'm certainly not starting a scene here now,' and turned to go.

'Don't bother, Signor Moreton. You'll not be seeing me again. But you're going to regret not following my advice. That Sicilian pimp you've grown so fond of has strange friends, and he and your precious Prince are cooking up a nice little racket now from all I hear. It could cost you quite a lot of money and I rather hope it does.'

I was angry. I was also hurt. Colombo was one of the very few Italians whose opinion I respected, and I had never dreamt he would react like this. Above all, I was worried. What could he be getting at?

Since settling the final details of the Prince's policy, I had dismissed it from my mind, but now all sorts of frightful possibilities haunted me, for I knew quite well that if the Prince and Avicenna tried to pull some smart insurance fraud with so much money involved, my head would inevitably roll.

I had been the expert on the spot; I had personally sanctioned the kidnap policy; ten million dollars might well be at stake, and it was on record that Colombo had warned strongly against the Prince and Avicenna from the start. Should anything go wrong, and word of Colombo's first report leak out, my career was over. Worse still could follow – an official Lloyds investigation, a reprimand for negligence, even a case for criminal complicity. Lloyds is not gentle with its erring brethren.

I had some sleepless nights in which I contructed imaginative scenarios of personal disaster, but then, as so often happens, my concern abated. Just as an oyster finally surrounds an irritant inside its shell with an insulating covering of pearl, so my mind grew a skin of boredom round the subject and I started to forget it. Then it was Friday. Work and worry over for another week and by six o'clock I was driving through the rush-hour traffic out of Rome. With the sun declining apricot and gold along the motorway, I headed for Toriella.

Diana seemed glad to see me. Pregnancy enhanced her with a sort of dreamy dignity, and she was in a private world of procreation, skin terra-cotta with the sun, hair bleached to palest gold, eyes very clear and unconcerned – *pezzi di cielo* (pieces of sky) as the Ripleys' Italian maid admiringly described them.

The Ripley house was by the beach, a long, low, battered bungalow, shaded with pines and raucous until night with children. Bunjy was welcoming and slightly drunk, Gladys as

119

fleshy as a bean-pole, flustered and bullied by her swarming offspring. I felt curiously at home among them all.

But something had happened to my wife. It must have been the pregnancy, but she had changed from the cosseted child-wife she had always been for me. How much she had changed I realised when I watched her walking up the beach with one of the Ripley children. She was barefoot, striding now with shoulders back and head held high, and suddenly I saw her as her namesake, Diana, Goddess of the chase. I had never remotely thought of her like this before, and this new vision of her troubled me. Again I had the feeling that I did not know her and all the unanswered questions of her affair with Petinacci were painfully revived. I did my best to keep them to myself, but she knew me well enough to realise that there was something on my mind.

That evening we all had a picnic supper on the dunes, then sat on, drinking whisky out of paper cups under a summer moon.

'Happy?' whispered Diana when the Ripleys had departed to see their progeny to bed.

'Of course.' I stroked her arm. It was covered with short very fine fair hairs and she was wearing the bracelet I had given her.

'What is it, Elly darling? What's the matter?'

How could I possibly explain? I shrugged my shoulders and said nothing. She took my hand and held it tightly.

'I know. You're brooding over what happened in the spring. I promised you it's over.'

'Is it? Are you sure? At times I'm haunted by it, and I'll never understand.'

I said this bleakly, and there was an edge to her voice as she replied.

'We agreed we wouldn't talk about it. Ever.'

'But I have to. There are things I have to know.'

'Elly, believe me. *I can't* tell you – and anyhow it's unimportant now. Please! Can't we leave it there?'

120

I shook my head miserably.

'Elly, listen. I love you, truly. And I'm carrying your child. For your sake it's best that certain things remain unsaid. He's dangerous, you know. It wasn't till I went with him that I realised just how dangerous. He'd stop at nothing – nor would those around him if they so much as thought we'd broken our agreement with them. You've simply got to trust me, and when we're back in England I'll tell you everything.'

I breathed deeply but still felt incapable of a reply.

'Promise, Elly. Promise!'

But before I could, there was a flash. We jumped.

'Got you both! Nice one!' someone shouted.

It was Bunjy Ripley. With his usual talent for being at the wrong place at the wrong moment, he was standing with his brand new Polaroid which he had been trying out all afternoon. For him it was one more joke in a joke-packed holiday.

'Wanted to see how this flash affair is working. Let's have a look. It could be interesting.'

He waited for the picture to develop, then offered it to us.

'A souvenir. Two love-birds caught together on a beach!'

He was laughing, but Diana snatched it from him before I could even see it. Later I asked to look at it, but she said it was so unflattering that she had thrown it away.

July turned into August and Diana stayed on with the Ripleys by the sea. She was obviously happy there and the routine rather suited me. Rome emptied, August ended, and September started with a heatwave. Summer that year was like some roaring animal that would not die.

I had hoped to be able to spend most of the beginning of September with Diana, but inevitable last-minute hitches kept on cropping up before I handed over to the stalwart Robinson: then came the rigmarole of organising the removal back to

London.

It should have been simple, but Italians are wary of simplicity, and overnight half the bureaucrats in Rome became personally involved in our departure, each requiring my presence in some dusty office – permissions to be asked for this, taxes to be paid for that, certificates, stamps, affidavits, lawyers' letters. Had I been purchasing the Vatican, there could hardly have been such finely spun negotiations.

Luckily it turned out to be an uneventful time – no more spaghetti factories in flames or unforeseen disasters at the airports. Rome remained as stifling and empty as some stately urban no-man's-land, but there were signs of autumn on its way. The leaves, which I had seen that springtime greening the plane trees by the river, now lay scorched and scuffed along the pavements. Restaurants reopened and the football season started. So did the violence. Three masked terrorists (back from their holidays as well?) shot a journalist in the back in Monte Mario; only the beginning, the terrorists proclaimed, of a triumphant wave of proletarian justice against imperialists. The journalist died and there were rumours in the press of a 'harsh black autumn'. I booked the removal men for 19 September, grateful we would soon be out of it.

I missed my wife, but saw her most weekends and kept reminding her that we would be totally united back in England where our new life would finally begin. Hugo had come up trumps for once, and even offered us his flat in Tite Street till we were settled. I told Diana the good news on the telephone.

'Elly, how wonderful! Perhaps we misjudged him after all. We'll be so happy. You're a saint, darling, taking care of all the beastly details of the move, while I lie here in the sun with my belly growing. I feel guilty, honestly I do. I should be back in Rome, looking after you.'

'Just look after your dear self. That's all that matters.'

'You're so good to me. I love you darling.'

'And I love you.'

122

I always felt much better after this sort of conversation with my wife.

And yet, perversely, now that everything was set for our departure, with a golden future once we landed at Heathrow, I began enjoying Rome again. I was not prepared for this, and felt it an obscure betrayal of everything I longed for, but the city would not go away: it was like a mistress, long discarded, who kept tempting me to visit her again, and I began to yield.

Sometimes I walked alone in early mornings through the piney stillness of the Borghese Gardens followed by lonely dogs. Come the evenings and I searched out restaurants I had never visited before and enjoyed unexpected food. There were even temptations of the flesh, but I resisted them: to quiet them I climbed the Capitol by moonlight and drove bumping over the ancient Roman flagstones of the Appia Antica as dawn was breaking. It was a dangerous, somewhat silly game to play, fueling nostalgia for the future, but I knew that by leaving Rome in two weeks' time, I would be burying some small insistent portion of myself for good.

Riciulous, of course! For I also knew that the sooner we were out of Italy the better now – particularly when I noticed a small paragraph in the European edition of the *New York Herald Tribune*, recording that His Highness the Prince of Santo Stefano was back in Rome, 'Bronzed, fit and eager to return to his various business interests' after a well-deserved vacation in the Caribbean. I wondered whether Dr Avicenna had gone with him. I also wondered what those business interests were.

Just a few more days and I would no longer have to worry. Friday 19 duly came, and everything appeared to be in order for our leaving – documents to 're-export' our furniture, tickets booked to London, first-class British Airways, for the following Monday afternoon, and I had arranged to drive up to Toriella for one final long-weekend, once I had supervised the packing of the furniture in the apartment, and seen it safely on its way.

That morning the removal men arrived at ten o'clock and I was there to see them in. (It was Luisa's *giorno di riposo*). There were six of them, monkey-like, muscular small men in spotless vests and gym-shoes forming what they called *una squadra*, which was paid an outright fee – I forget how much – for the horrendous task of moving every object we possessed down six separate flights of stairs and into the removal van below. The sooner this was done, the sooner they were paid, and I have never witnessed men outside the circus-ring working together with such skill and dedication: this made them seem more like scene-shifters than removal men, and as they went scurrying up and down the stairs, balancing away our bedding, wardrobes, carpets, lampshades, pictures off the walls, it was as if the whole background to our familiar life in Rome was vanishing before my eyes – as indeed it was. Soon there was nothing left save a pile of shameful rubbish in the kitchen, an old sofa I was offering Luisa, a water-softener, and three battered kitchen chairs.

I signed yet one more document – attesting to my total satis-faction with the *squadra's* work – tipped the leader twenty thousand lire, and surveyed the emptiness around me. The midday canon on the Janiculum boomed behind me, and the sun was shining on the empty walls: just two hours to remove all evidence of three years' living in a modern city.

I remembered then that moving house ranks seventh – after events like bankruptcy, bereavement and divorce – in the actuarial tables on the incidence of heart-attack among the middle-aged: but I felt quite well, slightly at sea but in the best of spirits, as I washed in the naked bathroom, changed my shirt, then left the apartment for one final lunch with Robinson. This time it was my treat, of course, a suitable fare-well gesture to my esteemed successor. The previous evening I had dispensed handshakes and champagne to the remainder of the office staff, but Robinson was due a little more than this, so

I had booked a table at Pancrazio's, a restaurant in the ruins of what was once the theatre of Pompey where Caesar was stabbed by Brutus – my own completely inappropriate little joke.

We ate well and drank better still. Robinson's small nose was peeling and the Barolo made him sentimental – also somewhat pompous.

'Henry, I must record my thanks for everything you've done. You've left a splendid legacy behind you.'

'Only done my job. I'm sure you'll do it better.'

'Impossible! It's only in the last few weeks I've come to realise how much the office – and the boys back home in London – owe to Henry Moreton. I'll do my best to follow his example.'

It was the drink, of course. His face was very pink and shinier than usual. We shook hands more warmly than we would have done in London; then I paid the bill, patted him on the shoulder, man to man, and left him to it.

One final task remained before I drove off to Toriella – collecting my false teeth from Professor Cocchi. For weeks I had been making do with the temporary set he had improvised for me while making the adjustments to that masterpiece of dentistry he had promised. There had been unseen problems, (probably no more than that his technicians too had been on holiday) and the Professore was, as he kept telling me, a perfectionist. But everything was promised for this weekend. My appointment was for 3.30 in the Via Stradivarius.

I had a hired car, a big grey Fiat, for the weekend, but with the Friday traffic already building up now in the centre of the city, I decided it was best to take a taxi. I found one easily enough, but the driver in his wisdom took a short cut through the narrow streets behind the Corso and we inevitably landed in a traffic jam. We inched forward – car fumes, tension, everybody hooting – but I was able to relax. There was no hurry, and I glanced out at the street. A newspaper kiosk was beside us, and the billboard for the evening papers caught my eye.

'*Principe Rapito!*'

This was in the customary big bold type. 'Prince raped?' I said, translating the headline. 'Odd!'

The taxi and the traffic had jammed tight by now, and my brain began to function in its usual jerky fashion.

Principe Rapito. Surely *rapito* is the past participle of the verb, *rapire* – to snatch or grab? 'Prince grabbed?'

It took a moment longer for my mind to make the necessary connections: seconds later I was in the street, the paper in my hand, and reading the headline story with mounting horror and alarm.

At 11.30 this morning, and in his family palace in the centre of historic Rome, the Prince of Santo Stefano was kidnapped by three armed men. During the shoot-out that ensued, the Prince's bodyguard, Elio Zanobetti, was severely injured . . .

The traffic had begun to move, and as the cars behind my taxi started hooting, my driver waved at me to get back in.

. . . the kidnappers made their getaway with the Prince in a stolen van. The Carabinieri were on the scene within minutes of the alarm, but so far there is no news of the criminals or their victims.

The hooting rose to a crescendo.

'Madman, are you standing there all day?' shouted my driver. I fumbled for money in my pocket, found a ten thousand lire note, shoved it in his hand, and walked away.

126

14

So this was what Avicenna and the Prince had been planning
all along! It was so obvious I could have wept – and almost did
until I saw a passer-by eyeing me strangely: I began to walk I
knew not where, clutching the paper like a talisman against
some further ghastly revelation. There was no question in my
mind that this so-called 'kidnap' was a put-up job, that 'nice
little racket' which Colombo had warned me of. I had feared
something of the sort. No wonder Avicenna had been so
desperate that the Prince's kidnap policy went through; and
now came the payoff, just as I was leaving Rome and thinking
the disaster syndrome was behind me.

'Idiot!' I raged. 'Weak, stupid idiot! Giving in to a man like
Avicenna. What are you going to do?'

Not a bad question for I needed to do something – fast, if
only to protect myself. The Prince's insurance had been my
primary responsibility – however anxious Hugo may have
been to push it through – and no one at Lloyds would pay out
ten million dollars on a kidnap without a very full investigation of the case. Searching questions were certain to be asked
when the kidnap squad arrived, and if the truth emerged, I was
ruined. So was my marriage. So was everything I stood for –
reputation, livelihood, and all those golden dreams of lifelong
happiness which had been just within my grasp.

All I could do at first was continue walking and I found
myself in the piazza opposite the Pantheon – loathesome
edifice with its great pockmarked pediment and absolute indif-
ference to my fate. It had been there two thousand years, one of
the greatest buildings in the world, but suddenly I saw it as a
sort of landmark of human misery, standing impervious like
Rome itself, to the millions upon millions who had slaved and

died here. Rome was a trap and a perpetual prison: I should never have come here, and had become inexorably caught.

But was I really? I found a bar, bought myself a drink, and tried applying my intelligence – instead of my disturbed emotions – to events. Panic and self-pity started to subside.

First things first, I told myself as I sipped my medicinal Campari soda. It would certainly appear suspicious to the investigators for the kidnap to have come so swiftly after the insurance was arranged – but suspicions were one thing, proof another, and why should anybody have to learn the truth? Who could betray me? Avicenna and the Prince, of course, but they wouldn't. Diana? Inconceivable – and anyhow she didn't know exactly what had happened. Nor did strange little Colonello Rossi. It went against the grain, particularly for me, to let a pair of blatant crooks calmly pocket a small fortune, but as long as I kept my head and bluffed things out, I still had a sporting chance of staying in the clear.

I finished my drink and as I started nibbling the slice of lemon left in the bottom of the glass – a habit which Diana detested – I noticed sunlight gleaming on the gold and brown façade of the church across the street: it was like a sudden glimmering of hope. My safest plan, I saw now, was to act as if nothing untoward had happened, forget about collecting my false teeth, and get to the haven of Toriella just as soon as possible, where nobody could reach me. I was about to leave when I remembered my former friend, Colombo.

He was the one weak link, my greatest source of danger, for he and he alone would realise the truth and would inevitably talk when approached, as he would be, by the Carabinieri or by the kidnap squad once they arrived in Rome. I had to see him first. So I telephoned his office. After our last encounter, this took a little courage and he was none too welcoming.

'Well?'

I mumbled about being desperate to see him, adding that something terrible had happened, that he was the only man in

Rome who could help me – and so on.

'When do you wish to see me?'

'Straight away.'

'My God! Very well then, but give me a quarter of an hour. You know my address. Of, and Signor Moreton.'

'Yes?'

'It had better be important!'

As far as I could remember, Colombo lived and worked in a tiny flat just off the Via dei Coronari in the heart of historic Rome. It wasn't far. I guessed I could walk there in fifteen minutes flat, so I set out on foot. By now I was coming to my senses and Rome was almost bearable again. I had to cross the Piazza Navona, one of my favourite spots in the whole city, with Bernini's great carefree fountain of the Four Rivers; water cascading over rocks, a lion, a horse and a sea-monster, together with a palm tree and an obelisk and four gigantic figures – all this in the middle of what was once a stadium for chariot races built by the Emperor Domitian.

Orange peel was floating in its waters, small boys careered around it on their bicycles, an old man held a cluster of balloons like coloured pebbles flung into the summer sky. Colombo's flat was just above a smart antique shop round the corner: typical of a good Communist like him to settle in the most expensive part of tourist Rome!

He had a 'Speakerphone' like mine, and when I pressed the bell and listened for him to answer, I merely heard an uninviting grunt. I gave my name. The door buzzed open and I climbed the stairs.

It was a curious apartment, the sort of place one might have expected of an antiquarian of eccentric tastes rather than a left-wing private eye – a fine Bokhara carpet on the floor, walls lined with books and eighteenth-century paintings, a blue and silver antique chandelier, far too large for the crowded little room, and a litter of possessions everywhere; the latest recording apparatus, a set of samurai armour by the balcony, weapons, dirty dishes, and a stuffed gibbon in a large glass case. An antique wooden staircase led to a small gallery above, and I heard him shouting.

'Hold on! Just let me fix this bloody leg of mine!'

An upstairs door was opened, and Colombo came limping down the stairs, scowling and resplendent in a crimson dressing gown.

'So, you are desperate, so desperate you interrupt a man's siesta!'

'You've heard the news?'

'What news? I've been in bed. They've killed the Pope?'

'Of course not.'

'Pity.'

'Be serious. I'm appealing to you for help. The Prince – they've kidnapped him. Or rather, they've staged a kidnap.'

'Prince? What bloody Prince? And who's staged what? Why don't you just sit down and calmly tell me what has happened?'

'So what am I supposed to do?'

I had given him the evening paper, and Colombo, after rummaging around to find his spectacles, had read the whole report in silence.

'I did my best to warn you but you wouldn't listen. I still don't understand why on earth you recommended the insurance in the first place.'

'I had no choice.'

'No choice? A man like you no choice? They must have bribed you. Now you pay the price. I said you'd have to.'

I kept my temper as I knew I must and patiently explained exactly what had happened.

'Ah! So it wasn't money but your wife. I told you that

Avicenna was a blackmailer and a pimp. What else did you expect from him? You should have let me deal with him you know.'

'Easy to be wise after the event, but nobody could find her and this seemed my only chance of getting her back. I love her.'

'Love, wives – the trouble that they cause! How many times I hear it in my business. Maybe one is better off without them.'

He paused and at last I was honoured with the beginning of a smile.

'So, Signor Moreton, because of this blackmail, you believe the disappearance of the Prince has to be a put-up job to get the ransom money out of Lloyds?'

'It must be. We know that Avicenna is a crook and the Prince is broke, and you warned me they were up to something in the summer. Why else all that effort to make me recommend that hefty policy with a kidnap clause?'

He lit a cigarette and exhaled a thoughtful cloud of smoke through the tendrils of the chandelier.

'The kidnap could be genuine. Unlikely, but it could.'

'You can't believe that after what you've told me.'

He shrugged impatiently, then glanced at his watch.

'It's time for the latest news on television. Let's see what they have to say about it all.'

Colombo's television was remote-controlled: with his love of gadgets he seemed proud of this, and spent some time pressing the buttons on the hand control before the colour screen beside the gibbon flickered to life. After a birth-control commercial – a naked couple on a beach, the new explicit Italy – the late afternoon news began with a full report on the kidnap of the Prince; shots of the Palazzo Santo Stefano, police vans in the courtyard, a brief old newsreel sequence of the Prince himself, then views of the *salone* and the marble staircase at the top of which reposed a shape I recognised at once, the unattractive corpse of Hitler, 'faithful guard-dog of the

131

Prince, who was gunned down by the criminals as he struggled to protect his master', as the reporter put it.

He was a lugubrious young man with an overlarge moustache who proceeded to recount how three masked men in a stolen plumber's van had entered the *palazzo* at 11.30, tied up the *portiere*, and taken the Prince at gunpoint from his first floor study. This was when poor old Hitler had made the supreme sacrifice, 'and the Prince's bodyguard, the ex-wrestler Elio "Pulcione" Zanobetti was also wounded. He is in the hospital of San Pancrazio, but as yet there is no news of his condition.'

'Poor Flea,' I said. 'Let's hope they paid him in advance.'

'One unusual feature of the kidnap is that the Prince, despite extensive family possessions, is not himself a wealthy man. He is known to have heavy gambling debts, and it is hard to see how the captors hope to gain the sort of ransom that will make their coup worth while. For this reason, informed sources are already speculating that politics may have been involved. The Prince made no secret of his support for the neo-fascist MSI party. There is also a possibility of Mafia involvement, as the Santo Stefanos have had possessions in Sicily for generations. I spoke to the officer in charge of the investigation, Colonel of Carabinieri, Ottorino Rossi —'

It was another nasty shock to see that dapper bearded figure preening himself in the courtyard for the television cameras. Not that he gave much away – but I would have rather had anyone but him.

No – too early yet to speculate on the affiliations of the kidnappers, but there were certain leads (surprise, surprise!) that he was following. No, he had received no communication yet from the kidnappers. Of course he had certain theories of his own about the case which had a number of unusual features. (He could say that again!)

'And could the Colonello tell the viewers what those features are?'

Not on your life! I recognised the knowing little smile as the Colonel shook his head.

'You must excuse me. There is work to do.'

'Of course Colonello! Thank you Colonello! And next for our viewers . . .'

Colombo extinguished the remainder of the programme.

'*Tesoro*,' wailed a female voice from the room upstairs. 'What are you doing down there watching television? It is not polite.'

'Business, dear heart! I will not take long. Be patient.'

He turned to me, and spoke briskly now.

'So, you have asked for my advice. I will give it, trusting that this time you will treat it more seriously than you did the last time you consulted me. As far as you're concerned the whole affair seems relatively simple.'

'That's the last word I'd have used.'

He waved his hand impatiently.

'I've been hearing rumours for some time that something of the sort was in the offing and these two friends of yours have clearly been preparing this for months. It was probably set up even before you finalised the Prince's kidnap policy, and today they made a good professional job of it. Your Avicenna knows exactly what he's up to and has left nothing to chance – the careful stageing of the kidnap and the escape, a safe hideout for the Prince and a neat way to collect the ransom. It's all been careful staging of the kidnap and the escape, a safe hideout for

'No chance of the Colonel and the Carabinieri catching them?'

'That little bearded monkey? Not a hope in hell, unless the Prince makes some daft mistake, which isn't likely. Take my word for it, even while we're sitting here, the Prince and your friend Avicenna are already safely tucked away in some cosy farmhouse in the mountains with everything they want to let them sit the whole thing out – food in the deep freeze, all the drink they want, television and a good-looking houseboy for

133

the Prince. Don't worry – they're all right. The media will soon be hearing from them. Then after a period of tedious negotiation, your friends in Lloyds will end up having to meet the cost of the ransom – or a fairly hefty part of it. After a little while the Prince's return will be faked as neatly as his kidnap was this morning. End of story and you will have been extremely fortunate.'

'Fortunate?'

'But of course: provided you are sensible. Had this been done by amateurs it could so easily have been bungled and that would have led to questions which could have been awkward for you, expecially here. Why did you arrange kidnap cover for an Italian citizen knowing it to be illegal under Italian law? Why had you dealt with men you knew quite well were crooked? But these so-called kidnappers will be discreet. You, dear friend, must be the same.'

'And if the Colonel questions me?'

'Say absolutely nothing. He's bound to have found out about the insurance on the Prince, but as long as you don't admit it, you're in the clear. As far as you know it was all arranged through London, and that was the Prince's business. What goes on abroad has nothing to do with you.'

'Avicenna?'

'Sure, you knew him slightly, but so what? You'd no idea that he was crooked. He was no more than a business acquaintance like hundreds more you know. But just one word of warning. I know this Colonello Rossi. He may not be the brightest man in Rome, but he takes his work seriously and he will certainly continue watching you. Remember this and assume that from now on your telephone will certainly be tapped in case the kidnappers attempt to contact you. If anybody tries to get in touch, keep right away. You understand?'

'*Caro mio*, how much longer?' wailed the voice. It sounded more impatient now.

'Coming, my beloved. Coming.'

Colombo rose, and to my considerable relief offered me his hand. I thanked him for his help.

'One final thing,' I said.

'Yes?'

'The insurers will be sending someone out to take charge of the case. He'll certainly want to see you. You will be tactful?'

'You think I might betray you? Signor Conte, you have been a fool but don't make things worse by trying to insult me.'

15

I felt considerably safer after my visit to Colombo and realised that it was probably unwise to rush off to Toriella, however much I longed to be there now. It could be misinterpreted. Much better act responsibly and be around to meet the members of the kidnap squad, if and when they arrived from London. So I telephoned my wife – from a callbox: after Colombo's warning I wasn't taking chances with tapped telephones – and got her straight away.

'Elly darling, we've just heard the news. Is it *your* Prince?'

'Afraid it is.'

'How ghastly! Poor Prince! And poor Elly! But you're not involved?'

'Could be, my love. Depends what happens. I'd better stay at least until tomorrow just in case I'm needed. Sorry it rather dishes our weekend.'

'Oh Elly, *what* a pity. The Ripleys have arranged a farewell dinner for us for tomorrow night. Promise to try and get up for that at least.'

'I'll try – but don't count on it.'

'Poor darling. And for this to happen after all the work you've been having with the move. You need a rest. Why don't I come back to Rome to be with you?'

'Better if you stay put. The flat's completely stripped.'

'How will you manage?'

'I'll be fine. It'll soon be over and we'll be back in London. I don't want to have to worry about you as well as all this other nonsense until we go.'

'Elly, you're the most wonderful thoughtful husband in the world. What would I do without you?'

'Stay good and think of me.'

'And you too, Elly dear.'

I thought I had better check with Robinson to see if he had any news so rang the office after speaking to my wife. He sounded as if he was coping rather well.

'Quite a facer, but not to worry. Don't see why it should have to concern you at all. I spoke to London half an hour ago. Strict instructions to stay absolutely clear and of course not a whisper to the press. Two of London's top troubleshooters arriving on the evening plane, and they'll take charge of all negotiations for the payment of the ransom. Glad to be getting back to London?'

'What do you think? Only sorry that this had to happen just as you took over.'

'Don't mention it, Henry. Good experience. And if there's anything I can do, you've got my number over the weekend. Just holler.'

Good old Robinson.

It was too late to go to Professor Cocchi now, but I couldn't bear the thought of returning yet to my stripped apartment, and suddenly I felt myself a homeless exile in a hostile city – simply because of Avicenna and the Prince. Why couldn't they at least have waited until we were back in London?

I felt angry now and having nowhere else to go began an aimless trek towards the river: it was nearly six o'clock, the loneliest time of day in any city, with the sun declining, people returning to their homes, and an hour or so to kill before the restaurants opened.

After that long dry summer, the Tiber was a muddy trickle, with a jolting wall of evening traffic grinding along its banks. I had the pavement to myself and as I tried escaping from the traffic fumes, I turned off down a backstreet and recognised hat I was near the Palazzo Santo Stefano. On an impulse I thought I would go to see it for myself.

The piazza was as I remembered it, with the same election posters peeling on the wall, but the palazzo gates were open wide, a television van was parked beside them, and several dozen onlookers were still gawping past the guard at the courtyard, waiting for something to occur. I joined them, sensing the strange attraction of a recent crime – although I knew it really hadn't been a crime at all.

I could see floodlights glaring through the first-floor windows – presumably police photographers and forensic experts still at work doing their best to reconstruct the morning's happenings. I wondered what they'd found. The whole great building seemed even more oppressive than I remembered and although I knew the kidnap had been staged, I found it hard to avoid the feeling that some act of violence and evil really had occurred. Several police cars – khaki painted Alfas with official markings – were parked inside the courtyard, and as I watched I saw uniformed *Carabinieri* entering one of them. It started up, and as it swung out through the gateway, passing a few feet from where I stood, I recognised the bearded figure by the driver – Colonel Rossi.

He was staring straight ahead, but as the car went by, his head turned and his eyes met mine. This happened very quickly and there was no sign of recognition or surprise on his face, but I am sure he registered my presence. It was a most unpleasant feeling, and as I turned away I was certain I had made a grave mistake by being there.

Pondering this, I ate a solitary wretched meal in a *trattoria* near the flat, incurring almost certain indigestion by worrying about the Colonel as I shovelled down *spaghetti carbonara* and a veal chop. Then I returned to what had been my home.

Total desolation greeted (or rather didn't greet) me – floor-

boards instead of carpets, naked light bulbs hanging from th
ceilings, and the ghostly imprint of where pictures had onc
been on the walls. Suddenly it seemed a foretaste of the los
that threatened me, for with the windows now uncurtained t
the night, even my privacy had gone and the echo of my foot
steps sounded like someone walking in an institution. Slee
was my only refuge – and I knew I would need to be feelin
fresh to deal with the London 'troubleshooters' next morning.

I found some blankets in Luisa's room (mercifully she wa
away for the night) swallowed two Mogadon and bunked dow
on the rump-sprung sofa.

I must have been asleep an hour or so when I was woken b
the buzzer to the downstairs entrance to the flat. It was
ghastly moment. The colonel was very much on my mind and
I was certain he must have come to question me. (I had reac
somewhere that the police arrest suspects in the middle of the
night when their resistance is at its lowest.) So I stayed where
was, trying to ignore the buzzer, and hoping he would go away.

No such luck. The 'Speakerphone' continued buzzing lik
an angry bee and in the end I answered.

'Moreton?' asked a very English voice. I was saved from the
Colonel for a while at least.

'Who wants him?'

'You don't know me, but my name is Platt. Hugo Goodwin
gave me your address. My colleague and I have just swanned in
from London and would be grateful for a little chat.'

'Can't it wait until tomorrow? I'm in bed?'

'Oh, I'm sorry – but it is a little urgent, and we won't take
long.'

'Very well.'

I pressed the switch to open the front door, and by the time I
had pulled my trousers on the lift was coming to a stop. I
opened the door and Platt and Mills entered the apartment and
my life.

One says Platt and Mills, like Jekyll and Hyde or Marks and

pencer, as if they were a sort of double-act, which in fact they were. Platt was tall and pale and thin, an Old Etonian with all the ruthless langour of the species: Mills was a silent, hairy man encased in tweed. In fact I did know them both by name as two of the 'troubleshooters' Robinson had mentioned. I simply hadn't realised they moved so fast.

Platt took command at once, offering an absent-minded handshake, and strolling over to the window.

'My, *what* a view! Fan-tastic! The Janiculum, isn't it? And a balcony as well. Lucky you!'

Mills ignored the view but sniffed suspiciously at the empty room, like an old animal nosing around an unfamiliar cage.

'What's happened to the furniture? Bailing out already?'

'Didn't Mr Goodwin tell you we were on the point of leaving Rome for London. It was arranged several months ago. My wife and I are booked on the London plane for Monday afternoon.'

'Oh!' said Mills, and sniffed again.

'But how too sad to be leaving Rome!' said Platt. 'Must simply break your heart.'

'My wife is expecting a child in the new year and we want it born in England.'

'But of course. Congratulations!' murmured Platt, and Mills sniffed again. I felt it incumbent on me to make at least a token show of hospitality.

'As you can see, the facilities are just a little limited. The removal men were here this morning. But there is a little gin.'

'Perfect,' said Platt, but Mills refused, reminding me that in England even ex-policemen never drink on duty.

I fetched the gin and offered them the kitchen chairs. Platt grinned and made himself at home, draping his lengthy body round the chair, and lit a Turkish cigarette. Mills remained standing as if still deciding where to hit me first. Neither seemed inclined to speak, so I took the initiative.

'Well, gentlemen, I realise why you are here, and you must

141

tell me how I can be of assistance. I'll help in any way I can of course.'

'Most kind!' said Platt. 'Since you mention it, there are just a few small points that we would like elucidated, and it would save a lot of time if everything was clear from the beginning. Between us, Mills and I do pride ourselves on having, well, a certain expertise in handling this sort of thing.'

His hand fluttered vaguely, and a smoke ring hovered by the window like a small unwanted halo.

'Right!' said Mills, and shifted on his feet. 'From now on we're in charge, and you leave everything to us. I mean everything. Police, press, family. You know nothing and say nothing. Clear?'

'Perfectly. But it so happens that I already know the Colonel from the Carabinieri in charge of the investigation. He'll probably want to see me.'

'You mean he already knows the Prince was insured against kidnap? That's all we want!' said Mills.

'Probably. He's not a fool, and the authorities are generally quite well informed about such things, as you should know. It's not illegal for Italian citizens to insure abroad to cover ransom payments.'

'Quite!' said Platt, still looking through the window at the view. 'But it is illegal in Italy to deal with kidnappers direct – at least in theory. Everything depends on the discretion of the officers involved. What sort of character is this Colonel friend of yours?'

'Zealous and I'd say that he is honest. Could be tricky.'

'Ah! All the more reason then to remember what Mills has said and be extremely cagey if he questions you. We'll have to have a little chat with him ourselves first thing tomorrow morning just to see which way the land lies. I'm sure we'll manage. But as far as you're concerned, everything about the kidnap policy was arranged directly between the Prince and his insurers back in London. Stick to that, and everything

142

should be all right.'

I nodded, stifling a yawn. There was something reassuring about this androgynous young man, but the Mogadon was working.

'Thanks for the advice. It's good to have you here.'

Platt smiled and lit another cigarette.

'Our pleasure. Frankly we don't see any great complications over this one, do we Mills?'

Mills shook his head.

'There's that other business that you wanted to ask him about.'

'Oh yes, I was forgetting. Tell me now, you met the Prince. What did you make of him?'

'Hard to tell. I only met him twice.'

'You see, old boy, what rather puzzles us is why you agreed to this whole deal in the first place. Awful lot of money, wasn't it?'

'Is that any of your business?'

'Could be.'

I realised that Mills was watching me and swallowed hard. Platt was now facing me as well.

'As you should know a sum like that is not all that unusual for the very rich. And a lot of influence was brought to bear from London.'

'So I gather. But he really wasn't very rich at all. According to this evening's papers, he was deep in debt.'

'That's what they're saying now. But it wasn't my information at the time, and I have my doubts about the debts. In Italy, everyone has debts, and the family are still the fifth or the sixth richest landowners in the country. When I saw the Prince, he was living on quite a scale.'

'Ah!' said Platt. 'I see. You must forgive us asking, but we have rather nasty minds. Must come from the work we do. Ah well, we must be going, and will be in touch tomorrow. We're staying at the Raffaelo. Always stay there when we come to

Rome. Friendlier than the Grand and a very nice barman. Know it?'

I certainly did. It was very chic – and just round the corner from Colombo's flat.

'You do yourselves very well.'

'If we don't, old boy, who will?'

He stood up, and nodded to his colleague.

'If this runs to form, we should be getting some sort of demand from the kidnappers tomorrow. If it comes to you, do let us know at once.'

'Before the Colonel?'

'Yes, it would be wise. And now good night to you and thanks for that refreshing drink. Sweet dreams!'

16

I had a rough night on Luisa's sofa, but awoke surprisingly refreshed although it took a moment to remember where all my furniture had gone. Beyond the river I could see the hazy early morning sunlight which generally preceeds a baking Roman day, and thought enviously of my wife beside the sea. With luck I might still be able to drive up to join her for what was left of the weekend: everything depended now on what had happened on the kidnap front during the night.

What I feared, of course, were the sort of revelations that could involve me or Diana and keep us off the Monday plane to London, so I soon padded off downstairs, unshaven and distinctly anxious, to collect the morning papers.

I need not have worried. There were no further shocks, thank God, and had the slimy Avicenna written the press reports in person, they could hardly have appeared more powerfully authentic. Just for once the capitalist *Messagero* and the Communist *Única* were in broad agreement, both carrying the story of the kidnap under banner headlines, flanked with pictures of the recumbant Flea being dragged to an ambulance by a pair of hard-pressed stretcher-bearers. Each paper also had the identical library photograph of the Prince – most flatteringly out-of-date – and the *Messagero* had scored with a picture of the kidnap van, found abandoned near the port of Ostia.

Reading the reports, I realised just how professionally Avicenna and the Prince must have planned it all. Nothing had been left to chance and it must have taken real nerve to have put a bullet in the Flea when he was in the plot – as he must have been. Traces of blood had even been left in the van for the police to find.

Apparently three men, all masked and armed, had driven up to the palazzo in the van that morning. Shortly before there had been a call to the *portiere* about a leaking water tank, and when he let them in he was swiftly bound and gagged. He hadn't seen their faces, but he heard Hitler's barking followed by several shots. A few minutes later he had heard the van driving off.

Not much to go on, and so far there had been no further news or ransom demand from the kidnappers. But scarcity of information never has inhibited your true Italian journalist, for whom imaginative speculation is the very stuff of life. Nobody mentioned Avicenna, nor the fact that the Prince was covered by insurance. There was precious little either about Colonel Rossi, who was still keeping very mum about those 'certain leads' of his. But there was column upon wordy column on the Prince and the Santo Stefanos and the potential motives and identities of his kidnappers. These ranged from the Red Brigades to a hit squad from the Israeli Secret Service. The one possibility which no one mooted was that the kidnap had been faked.

This was encouraging and with any luck now everything would quietly calm down and the rest of the affair tick on to its conclusion like an expensive watch. Once the ransom demand arrived, Platt and Mills could get to work, the money would be paid, and I would be safely back in London. Colombo's advice was proving sound again, and I even felt a sneaking sympathy for Avicenna and the Prince. They had beaten the system – which has always something to be said for it – and I could picture them comfortably sitting the whole thing out in their hideaway with their deep freeze and their television, waiting for the money to roll in. Platt and Mills would also be sitting, in still greater comfort, in the Raffaelo, and there was really nothing now to stop me doing the same with my wife beside the sea.

I tried ringing Platt and Mills at the hotel to tell them I was going to Toriella. They were out but I left a message for them, together with the Ripleys' number.

Luisa had reappeared by now. (The cool Roedean lady who sold us the apartment was handling the re-sale and was taking it for granted that Luisa had to be included in the deal.) Luisa seemed quite unaffected by the prospect: presumably she had witnessed many other families coming and going in her time and would see many more; but she was fairly amiable this morning, made me coffee and inquired after the Signora. She was well, I told her, and I was just about to drive up to be with her at the sea, before we left for London Monday afternoon.

'And when does the baby come?'

'In the New Year.'

'In the New Year, eh?' She started laughing. Luisa rarely laughed at anything, and I put her good humour down to the month's wages I had paid her in advance, and the fact that she would soon be rid of us for good.

I rang Diana to tell her I was on my way, spent some minutes packing my few possessions – shaving kit, shirts, lightweight suit – and reached the Ripley bungalow in time for lunch.

White wine, great plates of fried potatoes, and chicken cooked by Bunjy Ripley over a charcoal grill beneath the pine trees. I resolved never to be rude about his barbecue again. Platt, Mills, the Prince and Avicenna all seemed a continent away.

The air smelt of sea, of pine, of roasting chicken and a sort of gentle sanity seemed to be reestablished in my life. Diana sat beside me in a yellow dress, and from time to time she took my hand and held it tenderly. She seemed to have established herself among the Ripleys as a beautiful pregnant elder daughter I happened to have fallen in love with from afar. Most of her

147

conversation was with the Ripley children. They had a lot of jokes they shared in common, and inevitably I found myself engrossed in grown-up conversation with the inescapable Bunjy, who seemed pleased to find a fellow-spirit of his own age-group with whom he could discuss the things that really mattered – like the involvement of Leone, the ex-President of Italy in the Lockheed scandal, the flight of Italian capital abroad and the impending devaluation of the lira.

'How long d'you give it all?' he asked.

'Give what?' I was trying to pay attention to my wife who was giggling over something with the youngest Ripley daughter, a toothless, leggy, eight-year-old called Jo.

'The present set-up. Italy. How long before it all collapses and the Reds take over?'

'It'll survive. It always has. The Church and the family have always been the backbone of the state. A few more crooked politicians here or there don't make much difference.'

'But do you really *have* to go?' Jo was saying.

'You can come and stay with us in London,' whispered my wife.

'Promise you'll invite me.'

My wife nodded.

'You can't be serious,' said Bunjy, round face puckering at my stupidity. 'Didn't you read this morning's papers? The Communists have kidnapped the Prince of Santo Stefano from his own palace in the heart of Rome. How do you explain a thing like that?'

'Are you sure it was the Communists?'

'It has to be. Henry, you can't be so naïve. Know thine enemy. Red Brigade, Trotskyites, Red Army Faction – they're all the same, and we know where their money comes from. Have you read Lenin, Henry?'

His eyes bulged with extreme concern, but mine were on my wife who was hugging the gummy Jo and nodding.

'Promise *faithfully*!' implored the child.

148

'Lenin says it all,' continued Bunjy. 'It's there in black and white. Continuing revolution, the use of violence to undermine our capitalist order, followed by the irrevocable dictatorship of the proletariat. Read the bugger, Henry. You'll be in for a surprise.'

We finally escaped from Jo – and Bunjy's diatribe on Marxist-Leninism – and wandered hand in hand along the shore.

Far out a coaster spun a thread of lilac smoke from headland to indigo horizon. Yachts were wilting on the breathless summer sea. The sand burned my unshod instep.

'Darling, it's going to be all right?' she asked.

'What?'

'This dreadful business with the Prince? We won't be affected?'

'How could it possibly affect us?'

'Hugo insured him, didn't he? Against kidnap. You arranged it. Does this mean that you're involved?'

'How do you know what your brother and I get up to?'

'You'd be surprised what I know, Elly darling. But you're absolutely sure we won't have to put off our departure?'

'Absolutely.'

I could tell she was still anxious and upset and did my best to calm her.

'Does it mean so very much to you to get back to London?'

She nodded. Suddenly she seemed on the edge of tears.

'Elly, I'm scared. I just couldn't bear anything to go wrong between us now. Promise to be careful. And promise it will be all right.'

I kissed her slowly on the lips and did as I was told.

'Henry! Hen-ry! Telephone!'

Gladys was standing on the beach below the bungalow,

waving her arms and shouting. Couldn't one be free for just a moment from the curse of other people?

'Coming!'

My wife looked worried, but obedient as ever to the summons of the world outside, I went stumbling across the sand and was breathless by the time I reached the bungalow.

'Sorry,' said Gladys, 'but it sounded urgent.'

It was a bad line, and at first I failed to recognise the voice.

'Who?'

'Platt. Platt here. You remember . . .'

The telephone made him sound like Donald Duck.

'Yes. Yes, of course. How are you. Everything all right?'

'Top hole, though poor old Mills does feel the heat. Listen, there have been developments since we saw you, and I thought I ought to let you know. Just seen your friend, the Colonel. Not exactly cosy, is he?'

'I did warn you.'

'Absolutely! As you said, he obviously knows all about the insurance and about you as well, old boy. You don't seem exactly popular, but that's neither here nor there. What will interest you is that he's been interviewing the guard in hospital. The ex-wrestler johnny, the one they call the Flea. He's broken down.'

'He's what?'

The line was getting worse, and Donald Duck was being strangled now.

'Give me your number and I'll ring you back.'

I did, and this time heard him clearly.

'As I was saying the blighter's broken down. Confessed. The whole thing was a put-up job. Faked from start to finish. He was in it with the Prince and several others. The Colonel has offered the Flea immunity and got a full confession in return. Full marks to the Carabinieri, eh? Never knew they had it in them.'

'Pretty good! And what about the Prince and his accomplices? Any news of them?'

'He wouldn't say, though he's clearly got a good idea of where they are. Not that it really matters very much to us. A criminal matter now for the Italian courts. We're in the clear – fraud renders the policy null and void of course. I'd say that we've been pretty lucky.'

'How?'

'With our wrestler friend. But for him the Prince would have screwed our people for ten million bucks. To be honest with you, Moreton, I did have my doubts about the whole shebang from the beginning, but in a case like this it's usually impossible to prove anything although you guess it's crooked. I've had several cases in my time when we've paid out on a kidnap that we've guessed was rigged. Without proof, there's nothing we can do, but I tell you it goes against the grain.'

'I bet it does. What happens now?'

'Not a great deal, as far as we're concerned. I'll be making a full report of course for our people back in London. Could take a day or two and I expect they'll want to see you to inquire why the policy was recommended in the first place. Better have your story ready. Just warning you, old boy.'

He laughed but even on the telephone his humour sounded hollow.

'You won't be emphasising that aspect of the affair?'

'Good heavens no. But I'll have to mention it. To be honest though – and don't misunderstand me – I think it's probably as well you're leaving when you are. In your shoes I don't think I'd trust that Colonel friend of yours, and I've an idea he knows a good deal more than he let on to me. Once he catches up with the Prince I think he'll go to town on the affair. It could, just could, be slightly tricky for you.'

'Thanks for the warning, but as I told you, we're off on Monday and we can't leave earlier than that.'

'That's all right then, isn't it old boy? Nothing to worry about. Just keep your fingers crossed that nothing else crops up, before you leave.'

17

Perhaps he meant well, but there was something about the way that Platt conveyed the news that made me fear the worst. I didn't trust him and so much was going wrong that the Disaster Syndrome had clearly started up again. Who would have thought the faithful Flea, of all unlikely people, would turn out to be the one to ruin the whole affair? And what would happen now? Would the Prince be caught? And Avicenna? Would I be dragged in too when the whole case came to trial?

Probably. According to the Moreton Theory of Disaster, this sort of multiple effect invariably continues on from bad to worse until the full catastrophe is reached. I should have known better than to pin my hopes on the ability of an idiot like Avicenna to pull off a complicated fraud like this.

The strange thing was that suddenly I hardly cared. If the Disaster Syndrome was at work, there was nothing I could do about it now; and if the worthy Platt was all prepared to knife me once I was back in London (as I imagined that he was), I would do my best to deal with that when the time came. Sufficient unto the day is the Disaster thereof – and for a while at least I had Diana and these few precious hours of grace beside the sea. In my experience disaster victims are rarely quite so lucky.

'Everything all right?' my wife asked anxiously when I returned from the telephone.

'But of course. It was that chap I told you about from London. Lloyds have just saved themselves ten million dollars. The Prince's kidnap was a fake.'

Her eyes were wide with wonder as she stared at me.

'But Elly, how extremely wicked! You mean to say the

Prince would do a thing like that?'

I kissed her on her smooth brown forehead.

'Darling, some people will do anything for money.'

The news was on the evening television. I was relieved to see that there was still no mention of Avicenna, but there was several minutes on the Prince, who was now revealed to one and all in darkest hue – as spendthrift, drunkard, addict of low life and shady friends, and much besides. (Italian press and television have none of the ladylike inhibitions of our British laws of contempt: anyone accused of almost anything is assumed guilty, especially if finally proved innocent.) And next morning the Sunday papers really went to town on the wretched fellow.

It was front-page news, of course. The left-wing press predictably banged on about the whole affair as an example of the morals and corruption in high places, with the Flea as a hero of the working classes: while the right-wing journals did their best to treat it as a slightly far-fetched joke and the Prince as a sort of licensed scallywag from whom such behaviour was rather to be expected. The insurance policy was mentioned – although none of the papers had the correct sum involved. Colonel Rossi and his boys received honourable if condescending mention, but there was still no hint of Avicenna nor, thank God, of me. As for the Prince's whereabouts, most of the papers seemed to think he was probably abroad. The Flea had evidently not known whatever hideout had been planned, and for the time at least, the Prince and his accomplices remained uncaptured. Long might they so continue!

I felt somewhat safer after reading these reports, and hope – as is its nature when the sun is shining – rapidly revived. Perhaps this was one occasion when the Moreton Theory wouldn't work. Perhaps, who knew, the catastrophe I feared would float away, and Avicenna and the Prince would be quietly forgotten. It began to seem as if they might. There were no calls from Platt and Mills, no visits (as I still half feared) from Colonel Rossi, and that Sunday passed in a haze of Ripleys and regret at our imminent departure.

Come Monday morning and after an early breakfast on our own beneath a big pink oleander in the scruffy garden, the whole family was out in force to speed us on our way – Gladys in faded jeans and breastless sweat shirt, Bunjy with his Bermuda shorts, the children sunburned and barefooted, clustering round the car. They fought to hug my wife and I noticed Jo in tears. Bunjy and I exchanged a manly handshake and I kissed Gladys swiftly on the cheek, thanking her for all she'd done.

'Oh, but it's been lovely having her with us. She's one of the family. You will write quickly, promise.'

Promise I did. More kisses followed from the children. Then we were in the car, and making our final turn out onto the familiar main road by the sea.

'Come back next year!' the Ripleys shouted. Something told me that we wouldn't, and the last I saw of them was a fluttering of brown arms in the driving mirror.

'I'll miss them,' said Diana.

'D'you think you're really going to be happy back in England after all?'

'Of course I will. And so will you.'

Suddenly it seemed as if we both had doubts as the still deserted early-morning beach sped past the window like some fast-receding glimpse of earthly paradise, with sun umbrellas furled and on parade along the sand, and the headland golden in the freshly risen sun. The day was like a fortune waiting to be spent and had she said the word I would have stopped the car and shared it with her there and then. But the future was set like a machine and we were part of it. There was no stopping

now, and by the time we reached the *autostrada* it was as i
England had almost started.

But it hadn't quite. We reached the great hot rush of Rome just
before eleven – bells ringing, pigeons and fountains in the air,
the streets already choked with hooting traffic – and I had our
schedule for these last few hours carefully worked out. My wife
had an appointment with Alfredo, her faithful hairdresser,
near the Via Veneto, and while she was with him I would take
the car, make my farewells to Colombo, the drive on to the Via
Stradivarius for my teeth. I had a table booked at our favourite
restaurant, just round the corner from Alfredo, for 1.15. Diana
would meet me there, and after a last ritual blow-out as a fare-
well to our time in Rome, we would drive on to Fiumicino
with our luggage, dump the car with Avis, and be safely on the
London plane by five o'clock. Allowing for the London one
hour time-lag, we would be back at Heathrow at 5.45. So
much for our plans.

'Trust you to organise us to the final minute,' Diana said, as
I left her to Alfredo's tender mercies.

'And don't be late. I can't bear sitting at a table on my own.'

'Would I let you? Not in Rome.'

She laughed and as I watched her determined little sil-
houette swing through Alfredo's stainless-steel portals, I felt
how fortunate I was to possess such a very pretty woman for a
wife. This suddenly seemed far more important than all the
other silly dramas in my life. It was some time since I had seen
her wearing high-heeled shoes and I had quite forgotten what
excellent legs she had and how stylishly she walked.

Colombo was expecting me and seemed genuinely touched
that I had come to say goodbye. He even had a present for me –
a bottle of *Averna*, a bitter-sweet Sicilian liqueur he knew I

156

iked. The flat was in its usual state of chaos and he was in shirt-sleeves, typing at his desk with the stuffed gibbon by his side for company.

I thanked him sincerely for all he had done for me and felt embarrassed not to have brought him something in return. This could be rectified of course once I was back in London.)

'So I was wrong, Signor Conte? That wide-boy of a Prince and his Sicilian weren't as clever as I thought. But I can't see them causing you any trouble once you are back in England. Be warned though about that other couple, Platt and Mills. They could be difficult I think. They called on me, you know.'

'I didn't. What did they ask you?'

'All sorts of damn-fool questions – chiefly about the inquiries I originally made on your behalf over the Prince. Don't look so worried, Signor Conte. I told them nothing, and I made out I was pretty stupid, which wasn't difficult. They seemed to have a pretty low opinion of Italians. All the same, they know about Avicenna.'

'How? You didn't say I knew him?'

'Credit me with just a little sense. But they seemed well-informed, and claim he tried a similar racket a year or so ago in Canada – and got away with it. Only half a million dollars, still . . .'

'Did they ask anything else about me?'

'No, Signor Conte, have no fear. They seem to think you're even stupider than me, although the ugly one —'

'Mills?'

'Yes, that's right. Signor Mills did ask me if I thought they'd bribed you to recommend the policy. I became very angry then on your behalf. He soon shut up. You've seen the morning papers? Nothing new, but it's a good story and the press won't let it drop.

He had the *Messagero* and the *Corriere*, both of which ran front-page stories on the 'Kidnap that Wasn't' and the 'Trick that Failed', together with fresh pictures of the Flea in hospital

157

and a full account of his confession. It was being treated as something of a *cause célèbre*.

'And will they catch them?'

'Bound to in the end. Even your Colonel Rossi could hardly lose them after a lead like this. The Prince, of course is ruined. Not that he ever did have that much reputation, but no one will ever trust him now and he could well end up in prison. Avicenna may be smarter. My guess is he'll ditch his noble master and take off. We'll not be seeing him again.'

He glanced discreetly at his watch; he had work to do and it was time to go.

'So, Signor Conte, after all your problems, everything has worked out for the best, and you and the Signora will live happily for ever after. A family, a well-paid job in London. The bourgeoisie will finally have got you, and I won't be there to keep an eye on you.'

'You'll visit us, of course.'

'In London? Oh, I doubt it. All that fog and I'm told the food is dreadful. But we will meet again, for you'll be back. No Englishman ever escapes from Italy for long, once he has lived in Rome.'

Professor Cocchi seemed relieved to see me (for a lot of money was invested in my mouth).

'Made it at last, sport? Starting to wonder if you ever would. Must have been overworking by the sound of it.'

He beamed through his silver spectacles and patted me on the shoulder.

'Come on in.'

Smiling photographs of famous patients from the past greeted me in his homely surgery – Alcide de Gasperi (first post-war premier of Italy and founder of the Christian Democrats), Benedetto Croce (Neapolitan historian and philosopher), and wily old Pope John himself. I felt honoured to be included in their number, and the fitting session might have been a presentation specially to mark my leaving Italy. With a decided flourish, the Professor showed me a neat perspex box and lifted the lid. The new landscape of my mouth grinned at me like a *memento mori*.

'There you go then – absolutely latest thing in stain-free porcelain, each tooth separately gold-mounted. No kidding, but you won't find craftsmanship like this in London or New York. Please . . .'

He motioned me towards the chair, expertly removed my temporary teeth, and then with a decided flourish, installed first the top and then the bottom set.

'Attaboy!' he muttered, as if I had just performed something rather special, and handed me the mirror. I smiled at myself and bared my lips. Immaculate dentation gleamed from each corner of my mouth.

'Magnificent!' I said – a tricky word to use until my mouth adjusted to its new contours – but it pleased him and he gave an awkward little bow, like a conjuror at the finish of his show.

'*My* pleasure, Signor Moreton! It has been an honour working with you.'

I rose and shook his hand, congratulations being very much the order of the day, and it was with some slight embarrassment that I mumbled something about the bill.

'Ah, my secretary sees to that, if you would kindly have a word with her. No hat, no coat? No, of course not. So have a good day then, Signor Moreton.'

For the last time, Professor Cocchi patted my shoulder and withdrew, and as I wrote out the cheque for the sum (enormous) that his secretary tactfully suggested, I felt it was possibly as well that my days with dentists were behind me. I said goodbye and the professor's big mahogany front door closed silently behind me like a chapter in my life.

As I crossed the deserted landing with its dark tiled floor, its plastic imitation rubber plant, its nineteenth-century painting of the crucifixion, all my attention was upon my brand new teeth; as my tongue began to get acquainted with these new neighbours it would have to live with, I pressed the button for the lift. This was an old-fashioned affair of the type one often finds in Rome, with a big cast-iron wheel above that started whirring as the lift came grumbling up the full six storeys at my summons. The lift itself was a black iron cage with elaborate brass fittings and a latticed door which rattled in the silence of that deserted block of flats.

It came to rest, and as I went to step inside, I smelt something familiar – hair-oil, aftershave? I was still worrying with my teeth and there was no light in the lift, so I was actually inside before I realised that somebody was there already. The door closed automatically behind me.

'Ah, Signor Moreton. I am extremely well and how are you? I've spent the whole damned morning trailing you, but now I've got you.'

Just for once, Avicenna wasn't laughing, and we started to descend.

'Please not to think of any funny business, Signor Moreton!'

Avicenna glanced down at a neat black automatic level with my pelvis. It is hard to express outrage with a mouthful of new teeth, but I did my best.

'Not too loud now, *please* dear Signor Moreton. It is not good that we attract attention as we leave this place. I apologise a million times for this inconvenience, but it is unavoidable, alas. Things have happened since I saw you last.'

The lift had shuddered to the street, and he pushed me out, the gun jabbing painfully in my back.

'Just walk straight ahead, now, Signor Moreton, and please to have no fear. If there is any monkey business, I will shoot at once. You understand?'

'Don't be ridiculous.'

160

'Me, I am not ridiculous at all. I am most serious indeed. Walk to that green van parked by the pavement and get in. The door is open.'

'You idiotic bastard!'

'Walk!'

I walked. The Via Stradivarius is in the old commercial part of Rome and the wide grey street was crammed with passers-by, but no one seemed to notice us. The only green van I could see was a grimy old Fiat Commercial with a woman holding aloft a glass and a bottle of champagne painted on the side. Beside this was the legend, *Polli, Vini, Liquori.*

'That's it – the Fiat. Get in and close the door. No tricks.'

I did my best to pay attention to the world outside, where I had dodged around the van and was in beside me. He had the gun beside him as we started up.

'Not quite the sort of vehicle you are accustomed to, Signor Moreton. Nor am I, but it avoids suspicion. Should anybody stop us, I am Alfredo Polli, wine merchant from Arezzo, and you are a friend from England who speaks no Italian.'

I said nothing, and as the ill-used van merged with the mid-day traffic felt a brief temptation to grab the wheel; but Avicenna clearly read my thoughts and shook his head. I noticed that he hadn't shaved.

'No, Signor Moreton, I would shoot you through the head and we might have an accident. It would be no answer to our problems.'

'I have no problems, Avicenna. Stop this bloody nonsense straight away!'

We narrowly missed colliding with a large green bus.

'No problems? Signor Moreton, you think you have no problems?'

He finally began to laugh.

'You have even more than me – and that's saying something I can tell you.'

*

161

As I have probably made clear by now, I am cautious, not to say cowardly by nature. Threats upset me and firearms appall me. Before force I instantly collapse. But now, although Avicenna's frightful driving seemed to be bringing death a shade too close for comfort, I really couldn't take him seriously. We bumped against the pavement near some traffic lights, and I felt more annoyed than scared.

'You'll attract attention, if you go on like this. Stop being such an idiot!'

This infuriated him – as I hoped it would.

'Attention? Whose attention?' he shouted back above the clatter of the engine.

'The police.'

'What do I care for the police? They can go fuck themselves your damned police. They won't help you now.'

I did my best to pay attention to the world outside, where I recognised the line of cypresses and the big Esso garage at the start of the one-way system past the Via Salaria which leads on to the Florence motorway. I also made a great attempt at self-control.

'Now listen, Avicenna. I've not the least idea what you think you're up to, but I am due to meet my wife for lunch at 1.15, and she'll worry if I don't turn up. Would you please mind stopping so I can telephone and leave a message for her at the restaurant?'

He shook his head as we nearly grazed another bus.

'Why not?'

'Just use your senses, Signor Moreton. How do I know you wouldn't try some trick?'

'Avicenna, you would have my word. Look, we were having lunch together and are booked on the evening plane to London. I've simply got to be there.'

'Then you miss your bloody plane and your wife has to wait for you. Big deal! You catch another in a day or two. Are always planes, and your wife can wait.'

It was then I lost my temper and began shouting – obsceni-
ties I had almost forgotten that I knew – and he began to bellow
back.

'You shut the mouth!'

He was waving the gun at me like an imbecile.

'Shut up or, by Jesus Christ, I shoot.'

'Shoot away then!'

Luckily for me, the entrance to the motorway was looming,
and he realised that this could not continue, for the motorway
police were usually parked in a patrol car by the toll-gate. We
slowed down, and he took a ticket from a bored attendant at
the barrier who was listening to his radio and barely looked at
us. Then we were on our way again, driving north, courtesy of
Fiat, at fifty miles an hour.

After our little outburst, both of us were silent, and from the
corner of my eye, I could see that he had put the gun away. I
was still furious, picturing Diana waiting patiently for me in
that crowded restaurant, and wondered what on earth she'd do.

The road was crowded, and the countryside was brown and
yellow from the scorching summer. We passed a tile factory,
several down at heel farms, and in the distance I could see a
train with green and silver coaches snaking its slow way back
to Rome. Then came a tunnel, followed by a viaduct across
one of the upper reaches of the Tiber. I was damned if I would
be the first to speak, but Avicenna started chuckling.

'I fail to see anything to laugh about.'

'Excuse me, Signor Moreton, but it is your expression on the
face. You are still trying to be angry with me, but it does not
become you. Listen now, this problem that we have. I will
explain.'

'Avicenna, for the last time, I have no problem – and I refuse
to become involved in yours. You tried to fake the Prince's
kidnap, and it didn't work. It has nothing conceivably to do
with me. I am due to leave your God-forsaken country in four
hours' time, and I am still prepared to give you my word to say

163

nothing of this to anyone. Just drop me at the next exit from the motorway, there's a good fellow. There's still time for me to telephone my wife, and I can find myself a taxi back to Rome.'

He seemed to ponder this, and for a moment I thought he might agree.

'Believe me, Signor Moreton, nothing would give me greater pleasure than to do as you suggest – but it is not possible. It is essential that I have you with us for a day or two. I will guarantee your safety, but we have what you English call I think a fuck-up. There is a slight misunderstanding. You alone can sort it out. Permit me calmly to explain without you jumping off the handle.'

I saw then that there was nothing further to be done. He was determined and the gun was in the glove-compartment on the dashboard.

'Why should I believe anything you tell me?'

'This time I tell the whole truth. On my mother's grave I swear.'

'Let's keep her out of it.'

'Before my mother I could never lie. Listen now, Signor Moreton. You are right of course. His Highness and I did plan the kidnap, as you know. All beautifully arranged. A perfect job and no one going to be hurt. It would have taken place in three weeks' time when we knew that you would be safely back in England. You see, even then I was concerned to cause you no undue embarrassment. And it would have been so easy, Signor Moreton, a dream of an affair, a straightforward business deal between us and the insurers. We would be reasonable, you understand, negotiate, discuss things, make a good deal for all concerned. Not to be greedy, for it is not my way. We suggest a figure for the ransom. They suggest another. Finally we meet. We drink together. In the end we strike a bargain, man to man. This is how these things are done. Is business, simply business. What was wrong with that?'

164

'You tell me.'

'Exactly. That is what I do. As I tell you, I have the plans completed, each tiny detail carefully arranged. That big dumb idiot, Pulcione, he is in it as you know, and he is paid and sworn to secrecy along with several others I can trust. So beautiful a set-up that I tell you I could weep.'

'But it went ahead.'

'Sure it went ahead.'

'So why are you complaining now when things go wrong?'

Avicenna groaned.

'Signor Moreton. We did not do it.'

I looked at him. For once his face was set and serious.

'Didn't do it? Don't be ridiculous. The kidnapping took place.'

'Sure, it took place. But I am telling you we did not do it.'

'For God's sake, Avicenna, if it took place and it wasn't you, who was it?'

He groaned again.

'Unfortunately that is something that I cannot tell you. All I can say is there were others who took over. Serious people, you understand. Somehow they hear what we are planning and jump the bloody gun. These people do it, Signor Moreton, but for real.'

It was my turn to laugh – which wasn't difficult when I looked at his woebegone expression.

'Avicenna, come now! First you arrange a whacking fraud which then misfires. You're totally discredited, the police are after you, and now you try telling me the kidnapping was genuine. There are limits.'

Avicenna shook his head.

'It is exactly as I thought. You don't believe me, and that is why I have to force you to accompany me now – to witness for yourself that what I say is true. You will meet these people who now hold the Prince. Then you will not laugh.'

'But who are these people, and why should they trust you as

165

an intermediary?'

'They are dangerous. That is all that I can tell you at this moment. But they know we are friends, and they understand my feelings for His Highness. Therefore they let me come to find you, knowing that all I am concerned with now is the Prince's safety.'

'And what do *they* want?'

'Why, what do you think, Signor Moreton? Payment of the full amount of money His Highness was insured for. They have all the details of the insurance policy, and they are asking for it to be honoured by your friends in London. So is His Highness. So am I. That, Signor Moreton, is why I come to you today.'

I was slightly staggered by the man's effrontery, I must admit, but remembered I was dealing with a one-time conman.

'Really, Avicenna now, a joke's a joke, but this is perfectly ridiculous. You can't honestly believe the insurers back in London are going to honour that policy after everything you and the Prince have done? You must know that fraud invalidates the policy.'

'But there was no fraud. We did nothing, absolutely nothing. Sure, I have admitted to you we intended faking the kidnap sometime in the future, but so what? We didn't do it. These others do it and you'll see that there's no fraud with them. They're serious. The insurance policy is still in force.'

'But it's preposterous!'

'What does it mean, preposterous?'

'Outrageous, unspeakable, a bloody racket.'

'Ah, I am relieved you understand at last. It is all these things. These people stop at nothing as you will realise when you meet them. They are one hundred per cent genuine kidnappers, and you can tell your friends in London who insured His Highness that they have to pay the ransom as they promised legally.'

'And if they won't.'

166

'His Highness will be killed for sure. And so will you. Is very simple.'

18

I tried to argue and point out the absurdity of his demands, but it was like attempting logic on a chimpanzee: all he would do was shake his head and mutter,

'But that is not the point, Signor. His Highness is legally insured for ten million dollars against the possibility of kidnap. Now he *has* been kidnapped, and his life is threatened. The insurers are obliged to pay. As I keep telling you, no problem.'

He belched and rubbed impatiently at his moustache as if that settled it.

'But there is a problem, an extremely tricky one. They're certain to refuse.'

'You convince them then, Signor Moreton. Is your job, and why I bring you with me now. You are an insurance man. You see the truth and that Dr Avicenna is not talking bullshit any more. This you inform to your friends in London and they have to pay.'

'And I tell you that they won't.'

He shook his head and belched again, a sad sound that made me remember the lunch that I was missing.

'I think it will be bad for you then, Signor Moreton. Very bad indeed. These people who hold the Prince could be hard with foreigners who do not meet their obligations.'

'Can't you stop making threats? I'm tired of them.'

He sighed.

'For the last time please understand it is not I who make the threats, Signor Moreton. I am your friend and will always be a man of honour. I want the best for everybody, everyone rich and happy. Now what is wrong with that?'

I was so exasperated with him now I simply shrugged my shoulders.

'Ah, Signor Moreton, I can read your mind. You are saying to yourself that I am not sincere and this is another of Dr Avicenna's tricks. But you insult me. I have my obligations to His Highness and it is his safety that concerns me now – that before everything. Why else should I be here? When this happened I could have buggered off, to France or even to America. Me, I am in the clear and I have good friends everywhere around the world. But how could I leave him, tell me that? Perhaps you do not understand what honour means to an Italian.'

'Perhaps not.'

'Listen, I work my balls off making these people who hold the Prince let me come to you today. I get no money out of this, not a damned percentage, nothing. Do you think I enjoy it? But my honour tells me that the safety of the Prince is what concerns me. Have you no sense of honour either, Signor Moreton? And those friends of yours in London?'

'I hardly think you're in any position to lecture me on honour, Avicenna.'

'Don't you, Signor Moreton? Then you must be taught what honour is.'

There seemed no point in any more discussion and apart from the racket of the van's old angry engine, the remainder of the journey passed in silence. I hardly knew if Avicenna was a crook or a buffoon but despite his gun it was hard to take him seriously and I was really more concerned about my wife than myself. What would she do when I failed to arrive at that expensive, crowded, very fashionable restaurant, since I had our money, airline tickets, passports in my pocket? Presumably she'd end up telephoning the British Embassy and someone would find my car still parked in the Via Stradivarius with all our luggage in the back: the Embassy would find her an hotel – this being the sort of thing that Embassies are for –

and I would duly be reported missing, presumed kidnapped, fled, or murdered.

Then what? Once my true fate was known, would Platt and Mills fly back to Rome to resume the case on my behalf? *Could* the insurers conceivably be persuaded to fork out something for the Prince? Might Hugo even try a separate deal for my release?

All but impossible after the hoo-hah that had followed the Prince's disappearance, and no one could believe a word from Avicenna. I didn't myself, and was convinced that my own capture was a forelorn attempt to blackmail the insurers into paying something after all. I was not going to be bullied and would rely on my discretion whether to cooperate or not. I still imagined I would have the choice.

I knew the road we were travelling quite well, having been ferried up and down it countless times by Oliviero to the money-mountains of Milan, Turin and Northern Italy where so much of our real business lay. The *autostrada* is the one true masterpiece of modern Italy, a marvel of tunnelled mountains, viaducted gorges, nearly a thousand miles of steel and concrete, placing the rocky length of Italy at the casual mercy of the motor car. Driven along it in the Rover, I had previously seen each journey on it like the rerun of a familiar travel movie, interspersed with the occasional stop for coffee or for petrol – always the same old views in the same inevitable sequence, Mount Soracte like the drunken profile of a Roman Hilltop Orvieto, always seen but never visited then Hannibal's Lake Trasimene, stagnant and uninviting on the right.

But now in this battered van, the landscape seemed quite different, and I realised how little of this countryside I really knew, and as the green and white sign-boards for each exit swung towards us, I was wondering which one would mark our destination. But the van went toiling on towards the North, the faster traffic flashing by, and the sun lowered in the sky.

We were in Umbria now, with its worn hillsides and its tree-less valleys, and just before reaching Tuscany we came off the motorway, onto the secondary road towards Arezzo, then turning left and up into the hills. Then suddenly I recognised the road. We had driven up it early that summer on our way to the Prince's castle. Where were we going? I tried asking Avicenna but he shook his head.

'All in good time. You'll see.'

It *was* the road to Mariello: I recognised the little village where we had stopped for petrol, the red-domed church beyond, then the lonely switch-back road that went meander-ing for miles through woodlands up into the deserted hills. A little further and the first of the Santo Stefano lands began.

'Avicenna, this is ridiculous. They can't be holding the Prince here on his own land.'

He grinned, his gold teeth glinting under his big moustache.

'Exactly. That is what I knew everyone would say – and why I chose the castle. It was my very own idea. I admit it to you, and I had it all so beautifully worked out, everything arranged there to the final detail. Tell me the one place nobody would think of looking for a kidnap victim – inside his own house, am I right?'

'You mean he's in the castle?'

'Right. These others learn our plans and take over all our work and everything that we prepare. Me, I weep with rage at what has happened, but there is nothing I can do. Signor Moreton, it is the perfect spot. You will recall that it is miles from anywhere, and no one from Mariello ever goes there if he can help it. The peasants still say the castle is a *casa maladetta*, a haunted house.'

'But what of the couple who looked after it? Anna and old Adriano?'

'Both are there. They make Anna do the cooking and Adriano is so stupid that he doesn't realise what's happened.'

'But somebody must guess what's going on. You can't hide a gang inside the castle without someone noticing.'

'Wrong again, Signor Moreton. I arrange everything. Even if you walk inside the castle now, you do not think that anybody's there. You'll see.'

We had almost arrived, and as the van heaved itself in bottom gear to the summit of the final hill, I had a brief glimpse through the trees of the castle far below – the huge containing walls built in the thirteenth century, the terrace where we had breakfasted each morning, the tower and the dusty little road that led up to the gatehouse. It was as still and dreamlike as a castle in a picture-book.

It was quickly lost to view as we started to descend the road down through the woods: the gravelled surface was worse than I remembered, potholed and rutted from the early summer rains, and the only sign of human contact with this woodland wilderness was an occasional small notice nailed to a tree proclaiming that this was private property and hunting was forbidden.

It was eerie to be driving again down the avenue of cypresses with not a soul about. Before there had been several dogs but they had disappeared. The hedges were untrimmed now, the gardens parched and overgrown with weeds. The great castle gates were locked and barred and the windows firmly shuttered. I imagined someone would see us coming and open up for us, but the gates stayed shut and we drove on past, taking the track beneath a line of mulberry trees that I remembered leading to the lower ramparts of the castle. I had explored them briefly with my wife and remembered a spot below them where old Adriano came to store his wine in the castle cellars. It was a dumping ground for rubbish too – broken pots, packing-cases, the carcase of a long-dead tractor – and beyond lay the entrance to the castle cellars, two big green doors that opened at our approach. We entered.

It was dim inside the cellars, and all I could see at first was a line of enormous barrels like obsolescent locomotives rusting away in some forgotten engine shed. Then suddenly the lights went on, the doors were shut behind us and Avicenna switched the spluttering engine off.

'There is no need for fear now, Signor Moreton. Everybody here knows who you are, but perhaps it is better that you do not try to talk with anyone.'

As he spoke I noticed someone standing at the far end of the cellar, a slim figure dressed entirely in black and wearing what looked like a balaclava helmet with a mask across the face. Standard gear for aspiring terrorists the whole world over, and Normally I would have laughed: theatricals and dressing-up have always struck me as inherently absurd, but there was something inhuman in this apparition. Not a word was spoken, but the figure turned, unlocked a low door in a corner of the cellar and led us down an unlit corridor that reeked of damp. He had a torch, and I made out another massive door that looked as if it must have stayed unopened since the middle ages. The masked one had a bunch of ancient iron keys, and while he struggled with the lock, I turned angrily to Avicenna.

'Now, where do you think you're taking me?'

'This is the tunnel from the cellars to the dungeons underneath the castle. They go on for miles, but had been sealed up for years. So you have no need to worry, Signor Moreton. You will not be disturbed. Nobody knows that they are there.'

The door finally creaked open, and the guide went on ahead of us, gym shoes padding on the stone flagged floor. We reached some descending steps, slippery with moisture: at the bottom two more creatures in black masks were waiting. One of them gripped my arm. I tried to shake him off, but the other grabbed me too. I began struggling.

'Avicenna! Where are you man? Tell them who I am.'

But Dr Avicenna had disappeared.

*

The cell was lit by a small electric bulb, screwed to the wall: it was windowless, stone roofed and floored, and smelled like a monkey-house that needed cleaning out. There was a bucket and a camp-bed and a deckchair, nothing else, and as I was bundled in and had the heavy door slammed shut behind me, I had a nasty memory of a time I was shown round a meat-room in a cold-store. I felt distinctly meat-like now myself, frozen and safely shoved away until required – whenever that might be.

I spent several minutes then reacting as I suppose most captives do in their first moments of captivity – shouting, rattling the door, kicking at the bed, and inspecting every corner of this loathesome little cell. The scope for such activity was limited, and after several minutes I took myself in hand, sat in the deckchair, and lit a cigarette.

It was no comfort and tasted filthy. At this point it was not the discomfort so much as the indignity of my predicament which was the hardest thing to bear – this, and the certainty that after all he'd said, Avicenna had totally betrayed me. I felt exploited, tricked, and made a fool of – reactions I had experienced so many times before in Italy that I should have grown accustomed to them now. All the same, it hurt.

I tried to tell myself that Avicenna was a common criminal who would blackmail, kidnap, even kill for money if it suited him. Thanks to the Flea, his plan to fake the Prince's kidnap had misfired, and he was obviously using me in a forlorn attempt to force the ransom money out of the insurers. That was what it boiled down to: that talk about another gang muscling in on him had to be another of his lies, like all that wordy nonsense about his honour and his fears for the Prince's safety.

Clearly they were all in this together – the Prince included; for how would another rival gang ever have risked letting

175

Avicenna drive to Rome in search of me?

It was then I realised that I was well and truly caught. It was all wonderfully Italian – charm and muddle masking the deceit, a lot of windy rhetoric and then a brutal outrage when one least expected it. For the truth was, I had trusted Avicenna in a funny way, and felt some sort of bond between us, just as I had with Italy. This was the result!

Rage and hysteria assailed me: I began pounding on the door and cursing him and shouting his name. I bruised my fist and scraped my knuckles, but it relieved my feelings and I kept it up for several minutes. Nothing happened, but when I listened I heard someone moving on the far side of the door. Then the light went out.

I can't be sure how long those bastards kept me in that pitch black little cell, for my watch stopped after several hours. No one came near me. All I could hear now was the slow drip-drip of water like a sullen metronome. Then I heard something scratching, probably a rat, but when I flicked on my lighter I saw nothing and the noise stopped instantly.

It seemed that I had been forgotten, and with the possibility of rats around me, I could not sleep. Luckily I no longer had the slightest sense of hunger: I imagine I was past it.

Then at last I did hear something – what sounded like a powerful car somewhere above me. The noise was faint. It stopped and I heard someone shouting. Shortly afterwards the light suddenly went on. A key turned in the lock, the cell door opened, and a figure stood there in the doorway, staring in at me. Even in the dim light of the cell, I recognised him straight away.

19

My secretary had been right: he was better looking than in the prison photograph the Colonel showed me, but nothing could disguise the scar above the mouth.

'Petinacci!'

He nodded but said nothing as he entered the cell, carefully clicking shut the door behind him. He was an elegant, slightly foppish creature in his tightly cut beige suit: he was very slim and with his collar length hair, expensive shirt and casually scuffed suede shoes, reminded me of some of the rich men's sons I used to suffer from at Lloyds. It was an uncomfortable moment for suddenly I understood Diana's infatuation, and my dormant jealousy revived. Whatever else he was, Petinacci was clearly no casual criminal as I had liked to think. He had a certain style: I could almost picture him at Henley or disbursing his father's money in a West End night club. But whatever was he doing here?

'Sorry about all this!'

He spoke English with a faint Italian undertone, and nodded distastefully as if to disassociate himself entirely from my squalid cell.

'Some things just can't be helped. I take it they're treating you all right. You've eaten?'

I shook my head: he sighed.

'Again my apologies. These people! I'll see to it at once, but first we have to talk.'

He brushed something from his sleeve and walked to the centre of the room. Seeing me watching him he smiled and shook his head. There was something about the smile I didn't like.

'Please, no trouble. It would not be sensible.'

It was a very casual threat, but I felt he could enforce it, and anyhow I was far too tired and dejected to attempt to fight. He offered me the deckchair.

'Why not sit down? I'll not take long, and you will be more comfortable. You're looking tired. Cigar?'

He produced a gold-edged alligator-skin cigar case from an inside pocket, and offered me a large Corona. Seeing me hesitate, he took it for himself, giving another of his plastic smiles.

'I pride myself on smoking very good cigars. It's not drugged if that's what worries you. I want you with your wits about you. Please!'

He offered me a fresh cigar which I accepted. (Why not? It *was* a good cigar.) Then he sat on the edge of the bed, crossed his legs carefully to preserve his trouser-crease, and tossed across a gold cigar-cutter.

'Matches or lighter? I take it Avicenna has explained the situation?'

'You mean this bloody racket you've cooked up between the two of you?'

He frowned, pretending to be puzzled.

'Cooked up? What d'you mean, cooked up?'

'What d'you think I mean? I didn't realise that you and your bloody gang of murderers were in it with him, but it figures. I knew he had some connection all along with your MPM but I didn't know that he was actually one of you. Your first attempt at kidnapping the Prince went wrong, and so you kidnap me.'

He drew thoughtfully on his cigar before replying.

'Murderers? A bloody gang of murderers? Now that is not polite. I and all members of the MPM are people of principle. We are against the state, against foreign imperialism, and this whole corrupt society we have to live in – everything you represent – so do not call us murderers, please. We are all combatants. We fight.'

'By seducing my wife and living like rich men's sons. Some

178

bloody combatants!'

I was pleased by the gesture of impatience this produced. I was annoying him.

'*My* wife! Do you think you own her? You talk about her like a poodle. Do you wonder she grew bored to death with you? And you bought her back like the good businessman you are. A sound commercial deal, wasn't it? Now you and your rich insurance friends in London have to pay the price for her in full – ten million dollars ransom as legally agreed for the Prince's life. And yours too, while we're on the subject. I'm perfectly prepared to throw you in as well.'

I realised I had to keep my temper now.

'You're very keen on money, Petinacci, for a man opposed to capitalism.'

He looked away.

'Money provides the sinews of the revolution,' he answered primly.

'It also pays for your cigars.'

'And why should I not smoke good cigars? Castro smokes them. So do I. Why should fat businessmen like you enjoy a monopoly on the best things in life?'

He turned to face me and his voice had risen. I had him on the raw, so I shrugged my shoulders and said nothing. For a moment he was silent, then he jumped up and began haranguing me.

'Your whole generation have done nothing except keep the proletariat in poverty, so you imagine that a revolutionary must be a half-starved outcast with his arse out of his trousers. Admit it! Bourgeois hypocrites like you feel safer if you are able to despise us and treat us all like dirt. It is an old, old trick, but I tell you that with me it does not work. I refuse to play the game according to your rules. I have suffered enough for my beliefs. In the past I have been beaten, tortured, starved, but now I say to hell with it. Suffering is stupid for its own sake. As every capitalist knows, money is power, and it's power I'm

179

after.'

He stood glowering at me, his big eyes protruding with emotion.

'Your cigar's gone out,' I said. This annoyed him too.

'Stop trying to insult me. You think I am playing some sort of Anglo-Saxon game, but you will learn how serious I am.'

'But I have already. Listen, young man, I'm very tired and would like to know what I'm supposed to do. I don't profess to understand what you and your friend Avicenna have been up to: whatever it was you must realise you've bungled it. No one in London in his right mind is going to believe now that the Prince was genuinely kidnapped, so forget any plans you have for getting the ransom money out of them.'

He was beginning to calm down and shook his head.

'You must understand that Avicenna doesn't come into this, except that through you he arranged the Prince's insurance policy with London, which was very useful of him. But it was I and my followers alone who captured Santo Stefano, and we intend to hold him here until the ransom's paid. We'll hold you as well. We're not in any hurry, so it's entirely up to you to get this whole thing settled if you want your freedom.'

'Any suggestions on the subject?'

'Your problem, Moreton. Yours and Avicenna's. You're the experts. But I will make arrangements for you to speak to those two men from London – what are they called now?'

'Platt and Mills. They're back in London.'

'Wrong again. You're not so well informed as you imagined. Both are still in Rome at their hotel. I saw to that. I also made sure they knew instantly of your capture. I'm told that they are most concerned.'

'Will I meet them?'

'All in good time. It would need to be carefully arranged. We wouldn't want your friend the Colonel joining in the act. And in the meantime I suppose I must convince you that Santo Stefano was genuinely kidnapped. That shouldn't be too difficult.'

He paused then to relight his dead cigar and turned to go. I longed to ask for news about my wife, but wasn't asking him for favours. He was entirely the self-possessed young dandy once again, and even gave a little bow as if to show our interview was over.

'Dinner is on its way at last. My apologies for the delay.'

He rapped briskly on the door: when it opened I glimpsed another of the hooded figures in the corridor beyond. Then he was gone and the lock shut noisily behind him.

Food was the last thing I imagined that I wanted, but when the cell door reopened twenty minutes later, and Anna entered with a tray, I realised that I was very hungry. She gave a quick sly smile of recognition, but one of the hooded guards was standing in the doorway so she placed the tray quickly on the bed then, head down, scurried off.

'*Buon appetito, signore!*' she sang out as the door was slammed behind her.

I drew some comfort from the food, which came as a reminder of the pleasures that continued in the world outside, as well as the happy few days I had spent in the castle with Diana. There was the home-made *ravioli* (filled with cheese and spinach) which we had so enjoyed, together with a jug of Adriano's wine, a bunch of grapes, some bread, and *pecorino* cheese. As I ate my spirits started to revive. When I finished, I relit what was left of my cigar and prepared for bed.

I was about to settle down to sleep – unwashed but otherwise undaunted – when the cell-door opened yet again and two guards entered. Neither spoke and their masks made them look like anonymous executioners, but I did my best to greet them calmly.

'Good evening to you gentlemen! An unexpected honour!' Which was evidently not their style at all, for they made no reply, but stood there like a delegation from the Ku-Klux-

Klan. And then they pounced. I kicked out and struggled, but the two of them were too powerful for me: as they dragged me to my feet a pair of handcuffs clicked around my wrists. There was no further point in struggling. When I started shouting one of them cuffed me round the face.

'Shut up!' he said.

I did.

'You come with us.'

And once again I did.

Avicenna had not been exaggerating about the tunnels beneath the castle. The one down which they led me seemed to go on for miles. It was so low we had to stoop. It smelled of stale damp air and mushrooms and was lit, every hundred yards or so, by an oil lamp hanging from a nail. We passed through another door which had to be unlocked, before we reached our destination – a heavily nailed cell door, which took a while to open.

The cell was smaller and dirtier than mine, and lit by a solitary candle on a packing case. It looked like an ancient burial chamber for the roof was vaulted and in the dim light in the centre of the room there seemed to be a body stretched out on a bier.

'Your Highness! A visitor!' one of the guards called out and the body moved its head.

My eyes were adjusting to the light but at first I failed to recognise the face beneath the filth and stubble of a partly grown beard. The body was covered with a rough grey blanket and the arms handcuffed to the bed. Hearing his name, he tried to raise his head and it was only then that I recognised him as the Prince: the eyes were large and very bright, the cheeks emaciated, and there was dried blood on the chin and fore-head. If he was acting with the others he was putting on a most convincing show.

'Who's that?'

Like his face, his voice had aged fearfully since I heard it last. One of the guards obligingly shoved me forward so he could see me properly. Recognising me, he cowered away.

'Not you too!' the poor devil whispered.

I raised my wrists to show the handcuffs.

'Don't worry, Prince! We're in the same predicament. Your dear friend, Avicenna, kindly kidnapped me in Rome a few hours ago. But for that, I'd be safely back in London with my wife by now. Imagine how I feel!'

'Dear Lord protect us!' he muttered to himself, sinking back and staring at the ceiling like some expiring father of the church. This was all very well, but there were limits!

'Pull yourself together, Prince! What else did you expect from a criminal like Avicenna? The two of you planned a huge insurance fraud and he's double-crossed you. You've only yourself to blame.'

Silence followed this, and when at last he spoke it was in a pathetic whisper.

'But I did nothing, and I've not been allowed to see him since I've been here. These people took me from my home by force and they've kept me in this cell here ever since. They're going to kill me if the ransom doesn't come. Moreton, I'm begging you to get me out of this. It's what I dreaded, and you know the truth. I'm legally insured. You've seen the policy yourself. For God's sake, tell your people back in London that they've got to pay.'

I felt like laughing but it was impossible not to feel sorry for him too: so I did my best to spell out the difficulties, but the guards were growing restive and one of them pulled my arm.

'Enough!' he muttered. But for a moment more I stood my ground.

'And how are they treating you now Prince?'

He gave a tired laugh.

'See for yourself. These people here hate everything I stand

183

for – and that goes for you as well. They're fanatics, Moreton, so just be warned. If the money doesn't come from London, I'll be disposed of like that friend I told you about. So will you.'

The Prince's words were not a good beginning to a sound night's sleep. The guards would not remove my handcuffs either, and the light stayed on, so I lay on my bed for quite a while, brooding on my fate and what on earth to do. The guards were clearly hostile and like the Prince I was quite convinced that I would be 'disposed of' if things did go wrong. I could expect no mercy from Petinacci, and I could not imagine Avicenna stopping them, even if he wanted to. Some sort of deal with London was my only hope, but was it possible? I had my doubts.

For I knew quite well that Lloyds is not a charitable institution, and no one would conceivably pay out on what was to all appearances a blatant fraud. Should I actually meet Platt and Mills I would certainly do my best to make them see the truth, but even then the insurers were certain to be difficult. In their position I would have been myself. So what was to be done?

Ironically, Hugo seemed my best bet now, for with my wife to pressure him, as I was sure she would, he would have to make some gesture to secure my release. The amount the kidnappers demanded was impossible of course, but some sort of deal was on the cards, and I could only hope that Petinacci would prove reasonable. If he was, would the other members of the MPM agree?

I tried to drive such questions from my mind by concentrating my thoughts on Diana, trying to picture her as she had been at Toriella, lying on the beach or laughing in the sun. But Petinacci had spoiled that by reviving all my jealous fears for her: her face kept vanishing, and all I could remember clearly was that last glimpse I had of her as she walked off to Alfredo's.

Finally I dozed off, and did dream about her then. We were

back in England, and I had taken her to hospital to have the baby, but for some reason I was forced to leave her there. I remember freesias in her room as we kissed goodbye: her hair was drawn back in a pony-tail. I promised to return as soon as possible, but found I had forgotten the address, and for the remainder of the dream I was in a London taxi with a furious old driver trying desperately to find the hospital. We seemed to drive around for hours but never did.

20

I don't know what went wrong, but Petinacci had clearly been over-optimistic when he had promised to put me in touch with Platt and Mills – or some other emissary from London. I imagine there must have been difficulties over setting up a foolproof rendezvous and making sure that no outsider intervened. This is no more than speculation for I was told nothing and for several days saw no one but the guards: my handcuffs stayed in place, I was fed twice a day, my bucket emptied every evening.

Strangely enough, this routine wasn't as unpleasant as it sounds, for once I was over the first shock and sense of indignation at my capture, an almost grateful resignation took their place. My brain slowed down, my worries left me, and I seemed to pass my time in a sort of dream-world, half-awake, half-sleeping like a foetus safe inside the stone womb of my cell.

Early on I made a brief attempt at establishing some contact with my guards, but desisted when they made it plain it wasn't on. They were correct but rarely spoke. The masks and the black clothing were a uniform, effectively effacing any individuality: for me they were completely interchangeable, and it struck me how entirely different they all were from Petinacci. Devoid of any show of personality they could have been his zombies, and I wondered how relations really stood between them all. Did he dominate them totally, or did they unite in some shared belief in violent revolution? Had any of the guards conversed I would have asked how they reacted to his swinging lifestyle.

For the first few days my greatest problem was adjusting to the way time passed, since my light was permanently on and I was without any sense of night or day. But I had now rewound my watch and started to keep a tally of the days on the wall above my bed. According to this, it was on the eighth day of my captivity, sometime in the afternoon, that Avicenna came to visit me again.

He was the last person I wished to see, for far from wanting any fresh involvement in the muddles that he always seemed to bring, I simply wanted to be left alone. Besides, I was certain now that he had no influence or power over Petinacci and the guards. I couldn't see them trusting him any more than I did. So I made no attempt to greet him and turned my head away. But he took no notice and seemed as confident and hearty as if paying me a business call in Rome. One of the guards was with him, and Avicenna called out, 'Ready, Signor Moreton?'

I turned and stared at him. He was in an old patched jacket, stained dungarees, and gum-boots and a greasy cap. I tried to put my feelings into my expression.

'Ready for what?'

Then he began his infuriating chuckle.

'Why, for our meeting with your friends from London! Have you no wish to see them? I can tell you, Signor Moreton, that it took some setting up. They have a crowded social calendar, those friends of yours and they make many difficulties, but everything is now arranged.'

'They're here?'

'What, in the castle? Come, Signor Moreton! That would not be possible. I am afraid that we must drive to meet them and it will be a complicated journey for we can take no risks. But they are used to this, and so am I. We must be on our way.'

I shook my head.

'Not until you've taken off these bloody handcuffs – and I would like a shave.'

'No time for shaving, but that does not matter. It is better that you do not look too smart, but the handcuffs . . .'

He shouted to the guard outside the door, and a brief argument ensued. The guard seemed reluctant, but Avicenna got his way and my wrists were freed at last – a considerable relief, as the skin was getting raw. But the guard still wasn't keen to let me go and kept prodding me in the back with his automatic as I shuffled after Avicenna down the tunnel, then up the stairs leading to the cellar. When the door opened, I saw the cellar lights were on and the old green van was waiting where we left it. A smart, metallic blue Ferrari was parked beside it, but it was not for us. Several other guards had now appeared to see us off, and Avicenna climbed into the van. I followed him. The engine coughed then spluttered into life, the cellar doors were slowly opened, and we began to back out into the world of normal human beings. The last I saw of the guards was an automatic being brandished in a gesture of farewell as the big green doors closed behind us.

'Nice friends you have, Avicenna!'

'Signor Moreton, do not joke about them. Were it not for me they would probably have killed you quietly by now. They do not care for foreign businessmen and none of them thinks you have much value as a hostage. I have to plead with them for you.'

'You are too kind.'

'It is nothing, Signor Moreton. I am always pleased to be of service to my friends.'

After the dimness of my cell, daylight dazzled me at first: the heat was stiffling too and as we rattled up the track skirting the castle walls the whole place could have been a deserted ruin in a sun-scorched desert. Nothing moved. The white tower shimmered beneath the blazing sky and one would not have thought of such a place existing still in modern Italy, so totally cut-off, so dream-like in its lifeless isolation. It was a vision that receded as we went bumping on our way between the dusty cypresses. Then it was lost to view as we entered the still

189

coolness of the woods.

I tried to question Avicenna, but he no longer seemed to want to talk and I noticed the gun back in the glove compartment. When I asked about our meeting, all he would answer was,

'All in good time. You'll see.'

By now I was quite certain he was a member of the MPM and working hand-in-glove with Petinacci. Otherwise why should they have trusted him like this? He had betrayed the Prince, and all the talk about his plans being taken over by the terrorists was moonshine – like almost everything with Dr Avicenna. But now I no longer cared. I had been fed so many lies that the truth barely seemed to matter. All that I wanted was my freedom – and to be shot of Avicenna and his friends and enemies for good.

For the world outside my cell had never seemed more beautiful: it was a perfect late September afternoon, and as we reached the uplands, the woods began thinning out, and the countryside below was like a map rolling away for miles and finally dissolving in a heat-haze where the horizon met the sky. No rain could have fallen here for months, and through the open windows I could smell the dusty aftermath of summer. Far off, a pair of buzzards circled in the sky, and to the left I saw the faint thin glinting of the distant sea. I had forgotten how lovely the land of Italy could be. Avicenna seemed to have relaxed, and was humming to himself.

'And how's the Prince?' I asked.

'Ah, not so good. Not good at all. Of course I am doing all I can for him, but the others do not trust me, and he fails to understand. He is, you know, diabetic so those conditions are not good for him. We get this settled quickly, eh, now Signor Moreton? No good for anyone, this carry-on – not for His Highness, not for me, nor for you and your lovely wife.'

'Why has it been taking so long even to set up this meeting now with Platt and Mills?'

'Ah, you know how it is. Difficulties – everyone make difficulties. Nobody trust anybody else. And like you, everybody seem to think it is some sort of joke. Is Petinacci who finally convince them he means business.'

'How?'

'Is a long story, Signor Moreton, but that boy is smart and most persuasive when he wants to be. Also, your presence with us helps. Your people in London have now agreed to talks, but a word of warning, Signor Moreton. They are not going to be easy, I believe, so for all our sakes I count on you to be pretty damned persuasive when you see them. You talk to them some good sense, eh?'

'I'll try, but don't go expecting miracles.'

He laughed and slapped me on the knee.

'Now that is what we need, a miracle. Perhaps we both start to pray. You are not Catholic are you, Signor Moreton?'

'Church of England.'

'Pity! I think your church has no miracles today. Why not become Catholic like me? Is possibly a better deal.'

'I'll think about it.'

His face lit up.

'You're serious? I have a friend in Rome, a *Monsignor*, and a most religious man. In the past I have performed him certain favours. You will see him when all this is over and he will arrange that you will meet His Holiness the Pope. Who knows, Signor Moreton – perhaps the good God is behind all this so as to bring you to our Mother Church.'

'God moves in a mysterious way.'

'Exactly, Signor Moreton. Is what my friend the *Monsignor* always says.'

Now that he saw me as a potential convert to the faith, I tried pumping him about my captors. He was still wary of giving anything away about the MPM but when I observed that Petinacci seemed an unusual sort of terrorist he nodded.

'Yes, a strange one. Even I do not always understand him.'

191

'You've known him long?'

'For many years, when he was a boy in Sicily. Already as a child he was different from those around him.'

'How come you knew him?'

Avicenna frowned.

'Signor Moreton, I think you ask too many questions.'

'But surely he can't be politically committed like those followers of his?'

'You mean that he is not sincere? Signor Moreton, do not underestimate him. He is more ruthless than anyone I know. I tell you this in confidence. He has a streak of wickedness you could not possibly believe. Certainly he lives well and he likes money as you have noticed for yourself. He has money of his own invested in Switzerland, and you saw the Ferrari in the cellar? That is his. He is smart and most ambitious, and he would kill anyone to get what he wants. Is most unusual.'

'He sounds like a gangster.'

This annoyed him as I guessed it would.

'Gangster? I have known many gangsters in my time, in Sicily and in America, and I tell you they are not like him. He always tells me it is good to play the part of a wealthy man. It is a good disguise, you understand. And since he is a wealthy man he does it properly, with real style. He spends, he uses money, but he also has political belief. That is why he is not a gangster. Here in Italy we have a long tradition that our politicians they make money out of politics. Our President Leone does and so does Petinacci. That is what I think you do not understand.'

'And his followers? Do they understand?'

He glanced at me a shade suspiciously I thought.

'Signor Moreton, you also have to know that in Italy most of our *terroristi* are not what you think they are. They are middle-class children playing at violence. They dress up, carry guns, prepare explosives – sometimes they even kill, but at heart, like much in Italy, it is theatre, a part for them to play.

192

They are young and they are bored. They are soft and are trying to be hard. Sometimes they try too much. I think you have seen this with those people at the castle, but with this Petinacci there is no pretence, no acting. This they recognise. He has the real brains and daring for the business that they lack. If they are actors, he is the one who writes the play, and that is why they follow him.'

'And you?'

He laughed uneasily.

'I say you ask too many questions, Signor Moreton. We are both *Siciliani* and I understand the workings of his brain. He is wicked but he trusts me – to a point.'

'And you trust him?'

Instead of answering, Avicenna shrugged his shoulders.

By now we had been driving for about an hour through this beautiful deserted countryside, and apart from passing an occasional car, had seen no sign of human life. Avicenna was keeping to the backroads, and I was wondering if he really knew where he was going, when we reached a tiny hilltop village. The place was so small it didn't boast the usual blue and white signboard with its name. Avicenna kept glancing at his watch, and we stopped outside a flyblown café which seemed to double as the village store.

We entered. It was cool inside with a faint smell of sour wine and cheap detergent. Dusty hams and sausages and fat *provolone* cheeses hung from the rafters: an old woman, looking rather like a cheese herself, stood motionless behind the marble counter. Avicenna seemed to know her, and he bought us beer and sat beside me at a plastic-topped table.

'Hungry?'

I shook my head.

'Is this where they're meeting us?'

'Too risky. In a moment I must telephone to them. I have

the timing carefully worked out. By then they will have reached a callbox I have told them of just twenty kilometres from here. Of course they will not know where I am calling from, and I will give them the location of another callbox where they can take a second call from us in fifteen minutes time exactly. A lot of telephoning, but it makes it difficult for anyone to lay a trap. Not that they're likely to, but better safe than sorry, don't you say?'

'We do.'

I drained my beer, the first to pass my lips for over a week. I like beer but had never realised before how hops can taste of freedom.

I watched as Avicenna ambled over to the telephone. Again he was looking at his watch and waited before dialling a number. The telephone rang quite a while: then I heard Avicenna briskly giving fresh instructions before ringing off.

'A further beer for you, Signor Moreton? We have the time before we go.'

I shook my head.

'Off then. We have one further call to make from another telephone in case some bastard is trying to be clever and trace that call back here.'

'Could they?'

'Is doubtful, but who knows?'

He must have been over our route before, for his timing seemed to be exact. Fifteen minutes later we had drawn up at an isolated callbox and this time we got through at once.

'All right?' I asked him when he finished talking.

'Let us hope. This sort of thing is always risky, but we'll be able to observe them first when they arrive.'

'How?'

'You will see.'

We hadn't much further now to drive – five minutes or so, no more – when we reached the edge of an escarpment. It was a spectacular spot, behind us the high woodland and the little road, and down below the valley and the central plain. In the clear sunlight of that autumn afternoon everything beneath us stood out like details in a panoramic colour photograph – a toy village with a neat square factory and smoke drifting from a chimney, a railway threading like a silver wire to the horizon, a patchwork of fields of ripening maize and vines and, slicing through them all, the main road to the south.

Avicenna parked the van beside the road and we got out. I noticed that he kept the gun. He also had a brand new pair of expensive Japanese binoculars, and as he stood there, gun stuffed into his belt, spying out the countryside below, there was something of the bandit leader I had seen in him that first morning when I met him in my office. Unlike his behaviour at the castle, he seemed in full command again. He turned and offered me the glasses.

'Watch that main road, Signor Moreton. They should not be long.'

The glasses were extremely powerful, but at first there was nothing to be seen except an old blue tractor with an empty trailer which soon turned off, then vanished down a track between the vines. Then I did see something, a red car in the distance driving towards us from the south. Through the glasses it looked like a ladybird crawling up a long white ribbon. Avicenna had already spotted it.

'Here they come, Signor Moreton. And right on time. Soon you will see them stop, and then we shall descend to meet them.'

He took the glasses, but by now I could see the car quite clearly with the naked eye. It was travelling at speed, then suddenly it stopped below, as if at his command. He was watching it intently with the glasses: even without them I could see two tiny figures emerge, open all the doors and raise the boot lid at the back. Avicenna was sucking noisily at his moustache and gave a decisive nod.

'You see, Signor Moreton. They act exactly as per my

195

instructions. Now we both go to meet them.'

Rather to my surprise, I realised my heart was beating loudly as we climbed into the van and started grinding down the hill in bottom gear for our appointment on which so much depended.

It was not exactly the reunion with one's fellow-countrymen a kidnap victim dreams of. Platt and Mills were standing together stiffly by the car, and as we drew up beside them, Platt smiled his frostiest OE smile, and dear old Mills, all pink face and sardine-and-tomato suit, just stared at me and glowered. It was probably the heat.

'Long time no see,' said Platt.

Mills cleared what sounded like a very nasty throat, and we got out and walked towards them. There were no handshakes, no demonstrations of undue emotion. I suppose it was very English and we stood there awkwardly beside the road like motorists after a slight collision.

'Extremely kind of you to come,' I said, unable to think of any other opening remark.

'Not to mention it, old boy!' said Platt. 'Are you all right?'

'Fine thank you. How's my wife?'

'Great form. Sends her love of course, and says you're not to worry. Staying with friends called Ripley. Terribly decent family.'

'Good. Tell her I'm missing her.'

'But of course, old boy. Of course.'

There was another awkward silence, and I could hear the tractor somewhere in the distance.

'So,' said Avicenna finally. 'You two gentlemen come here to discuss the details of the ransom. Let us get down to the brass tacks, right?'

Mills cleared his throat again, and Platt looked positively pained.

'Are we not being just a little previous?'

'Previous, Signor! I do not understand.'

I glanced at Avicenna, and suddenly realised how he must appear to Platt – the big shifty rather bloodshot eyes, the greasy face with the ingratiating smile, the grey hair fuzzing out from each side of his silly cap. I would have thought twice myself before discussing anything important with such a character.

'What I mean,' said Platt, 'and I'm sure you take my point is that this is a most unusual situation.'

'Unusual, Signor? I do not see it is unusual. His Highness, the Prince of Santo Stefano is kidnapped, and your associates in London have already insured him for the ransom. So you will pay and I will arrange delivery in safety of the Prince's person. Also of Signor Moreton.'

Platt gave what one can only call a hollow laugh.

'But Signor Avicenna —'

'Dottore Avicenna.'

'Quite. Dr Avicenna, as you know quite well, you and the Prince himself originally arranged his disappearance simply to defraud the insurers of ten million dollars. This is not the first time you have tried this sort of thing, so you must also know that fraud releases the insurer from all liability.'

'But it has been explained at length to you that our own plans were not carried out. We had no part in what occurred. It was the urban terrorists of the MPM who kidnapped him and are now threatening his life.'

'Then why are *you* here, Dr Avicenna?'

Avicenna was beginning to sweat profusely and raised his hands in supplication.

'All this I have explained to Signor Moreton, and he knows the truth. I am acquainted with these people in the MPM and still I have my duty to the Prince. I am here on a mission of humanity and begging you to help me save his life. Listen, I can arrange a deal. Is not impossible. I explain to them that ten millions is too much. Possibly I make them accept eight million, or even less. I argue, I am good at arguing. As I say, I know them and at heart they are reasonable people. Seven million. Even six. I am impartial in this. Just tell me what you are prepared to pay so I can start the bargaining with them.'

Platt glanced at Mills who was blowing his nose in a large red and white spotted handkerchief. I saw him shake his head.

'Not on,' said Platt.

'What you mean, not on? Me, I am asking no commission, not one bloody thing. I want the justice done and everybody happy. Five million.'

'Sorry, old boy. No deal.'

'You are a bastard. Four.'

Platt shook his head now, smiling like a poker-player with a winning hand. Avicenna seemed close to tears.

'You mean you let His Highness die?' he whispered unbelievingly.

'Should these so-called acquaintances of yours take the regrettable step of putting him to death, it's their responsibility, but I'm sure they won't. I'm sure you all know what you're up to, and I can only tell you, Dr Avicenna, that the insurers are quite adamant, and refuse to pay a penny.'

This was said very coolly and politely. The English upper classes are extremely good at saying no.

'And you brought us here, to tell us that?' said Avicenna.

'Everyone thought it best to tell you face to face and so avoid any subsequent misunderstanding.'

Avicenna muttered something I failed to catch, and Mills turned to the car, the day's business over. For me, of course, it wasn't.

'But Platt, where do I come in in all of this?'

I was embarrassed to be posing such an unprofessional question, and Platt looked mildly puzzled.

'You, old boy?'

'What about *my* release? Is nothing being done for me?'

'Ah! Nothing was actually mentioned, I'm afraid. I'm sure you'll appreciate that it was this business with the Prince that had the boys in London flapping. All that publicity – and ten million dollars isn't peanuts, even today. The implications of the case on the whole insurance market could be tricky. Very, *very* tricky – particularly with the press involved. It's felt we simply have to take a stand. You do see that, old boy?'

'Even if they blow my head off in the process?'

'Oh, I'm sure they won't do that. Come, come now, Moreton! I realise that you've been going through it, but you really mustn't let it get you down. You're an insurance man yourself, and must have learned that these affairs do have a knack of working out.'

He flashed another of his brittle little smiles, then paused and seemed to have an afterthought. He turned to Avicenna.

'Now how's about it, Dr Avicenna? Any chance of doing something for our Mr Moreton here? You have rather been putting the poor chap through it, haven't you? And I do assure you that it's not his fault that there's no deal. I know it would be extremely well received by the authorities in Rome if you released him now. Count in your favour.'

'You must be mad,' growled Avicenna.

'Please yourself then. Just a suggestion. Trying to be helpful.'

He turned to me.

'Bye, old boy, and keep your pecker up. Take it from me that it will all work out.'

Mills was in the car by now, revving the engine hard, and Platt raised a last lethargic hand.

'*Nil desperandum*! Any messages, old boy?'

'Just tell my wife I love her. And to take care of the baby when it comes.'

'Right! Right you are! Of course.'

The car door slammed, Mills spun the wheel, and I watched my hopes of freedom rapidly receding down the road to Rome.

21

The van seemed smellier and slower on our journey back, and the golden landscape which had been so open and entrancing on our outward journey, had now turned hostile, the woodlands threatening and full of shadows, and the sunset when it came was a reminder of my own descent into the castle dungeons that were waiting for me when the journey ended.

Avicenna seemed deflated. It was all too easy to understand his loss of face with Platt and Mills: he must have staked his reputation with the kidnappers on getting a final settlement with me to back him up, and had failed completely.

What would happen to me now? Being realistic, I didn't give a great deal for my chances now that my usefulness was over. I was patently expendable – to London and the MPM alike. In no way could I count on Avicenna, whose own standing with the gang would now be very shakey, and Petinacci could hardly be expected to have any scruples about killing me. Still less his followers. They might still think it worth their while to keep the Prince alive and finally succeed in screwing some sort of ransom out of his family. But now that Platt and Mills had given such a cast-iron refusal from the insurers over the Prince's kidnap ploicy – and in the process shown how little any of them thought of me – I had no market value any more. Worse still, I was a positive encumbrance to both sides now, and could not see anybody worrying too much about my fate.

Avicenna must have realised this too, for as if to make my lowered status absolutely clear, he insisted on binding my wrists and ankles when we were back inside the van. He was not stupid. Had he not done this, I felt so hopeless that I would certainly have made a bid for freedom, gun or no gun, and damned the consequences. Instead I had to sit beside him, trussed and powerless, being driven back to what appeared a very doubtful future.

For a while neither of us spoke and as I thought about my situation, I admit to feeling somewhat bitter, particularly over Platt and Mills – and puzzled by them both. I could understand the insurers' attitude perfectly, of course. Their reply had been predictable, and in theory they were justified in acting as they had. But why had they taken so much trouble sending Platt and Mills to spell it out? And why their total unconcern for me? Didn't I count for anything after those years of long devoted service to insurance? As for my wife and Hugo, their behaviour seemed nothing less than heartless. Perhaps I was being unfair to both of them, but surely there was something they could do instead of abandoning me like this?

I could rely on no one but myself, and the more I thought about them all, the more determined I became not to end up an unappreciated martyr to our great insurance industry if I could help it.

So then I tried arguing with Avicenna. For once it was hard to make him talk, and I pleaded with him outright to have done with it and let me go. I had no pride now and was soon begging for my life, using every argument I could think of. All he would do was sigh and shake his head.

'No one will kill you, Signor Moreton. Trust in me. You have my word and I have never let you down. Your life is sacred.'

'So is your friend, the Prince's – yet the MPM are threatening to kill him if the ransom isn't paid. Do you want me on your conscience too?'

He continued to shake his head, and had started sucking his moustache, but I wasn't giving up.

'Look Avicenna, be sensible for once. I know you're a decent man at heart. I even believe you're trying to sort this mess out and do the best for everyone, but it's impossible.

Everything's gone wrong, your great plan has failed and no one trusts you. People will soon start getting hurt, you included. Why don't you cut your losses?'

He reacted angrily to this.

'No more! I've heard enough.'

'Listen! I'm not a rich man, but I'm not exactly poor. I have influence in London and a lot of wealthy friends who'll help me. I can borrow quite a lot, and I'll guarantee a quarter of a million pounds, no questions asked, in any country you care to name if you'll let me go.'

He frowned and answered quietly,

'You, Signor Moreton, are the one who should be sensible. Even if my honour would allow me to agree, how could I be certain of the money? Once you are back in Rome why should you honour any obligation to a man like me?'

'You'd have my solemn word. I'd put it down in writing – anything you wanted.'

He eyed me with the sad suspicion of a smile.

'I wouldn't trust myself to pay, so why should I trust you? Besides, you would obviously inform your Colonello Rossi of our whereabouts.'

'Not if I promised that I wouldn't.'

'It would be your duty, and the pressures would be very great.'

'Very well then, come with me. You've committed no real crime yourself. I'd vouch for you to the authorities, and you could help them in every way you can. I'd help you make a deal with them and would make sure you got the money. It's your best hope of getting out of this intact.'

'Signor Moreton, you are talking nonsense. There are certain things about this situation that you cannot understand. I have my duty to the Prince and I cannot betray the others either. Trust me, Signor Moreton. I will still make everything work out and you will not be harmed. I, Avicenna give you my solemn word on it – and now we change the subject, eh? I was glad to hear the good news about the Signora Moreton. You had not told me of the interesting condition she is in.'

'What has it to do with you?'

'There you are, Signor Moreton! One minute you tell me that if I let you go, I can count on your gratitude for ever, and the next you say I must mind my bloody business when it was I who brought you back together with your wife. Human nature, Signor Moreton! It is not wise that we rely on it.'

I was not starting a discussion on human frailty, particularly with my wife involved, but he went on chuckling as if he had proved some point of deep philosophy. We were nearing the castle now, and while Avicenna's spirits seemed to have revived, I felt more hopeless and abandoned than I can remember. The sun had all but set and in the twilight I sat gazing at the fading countryside as if at my last glimpse of the world. The sky was flawless, merging in the West from apricot to deepest indigo, and below us the whole valley was dissolving into dusk. Nothing moved as we drove past and it was difficult to credit the existence of the castle and a gang of terrorists at the end of such a scene.

Then an unfamiliar noise caught my attention. At first I thought it was a thudding from the engine and I weighed my chances of escaping if the van broke down. The noise grew louder, and I realised it was not the engine, but a steady pounding from outside, like a carpet being beaten overhead.

Avicenna jammed on the brakes and grabbed the gun. I asked him what on earth was happening. He started swearing and I could see that he was staring at the sky above the trees. I looked – and then I saw the source of the noise and his alarm: a dark green army helicopter hovering above the road. It was very low. Even in the failing light I thought I could see the pilot in the perspex bubble of the nose. It must have seen us, for I could even feel the faint downdraught from its rotors like the wind of freedom.

It was an uncanny moment, we and the helicopter motionless, watching one another. Then the machine began to edge towards us, like some strange prehistoric bird about to swoop. At that moment I thought I was saved. Platt and Mills had not been as useless as I had imagined: somehow they must have given the authorities our position, and they had trailed us back – and this had happened when I thought the outside world had quietly abandoned me!

Trussed as I was, there was nothing I could do but sit and watch. Avicenna sat beside me, silent now, still clutching his automatic. What he intended doing with it, I had no idea. The helicopter was almost overhead by now and the noise was deafening. Then suddenly the noise increased, and the machine rose, banked and sailed away above the trees.

I don't know what I had expected but it wasn't this. Help had appeared so close at hand, then vanished so swiftly that I felt like some mid-Atlantic shipwreck victim watching a liner steam straight past his raft. Avicenna appeared in something of a state of shock as well.

'Well, and what do we do now? They know we're here.'

I hoped I sounded calm but felt like weeping. He nodded but sat sucking his moustache, clearly undecided what on earth to do. Then in reply he thumped his fist angrily against the wheel and switched the engine on.

'For God's sake, man! We're not returning to the castle?'

We started moving.

'We have to.'

'But the helicopter's bound to track us with its radar. We'll lead it straight to the castle and give the game away.'

He nodded.

'That is a risk that I must take. I think that they must know we're in the castle if they have got this far. If there will be trouble now, it is important I am there.'

'Avicenna, you're madder than I thought.'

205

'Quite probably, Signor Moreton. But no more talk now please. I think I have to concentrate.'

The castle wasn't far from where the helicopter spotted us – twenty minutes' drive at most – but we took longer since Avicenna drove without lights and the road beneath the woods was dim and dangerous. As it was, at one point we ended in a ditch, but Avicenna backed us out, and we continued on our slow, distinctly scary way. Once I thought I heard the helicopter in the distance, but it was hard to be certain with the racket that the car was making. By the time we were through the woods, darkness had completely fallen.

A full moon, like a great dull copper gong, was rising from behind the castle; by its eerie light we drove down the avenue of cypresses and round the massive walls. It was an enchanted castle now, a place of lonely magic which one could easily believe had stayed untouched since its last medieval owner rode away. There were no lights, no sign of any life, but one of the terrorists must have been keeping watch, for as we reached the courtyard by the cellars, the big doors started opening.

We drove in. The cellar was in darkness, and not until the doors had closed behind us did the lights go on. Three of the masked terrorists were standing in a line to welcome us – all armed with their automatic rifles. There was no sign of Petinacci. Avicenna switched the engine off, shouted a cheery greeting, and got out. No one answered, and none of the reception committee moved. I could see Avicenna smiling at them – rather nervously I thought – as he walked towards them. He had his own gun shoved in his belt, and one of the guards stepped forward, grabbed it and threw it behind him.

Avicenna stood there looking puzzled and a shade pathetic.

'Gentlemen!' I heard him saying. 'Gentlemen, what's going on?'

No one answered, but one of the terrorists struck him across the mouth.

206

He made no effort to defend himself, but still stood there with his feeble smile as the blood started trickling from his lip.

'Easy, now, gentlemen! A joke's a joke. Please!'

The guard struck him in the face again, this time with his fist and the blood began to flow.

'Traitor!' I heard the man mutter as the blow went home. 'And we are "Comrades" not "gentlemen", you bourgeois pig. Say it!'

'Comrades!' Avicenna groaned out through his bleeding mouth. 'But why are you doing this?'

The other guards joined in now, one of them pinioning his arms, the other slamming his fist into Avicenna's unprotected stomach. More blows followed, to his face and groin and I could see he was ready to collapse.

'Why do you think, filth? You drive off, you betray us to the enemy, and you think you can return.'

Tied as I was there was nothing I could do but watch as the beating-up continued. It was quite horrible, for I could feel the hatred of those muffled figures, while Avicenna still seemed unable to comprehend why he was being so maltreated by his friends. By now they had let him fall, and on the ground he was at their mercy as they started kicking him. I suppose they would have killed him – but suddenly I saw them stop and draw back from his writhing body.

'That's enough!' I heard someone say, and I saw a figure standing in the far corner of the cellar, framed in the doorway from the corridors below. It was Petinacci. He was like the others now, dressed totally in black, but his head was uncovered and he seemed to be unarmed. He stood a moment longer, watching what was going on, then walked slowly to the silent tableau lit by the bare bulb in the centre of the cellar. None of the three guards moved and Avicenna too was motionless, lying with his legs drawn up and his arms shielding his face. Not a word was spoken.

Now I could see him clearly, Petinacci seemed transformed

from the overdressed young playboy I remembered: I recalled what Avicenna had told me about him on our journey, for the face was set and hard and the scar above the mouth stood out like the weal from a whip-lash. He paused for a moment, quite expressionless, looking down at Avicenna. At that moment I imagined he was about to take a gun from one of his comrades and execute him where he lay. Instead he looked at the leader of the guards and slowly shook his head. Still no words were spoken, but I heard a quick drawing-in of breath. Then Petinacci raised his hand and made an impatient gesture of dismissal.

I saw the figure hesitate, but the other two had already turned away. Petinacci gestured at him once again, angrily now, and the figure shrugged, and started following the others, who went off through the doorway down to the corridors below.

Petinacci still seemed oblivious of my presence in the van and I sat there, fearful and fascinated by what would happen next. If, like his followers, he believed that Avicenna had betrayed them would he kill him? I still thought he might, for I saw now that he did possess a gun, and was standing over the recumbent Avicenna like some stern avenger. Then he was suddenly kneeling down and gently easing Avicenna's arms away from his battered face.

I realised that Avicenna must be conscious, for his shoulders moved, and I saw him try to raise himself to look at Petinacci. Petinacci had his arm around him now, and was trying to lift him to his feet. He was talking to him too, in some dialect I couldn't catch – apart from one word which I heard distinctly. The word he used was *babo* – the common Italian word for 'father'.

22

So Petinacci was Avicenna's son! I should have guessed, for now that I knew, I could see a certain similarity between them. (Or was I imagining this? Father and son resemblances are notoriously misleading.) And at last some of the unexplained events of the last few troubled months were falling into place – Avicenna's shadowy connections with the MPM, the way he had known so much about my wife's affair, and settled her return to me so smoothly as part of the deal over the insurance policy on the Prince.

I could still only guess at how the affair had ended between Petinacci and my wife. Had Petinacci cynically dumped her on his father's orders? This I somehow doubted. Petinacci – I still thought of him as Petinacci – hardly seemed the sort of son a man like Avicenna could order to do anything. No, my wife's own explanation, such as it was, still seemed the most probable account of what had happened. Having run off with Petinacci, she had found out the truth about him, promptly had second thoughts, and decided that she wanted to come back to me. Knowing what was going on, Avicenna had resourcefully exploited the situation to blackmail me, and manipulated my wife's return to his advantage.

So much seemed fairly obvious, but I still failed to understand how the whole muddle had occurred over the kidnap of the Prince. Had Avicenna and his son been hand in glove from the beginning, cynically setting up the whole affair? I would have said so, had I not known the two chief characters involved. I simply could not credit Avicenna with that degree of treachery towards the Prince: besides, all his subsequent behaviour had been too tortuous and tortured to fit in with such a theory. For once, I believed Avicenna – that he really had planned the kidnap with the Prince, only to have his great scheme taken over by his own son and the members of the MPM.

Poor wretched Avicenna – what a situation! I was almost sorry for him, for if this really was the case I could understand his desperate attempts to sort things out and somehow satisfy his twisted code of honour. He had been trying to do his best by everyone involved – the Prince, his monster of a son, me, even the members of the MPM – and at the same time steer clear of the clutches of the ever-watchful Colonel Rossi. Small wonder he had been in such a state! And small wonder he had failed.

What would happen now that the MPM had turned against him? I was left in peace to sort out the various possibilities, for nobody appeared remotely interested in my existence in the van. I saw Petinacci point in my direction, but Avicenna shook his head, and father and son went down to the corridors below, Avicenna limping and holding a blood-stained hand-kerchief to his face, and Petinacci with his arm around his shoulders. In any other situation it would have been a touching sight.

In a way I felt more hopeful now than after meeting Platt and Mills. I was not being quietly abandoned by the outside world as I had imagined. The authorities knew where we were, Platt and Mills would be at work on my behalf, and the people back in London must realise by now that this was a serious affair, and not some far-fetched slightly comic fraud that could be left to its own devices.

But in other ways, these new developments could make matters worse. As I had just seen myself, the terrorists were turning nasty and I was none too sure about Petinacci's power to control them now. Everything was coming to a head. If the authorities had brought in a helicopter, they must presumably be ready to deploy substantial forces round the castle. We could soon find ourselves besieged – then what? A trial of strength between Italian troops and terrorists?

What I had just observed was frightening enough, but if Colonel Rossi grew impatient and attacked, the final act could prove hideous beyond belief, with the terrorists trapped underground like rats, and both sides set on fighting to the last, with me in the middle of it all! Not the happiest of prospects, but as usual there was little I could do, for whatever his other inadequacies, Avicenna had certainly known about tying up a captive, and I could only sit and wait and see what happened next.

For half an hour or so, nothing did and my legs began to lose all sense of feeling. Then two of the terrorists appeared and dragged me from the van. I half expected to receive the same treatment they had meted out to Avicenna, but they were actually quite gentle with me, cutting the bonds around my ankles, holding me when my numbed legs buckled and helping me shuffle back along the corridor to the familiar refuge of my cell.

I would have liked to have asked about Avicenna but didn't risk it. Presumably Petinacci must be looking after him, and he would have told them something to allay their wrath – for a while at least. To my surprise I found some food waiting for me in the cell – water, salami, olives and a stale roll: it was not a feast, but I was actually quite hungry and the food gave me hope. The guards evidently wanted me alive. At that moment this was almost all I cared about.

I slept fitfully that night, constantly imagining I could hear the sound of fighting from above as the Carabinieri stormed the castle, but they didn't, and next morning I was still alive, and the gaol routine seemed to have been reestablished. Just after seven I received my usual cup of coffee from my usual silent guard, and smoked a cigarette. I had observed that I was always at my most optimistic at this time of day, and certainly the terrors of the night had started to recede.

I had read somewhere that in such situations the police usually attempt to make some sort of contact with terrorists rather than resort to outright force. With luck this would happen now and Petinacci surely had a strong incentive to bring things to a swift conclusion if only to protect his father from his followers? The more I thought about it, the trickier the young man's situation seemed to be. But when I saw him, later that same afternoon, he showed no sign of strain or tension, and seemed more confident and truculent than ever. This annoyed me, and we started arguing almost at once.

He had come to visit me alone, still wearing the black uniform I had seen him in the night before. (I noticed, incidentally, that the trousers were far better cut, the sweater of finer quality than those of any of his followers.)

'Ahah, the Gucci terrorist!' I said. 'Everything going according to plan?'

He could have smiled, the bloody man. Instead he made sure the door was locked behind him and stood stiffly facing me. I was lying on the bed.

'Of course! But it was a pity that you failed to make your friends see sense. A pity for you, old chap, for it makes you position far more difficult, and none of us likes the way they tried to use you so that the Carabinieri could discover where we were. Not that it makes the slightest difference. Things have become more ocmplicated, that is all. Your friends still have to pay – and rather more I think to cover our extra effort.'

'You must be joking!'

'Moreton, you should have learned by now I never joke. It is not my nature. But since you evidently doubt my seriousness in this, I will explain. Colonello Rossi and his men know we

212

are here. So what? They are not fools and our brave Carabinieri here in Italy have no taste for risking their lives unnecessarily. Some hours ago I got a message through to them explaining what I imagine they have guessed already – that we are virtually impregnable here in these tunnels underneath the castle and that it would be inadvisable, to say the least, for them to attempt to reach us. As I told them, we have explosives ready for them in the tunnels, which we will use if they attack. I also said that if they risk it, you and the Prince will be the first to die.'

'How thoughtful!'

He ignored this, but my sarcasm served to make him more humourless than ever, and he began pacing round the room, lecturing me as he had done before.

'I also told them, which is true, that we have food to last us several weeks, as well as the Prince's wine and there is water from the castle well. For myself, I am perfectly prepared to sit things out and wait, and I'm sure that Colonello Rossi and his men will do the same.'

'And what about your followers? They won't stand for that. After what I saw last night, I'd say you'll soon be having problems over discipline.'

He shook his head impatiently.

'Wrong again, Moreton. You don't know as much as you think you do about my people. We know we are all in this together, and are more united now than ever. This morning we discussed the whole situation democratically and I can tell you our morale could not be better. I have promised that we will win, and they trust me. I won't let them down, and we'll sit this out until your friends in London meet our just demands. For your sake I hope they don't keep us all waiting here too long.'

He smiled unpleasantly and I was fairly sure he wasn't bluffing – any more than Platt and Mills had been – and my heart sank as I envisaged weeks, perhaps months, of further tedious captivity with no certainty at the end of it. Petinacci

213

looked extraordinarily smug.

'And what about your father? How does he come into this?'

I hoped I had shaken him by mentioning Avicenna, but if I had, he managed to disguise the fact quite cleverly. The smile remained.

'My what? I fail to understand.'

'The unfortunate Dr Avicenna – or is his real name Petinacci too? He is your father, isn't he? I can't think even he deserves a son like you.'

He drew back and the smile had vanished now.

'Mind what you're saying, Moreton.'

I was still on the bed, but swung myself round towards him. Faced with the prospect of continuing captivity, I was past really caring what he did to me. I had a brief advantage, and I meant to use it.

'Aren't you ashamed at how you've treated him, Petinacci? Your own father, flesh and blood. I thought that in Sicily, such things counted. Yet you cheat him, bring him dishonour with his friend the Prince, and allow your own followers to beat him up. Have they killed him yet, Petinacci?'

I knew my words went home: the scar was showing, and his eyes were wide and staring as I had seen them once before when he was in a rage. For a moment I wondered if he could be slightly mad. But he managed to control himself.

'You must not speak to me like that. It is most unwise. Were it not for the ransom, I would kill you for those words of yours. Instead I will show that you are lying. I will prove it to you myself. But do not try me too far, Moreton, for I warn you that the point could come where ten million dollars would seem cheap for the pleasure of killing you myself.'

I wondered what Petinacci meant about proving I was wrong over Avicenna, but hadn't long to wait. A few minutes later I heard a faint commotion from the corridor outside, the cell

214

door opened, and Avicenna was standing there in person, flanked by one of the ever-present black-masked guards.

For some reason I was relieved to see him. He tried to smile, but his swollen face produced a grotesque leer instead. One of his eyes was closed completely, a front tooth missing. He looked terrible.

'Ah, Signor Moreton, such pleasure seeing you again! I hear that you are concerned about my state of physical well-being. I must assure you I am very well indeed.'

'You look it. How are they treating you now?'

'No complaints. As you perhaps observed, there was a slight misunderstanding when we return last night, but all is now ironed out and hunky-dory. You permit me to enter?'

'Be my guest. The amenities are not quite as I'd wish, but the welcome is sincere.'

He started laughing, but it evidently hurt for he stopped abruptly.

'Signor Moreton, not to make me laugh, I beg you. Several of my ribs are bruised and so I must be serious. I fear that we must have the company of this unattractive companion, but no matter. The idiot speaks practically no English and is important now that you and I converse. The time has come, I think, to sort this bloody muddle out.'

It was my turn to laugh.

'Isn't that what you've been trying to do ever since we met?'

'True, Signor Moreton. But now we shall do it properly – for once and always. Suddenly there is the chance.'

He walked with a certain cautious dignity across the cell and lowered himself into the deckchair, wincing as he sat. His guard squatted by the door and lit a cigarette. Avicenna started talking quickly in an undertone.

'We must cut the cackle, Signor Moreton, for we have not long. This morning I had a most profound discussion with Petinacci over what to do. He is very open to suggestions.'

'You mean you're actually on speaking terms with that son

of yours after the way he's treated you?'

He showed no surprise that I had learned his secret.

'Ah, so you've guessed the truth. I should have told you earlier myself, but it was not possible, for my son and I have not been on the best of terms. It is a bad relationship in many ways. I blame myself. For many years I have hardly been to him the ideal father, and he has learned too well perhaps from my example in the past. Nor have his mother's family helped. They despise me and have tried to make him do the same. There is not too much respect for me, you understand?'

'I've not seen much sign of it, since you mention it.'

'True, alas! Sometimes one has to pay for one's mistakes through one's children. The sins of the son visited upon the father. It is a little trick God often uses. Many times I have seen it happening in Sicily, but never did I think that it would come to me.'

He sighed and raised his hands.

'But also, Signor Moreton, you must understand I love my son. In spite of everything I love him. I forgive him, and I think the time has come to save him from himself.'

The guard was beginning to look bored. He stretched his legs and lit another cigarette.

'How much longer?' he grumbled.

'Just a few minutes, comrade. There are still certain points to be discussed about the ransom payment with the English capitalist.'

The guard puffed his cigarette and grunted. I exploded.

'Save him? Really Avicenna, talk a little sense.'

'Exactly what I attempt to do with you. If this continues, I foresee disaster for us all, and particularly for him. Few of the MPM trust him any more. He won't believe me when I tell him this, but it is true. I know them. They are frightened and they now feel they are trapped. They are getting desperate and angry as you saw with me last night. So we must both act quickly while there is still the time.'

216

I detected the beginning of another of Avicenna's little schemes and answered tartly.

'Rather a limited field of action for us, I'd have thought.'

He shook his head slowly.

'Not so, Signor Moreton. Only this morning, as I discuss these matters with my son, in a flash it comes to me that we have still one trump card we can play.'

'We could do with a few. What is it?'

He squinted at me through his one undamaged eye before whispering his reply.

'Your wife, Signor Moreton.'

23

'Signor Moreton, you will forgive me digging up again this painful subject which is dead and buried, but it is necessary you understand the truth.'

Again the same old promise Avicenna had been making almost from the day we met. Truth! Did he know the meaning of the word? And could he tell me anything about Diana I didn't know myself? If he could it was the last thing I wanted: at all costs I needed to preserve the happy memories I had of her until we were safely reunited. Then we could see about the truth.

So I shook my head.

'Please, Avicenna. Keep her out of it.'

'Signor Moreton, if I could I would respect your wishes. I understand your feelings and have no desire to cause you any pain. But too much is now at stake, and I believe your wife could be the answer to our troubles. I am serious.'

'Avicenna, I'm not listening.'

'Do you know why your wife returned to you?'

'Because she loved me, and because she realised that she had made a terrible mistake leaving me for someone like your son. Once she found out the truth, she couldn't wait to get back.'

He shook his head and sighed.

'That is not exactly how it was, Signor Moreton. Your wife knew what my son was doing when she left with him. Also, although it pains me to tell you this, she truly loved him, just as he loved her. I am afraid that this is something you must understand.'

'Nonsense, Avicenna! It was a brief infatuation, nothing more. She told me so herself.'

He continued to shake his head.

'That is what women always say to their husbands when an affair is over, but it is rarely true. And how does one define infatuation?'

'An overwhelming physical attraction that soon passes.'

'Then they were not infatuated. My son was deeply and seriously in love with her – and he still is. It was the same for her.'

I felt a chilling sense that he knew something that had been kept from me, and that if I went on listening, my life could never be the same again. But now I had to know whatever he had to tell me.

'Then why did she come back?'

'Because I arranged it, Signor Moreton. For no other reason.'

His one good eye was watching me, his swollen face giving an impression of bloated melancholy.

I began laughing.

'You, Avicenna? You flatter yourself. You couldn't arrange a night out at the opera without something going wrong.'

'Perhaps. But just the same, it is thanks entirely to me your wife came back. You see, I needed her to return as part of my deal with you over the ransom policy.'

'So how did you do it if she was so deeply in love with your son?'

'Such things are not difficult if you understand women, Signor Moreton, and believe me, I do understand them. Perhaps not much else, but the female mind to me is something of an open book. Your wife, for instance, she is proud, strong-willed, not someone to be mucked around. Am I right?'

I nodded.

'And such a woman would not willingly put up with too much nonsense from the man she loves. Signor Moreton, with my son there was a lot of nonsense in the past, and I knew about it. Like me he is *donnaiolo*, womaniser, almost from the day his testicles descend, perhaps before. When he is with your wife there is still another mistress he has had in the MPM, a girl from Bergamo in the North of Italy, a passionate crazy girl with red hair. Redhaired girls are often crazy, Signor Moreton, and this one is insane with jealously. He gets rid of her, you understand, because of the Signora, your wife. But this girl makes trouble. He tries to keep this from your wife, but I tell her. Also I tell certain things to the girl as well. I lay it on. I make sure that your wife think he is two-timing her with the redhead. There are rows, arguments, which I make sure grow worse. Finally, as you know, I arrange that she returns to you. The redhead helps me, thinking my son will then return to her.'

'Did he?'

Avicenna shook his head.

'My son is mad with grief when your wife deserts him. Me, I have seen nothing like it in my life. Never. For days he eat nothing. He is wild with fury, and in the end the redhead tells the truth to him.'

The guard was growing increasingly impatient.

'For God's sake, how much longer?'

'Not long, now, comrade. But it is difficult arranging matters with these capitalists. Have another cigarette.'

The guard took one reluctantly.

'After this we go.'

Avicenna nodded.

'So what happened then?' I asked. 'Weren't you frightened?'

'Of my son? That he might hurt me? No, he is not like that. He is more cunning. He is Sicilian and he wanted his revenge. He got it, as you know. Stupidly I had told him something of my plans with His Highness. You know the result.'

'The kidnapping took place because of that?'

Avicenna nodded.

'The money was also a consideration, but that was the real reason.'

He looked at me and did his best to smile. I noticed that his

221

lip was badly cut as well as swollen.

'Poor Signor Moreton, I am sorry to be telling this to you, but as I have said, it is necessary.'

'Why?'

'Because of something that you tell me yesterday, about your wife. That she will have a child.'

I had a premonition then of what was coming.

'The child is mine. Definitely mine. It was conceived after she came back to me.'

He made a clicking noise of disbelief and shook his head.

'How can you know? How can men ever know? It is an old game women play on them. My son insists the child is his.'

'You mean you told him?'

'It could be my grandson, Signor Moreton.'

'Avicenna, get this absolutely straight. The child is mine.'

Even as I said this, I felt the first uneasy glimmering of doubt. Avicenna shrugged his shoulders.

'At present it is neither here nor there who the father is. What matters is that my son believes it's his. He wants it, Signor Moreton. The unborn child and the mother. He will do anything to get them back.'

There was silence. The guard had nearly finished his cigarette, and I understood what Avicenna meant about his trump card then.

'There is one person and one person only who can settle this,' he said.

'And who is that?'

'Your wife.'

'But we can't ask her.'

'There you are wrong, Signor Moreton. My son still has his ways of contacting the world outside. She could be brought here.'

'No.'

'Signor Moreton. I have discussed this with my son at length. It is a family matter, and since I am head of the family,

222

finally he listens to me. He has agreed to what to me seems sensible and fair. Your wife will come here. It can be arranged.'

'I won't agree to it.'

'Agree or not, Signor Moreton. It will be arranged. And the three of us, you, me, my son, will ask of her the truth about the child she carries. If it is his, you will relinquish her completely, Signor Moreton, and my son will make an end of all of this.'

'He'll surrender?'

Avicenna almost laughed.

'That would not be necessary. Luckily the men who built this castle were a cunning lot, and there are ways out of these tunnels no one knows about. He and your wife would disappear. So would his followers. He would tell them it is over. My son and your wife would make their way abroad, leaving us and His Highness behind them. There would be no more talk of ransom.'

'And if she says the child is mine?'

'He would also go. Alone. It would be necessary to make some deal with his followers I think, but that would not be difficult. Lacking a leader, they are nothing.'

He looked up at me. The swollen face was definitely smiling now.

'Be sensible, Signor Moreton. What have you to lose? Either way you get your freedom, and if you have to lose your wife you wouldn't want her anyhow. If you keep her you will know for certain that the child is yours.'

The guard had finished his cigarette and stood up, jangling his keys.

'Come on,' he said. 'Time's up!'

'Coming, comrade. Coming. Signor Moreton, just one further thing. Is there anyone in Rome that you can trust who also knows your wife? It may be necessary to employ a go-between and I refuse to have any dealings with your friends Platt and Mills.'

223

I thought a moment then gave Colombo's name.

I learned later that the castle was under a virtual state of siege by now, with several hundred men positioned in the grounds, along with helicopters, armoured cars, and a group from the Carabinieri's specially trained anti-terrorist squad under the personal command of Colonel Rossi. During the hours of daylight, helicopters hovered overhead. At night every inch of the castle walls was lit by army searchlights.

But no one seemed inclined to make a move. No one was risking entering the castle cellars after Petinacci's warning and a state of stalemate ensued, for kidnappers and police alike. Within the castle, the routine continued as before. The food grew worse, the guards seemed jumpier, but I had no idea of all the activity outside. For two days after Avicenna's visit I heard nothing and saw nobody except the guards.

Curiously enough I gave little thought to Avicenna's words about my wife, after he had gone. At the time they had upset me, but I soon lapsed back into my previous state of goal-bound inertia. The world outside seemed so unreal I found it hard to take its problems seriously – still less the plots and strategems of Dr Avicenna. I also found it hard to think about my wife, except as the woman I loved. The ins and outs of her affair with Petinacci seemed irrelevant beside this. So did the ultimate paternity of her unborn child to tell the truth. For me she embodied freedom, love and earthly happiness, vague enough ideals I know, but it was my memories of her that gave them meaning in that meaningless captivity. So I closed my mind to Avicenna's various insituations and went on waiting. On the third day after our conversation, early in the evening, the guards came for me again.

I had never seen the room they took me to before. It was stone walled and windowless, like my cell, but bigger, twenty feet or so in length with a high timbered ceiling. It may once have been a torture chamber, for there were iron rings along the walls and hooks fixed to the heavy beams. But unlike the other parts of this subterranean prison I had seen, this had been furnished with a touch of style and even luxury – white fur rugs on the floor, an overstuffed modern sofa, ghastly chrome and plastic chairs, and bottles and a portable television on a small table set against the wall. Lighting was provided by spotlights hanging from the roof, which made the room seem rather like a set in a television studio.

The whole scene was theatrical, for Petinacci was already there, seated like some sort of grand inquisitor in a swivel chair with a light behind him, legs negligently crossed, arms folded on his chest. Seeing me, he scowled but said nothing. I was relieved to see that Avicenna sat beside him. Two of the guards were also there.

'Ah, Signor Moreton,' Avicenna said. 'How are you? It is very good to see you. Everything has been arranged to our mutual satisfactions in accordance with our conversation. Our friends are arriving shortly.'

'My wife is coming here?'

'Exactly. There were problems, but that friend of yours, Signor Colombo, finally managed everything. Without him it would have been impossible. He is a useful friend to have.'

'You explained everything to him?'

'Everything. He is no fool that one, and I could hold nothing back from him. From the first instant that I speak to him I trust him. I hope my trust will be respected.'

'It will be – with Colombo. He told my wife?'

Avicenna nodded.

'Naturally. She understands the situation.'

Avicenna's face seemed much repaired since I had seen him last, the swelling had subsided, but there were bruises on his cheek and he sported a spectacular black eye. This didn't seem

225

to worry him, and he really did seem in the best of spirits, hearty and confident as ever. If the room was like a studio, he could have been some way-out television personality, bouncy and imperturbable, hosting a fraught encounter for the cameras. Petinacci too had considerable 'media appeal' as I think they call it, with his black garb, saturnine good-looks, and the way he sat there, smoking and ignoring everyone. Nothing more was said and we must have waited on in silence then for several minutes. Then I heard steps from the corridor outside, and someone shouted for Petinacci.

'Enter!' he replied.

The door opened, and my wife was suddenly before me. Colombo limped in after her. She was wearing an old blue anorak and jeans. Her hair seemed longer than I remembered. She was even prettier than my memory of her, but there was a hardness to her face, and she held her head defiantly as she stared around the room. She caught sight of me, nodded, but did not smile.

'Elly! How are you? You're looking thinner. I feared that something like this would happen, and it has. It can't be helped. At least you'll be all right.'

I raised my arms to her, but she shook her head, then she faced Petinacci, giving him the briefest nod of recognition. He returned it – just as coolly. Avicenna, on the other hand, came bustling towards her, taking her hands in his, and giving her a chair.

Colombo looked at me and winked.

'Surviving, Signor Conte? That is what matters.'

He said this in his usual whisper which everybody must have heard. Avicenna grinned, and offered him a seat. The meeting was becoming positively cosy.

'Any problems getting here?' he asked him.

Colombo yawned and shook his head.

'Everything was taken care of. I congratulate you on the arrangements. Very useful back door you've found yourselves.

None of the Carabinieri within a mile of it.'

While this was going on, I had eyes for no one but Diana, but she still ignored me, sitting very upright in her chair, smiling cryptically at those around her and totally detached – an ice princess in an anorak.

Petinacci clapped his hands together, and motioned to the guards behind his chair. I saw them hesitate.

'Out!' he muttered, and they filed from the room. The door slammed shut behind them.

'So,' said Petinacci, stretching himself, then lighting yet another cigarette. 'The time has come to talk and bring this nonsense to a sensible conclusion. It has gone on too long and has been getting out of hand. It all began because I was lied to about somebody I loved. If I can now be told the truth, and my followers can be taken care of I am prepared to go. But there must be no more lies. You understand?'

Avicenna cleared his throat as if about to speak, but then thought better of it. Colombo leaned back, staring at the ceiling. I watched my wife. The smile had vanished but she sat immobile and expressionless as ever.

'Well?' said Petinacci softly.

'Well?' said my wife, meeting his stare at last. 'What do you wish to know?'

'The truth about the child.'

She must have been acting for she managed to look puzzled.

'Child? What child?'

'The child they tell me you are bearing.'

'Yes?'

'Whose is it?'

'Mine,' she replied with gentle dignity.

'And mine too,' he shouted. His face was suddenly alive, the scar showing white and clear above his mouth.

She did not answer him at once and when she did it was in the small clear voice that she had used before.

'Why do you ask? Do you still want me?'

He said nothing but I saw him nod.

'And if I come with you, you are prepared to end the siege and let the hostages go free?'

'Provided that the child is mine. It is mine, isn't it?'

There was a pause. All eyes were on her now.

'Of course,' she said.

Then she did look at me. Her face had its sad mysterious smile again. She shrugged.

'Sorry, my dear old Elly!' was all she said.

I don't know what happened then, for Petinacci was shouting for the guards, and I was hustled off before I could make a scene.

My release was not as swift as I had expected. I had to spend the remainder of the night in my cell – tormented by such thoughts of bitterness and jealousy as I had never known in my life. In the morning, no one came to feed me, and it was not until late afternoon that the cell door opened. It was Avicenna and he was alone.

'Signor Moreton. You are a free man once again. Everything is over.'

'They've gone?'

'Everybody. They all escape, leaving us and His Highness to welcome in the Carabinieri.'

'My wife?'

'She went with my son.'

I found that I was weeping, though whether from relief or loss I wouldn't know.

24

I found it hard to understand that I was completely free. I had grown so accustomed to living underground in that tiny cell that leaving it was like leaving hospital after a serious illness; following Avicenna up the stairs from the cellars to the ground floor of the castle, I had to pause for breath, feeling slightly dizzy.

We emerged into the main entrance hall of the castle. It was empty, but the big outer doors were open and the daylight dazzled me at first. I could see several cars belonging to the Carabinieri parked outside on the terrace, and the whole valley and the countryside beyond were golden in the last glow of the autumn sun. After my time entombed below, it looked like paradise and totally unreal.

'Have they all gone?'

Avicenna nodded.

'My son did not have too much difficulty persuading his brave followers the game was up and that they'd better save their skins while they still had the chance. The escape route was there along the tunnel. They were glad to go.'

'And the other two?'

'They followed them. They were the last to leave.'

'They were together?'

'I'm afraid so.'

I suppose I was still hoping Diana had changed her mind at the final moment. I would have had her back – whatever the truth about the child.

'What will happen to them now?'

'Those two will always be all right, believe me, Signor Moreton. My son has several foolproof ways to leave the country, and they will be across the border by this evening. So not to worry further now about your wife for in his way he loves her and he will certainly take good care of her and the child when it is born. The lady is not exactly weak herself.'

'Where'll they head for?'

'First Switzerland where he has money, then, who knows? America? New York would suit him. Americans like men with enterprise I think.'

'And the rest of his followers?'

He spat.

'Those idiots! They have been lucky to get out of this, and can now give up playing terrorists. Your friend the Colonel and his men have no idea how they escaped. They are scouring the country but they should not find them. Already they will be scuttling back to their loving families and their mothers' cooking. Tomorrow they can go back to university or get some relative to find them a respectable well-paid job, while my son is obliged to leave the country like a criminal.'

'He's got my wife and a bank account in Switzerland.'

'True.'

He must have seen my woebegone expression for he started laughing and put an arm around my shoulders.

'Poor Signor Moreton! Poor Avicenna too! Look at us both. Two sad old men who try their best but both end up with nothing while the wicked prosper like the green tree in the Bible.'

I began laughing too, without exactly knowing why. It was probably the sight of his face. With his black eye and the purplish bruises on his cheeks, he appeared a sort of doom-struck clown. A clown with his arm around a cuckold preaching the consolations of acceptance: a situation not without its comic elements and I went on laughing.

'Ah, Signor Moreton, who would have thought that it would all turn out like this? Is it not like life itself? We make such careful plans, we have such dreams, yet men like us end up with nothing. I think it is a sort of joke.'

230

'Rather a tough one.'

'True, but we see the joke, and we can laugh. That is what matters. It is those who cannot laugh we should feel sorry for, even if they seem to win. Poor Colonel Rossi, searching for ever for the MPM – and that wife of yours, after everything that's happened, ending with my son.'

'Surely they deserve each other.'

'That is the point. Of course they do, but they will never laugh like us at what has happened. They are not humorous by nature. I have an idea, Signor Moreton. I will find you a woman of your own age, a rich Italian widow with a sense of humour who will cook for you and be experienced in bed and make you happy. That would be a kindness, eh?'

'If you'll let me find you an English woman in return – a policeman's widow with artistic tastes who would keep you out of mischief. That might be an even greater kindness, come to think of it.'

'Perhaps too great, but I'll consider it. Let me show you to your room; then I return to His Highness, for he needs me.'

'How is he?'

'Better than I expected, and very happy to be free. Already he is making plans for us to dine together here this evening. You can see Signor Colombo when he returns. In the meantime take a bath and rest and look forward to dining here tonight to celebrate.'

I wasn't certain what there was to celebrate, but nodded, and we climbed the stairs together, arm-in-arm, like two old troupers at the conclusion of a play.

Upstairs the castle had been totally transformed: Anna and Adriano must have been hard at work and with the windows open and the sunset lighting up the rooms, the main apartments were lovelier than I remembered. My room looked across the gardens. (Someone had had the sense not to put me

231

back in the room I had occupied here with my wife.) This was more suited to a single gentleman, with its neat four-poster, frescoed walls, and a bathroom leading off. Anna had already laid me out a clean shirt, slippers and a towelling dressing-gown: Avicenna ran the bath for me, then left me to it.

There was an enormous antique marble bath in the centre of the room, with great brass taps that splurged a torrent of hot water. I took some time making sure the temperature was right, then lay there marinading with the windows open, watching the swallows fluttering beneath the eaves and then the bats succeeding them as evening started. As the dirt of captivity soaked away, my fears and my anxieties floated off as well, and I began to wallow in the sheer relief of luxury, curiously at peace and glad to be alive.

The bathroom ceiling had been painted, rather badly, in the late nineteenth century with a mythological scene. Suddenly I recognised it. By a strange coincidence it was Diana and the stag – the powerful young goddess striding forth across the centre of the ceiling, bow in hand, eyes flashing, ample breasts exposed, and the wretched stag already stricken with an arrow, and cowering in the corner of the ceiling by the hot water tank. Something about this Diana even reminded me of my wife as I had seen her striding up the beach at Toriella and had felt for the first time that she had changed. She had indeed. This Diana was a huntress and a destroyer, not the child-wife I had loved and cossetted so long. Suddenly I was glad that she had left me. Diana had another target for her arrows now. They were welcome to each other.

There was whisky in the bedroom, and by the time I had dried myself and shaved and poured myself a drink, it was almost dark. Lights were twinkling along the terrace, voices echoing from below, and I was feeling almost human once again.

*

232

'His Highness awaits you on the terrace, Signor Moreton,' Anna announced as I came downstairs. Of us all, she was the only one who seemed completely unaffected by the ordeal of captivity – same crafty smile on the same beautiful old wrinkled face – and when I asked her how she was, she simply shrugged and answered, 'well enough, thank you, Signore' and pointed to the terrace.

At first I thought some sort of celebratory party really was in process; candles in glass jars had been lined along the balustrade, the tower was floodlit, and a long marble table had been laid beneath the pergola. The crickets had already started up their evening racket and a breeze was moving fitfully along the valley, making the candle-shadows flicker, and bringing up the scent of thyme and brushwood from the parched countryside below. Two or three people were on the terrace. A cork popped from a bottle of champagne and to my surprise the Prince came forward, glass in hand, to welcome me, miraculously resurrected from the figure I had last seen in that burial chamber of a cell.

'Ah, Moreton, here at last! Welcome to our little freedom party!'

He limped slightly, and his face was still painfully emaciated, but he was now dressed in a dark blue Lacoste shirt and pale blue slacks, and it was extraordinary the difference that clean clothes and a shave had made.

'And how are you feeling, Prince? Somehow I never quite believed we'd meet again.'

'Oh, one is tougher than one thinks. Clean living and pure thinking are the secret. Feeling all right yourself?'

However much I disapproved of him, the charm was working as it invariably did, and I nodded, gratefully accepting the champagne. There was a sort of bond between us now – our shared survival – and it seemed distinctly pointless judging him any more. He gripped my arm and I noticed that those curious dark eyes of his were twinkling beneath the overgrown

233

eyebrows.

I recognised Colombo talking to Avicenna: catching sight of me he turned and raised his hands in greeting.

'Signor Conte! So it is over! Welcome!'

He was immaculately dressed – pale yellow linen jacket, white flannel trousers and a beautifully tied pink silk cravat. With his fine profile and the silvery hair, he was the only one of us who really looked at home in these sumptuous surroundings. He took my hands in his. The castle and the surrounding countryside could have belonged to him.

'I never realised you had a title, Moreton,' said the Prince.

'A courtesy title,' said Colombo. 'I gave it him and am the only one who uses it.'

The Prince looked puzzled at this explanation, but did not pursue the subject. Instead he asked,

'And how did it all go at the end?'

Colombo rolled his eyes and shrugged.

'Tricky. Touch and go to the last minute as these things often are. Everyone terribly excited and several of the MPM were all for fighting it out against the Carabinieri. Death or glory. There was a furious discussion. Some of them accused Petinacci of betraying them. He kept his temper and finally convinced them, although he more or less had to force one or two of them back down the escape tunnel at gunpoint.'

'Did he now?' said the Prince. 'Thank God he managed it. Tell me about this famous tunnel – I never knew of its existence. Where does it emerge?'

'Over there.' Colombo pointed across the valley to hillside opposite. 'You can't see it now, but there's a ruined farmhouse with a track that leads down to the road behind the hill. The tunnel comes up through the cellar.'

'Who'd have thought it?' said the Prince.' I used to play there as a boy. The place was empty even then, and I've always meant to do something with it. Too late now of course.'

'How was my wife?' I hadn't meant to ask, but the question somehow phrased itself.

'She was fine,' Colombo answered quietly.

The Prince had opened another bottle of champagne, and was carefully topping up my glass.

'Signor Colombo is a genius. He has already seen Colonel Rossi on our behalf. Unofficially he has told him there will be no charges.'

'Nor against me,' said Avicenna. By candlelight his face looked less alarming.

'A toast to Signor Colombo!' said the Prince. 'It's because of him we're here at all.'

We raised our glasses but Colombo looked embarrassed.

'Please do not thank me, gentlemen. I did my job for which I have received my fee, which was more than adequate. I didn't want anybody killed, but don't imagine I approve of you or anything you did.'

'Quite right,' the Prince said gravely. 'Now that I've thought about it I don't particularly approve myself. But we failed, so why not look upon us all as proof that crime doesn't always pay, even in Italy, and accept our gratitude?'

'As long as you understand my feelings.'

'But of course we do – and they do you credit. We can at least eat together and your integrity will stay intact. Rather a scratch meal, I'm afraid, but Anna has done her best and in the circumstances I'm sure you'll make allowances.'

The Prince was being over-modest, for the dinner was a feast – more for the eye, alas, than for my out-of-practice stomach: quails, young lamb and the last of the year's asparagus, a delicate cheese soufflé covered with thinly sliced white truffles, figs and delicious cheese. We drank very old chianti, pale with age and tasting of straw and roses. Colombo was soon over his pomposity, and before long he and the Prince were swapping stories about crooks and celebrities they knew. For once Avicenna seemed distinctly muted, and I am afraid I drank too much, as usual. By the time we had reached the brandy and cigars the world appeared detached and beautifully unreal. A slender moon had risen high above the valley, and with the starlight the whole countryside was clear as day.

I heard Colombo ask the Prince about his plans for the future.

'Who can tell? After this trouble I think it best that I leave Italy for a while at least. My cousin can take over the estates. You'd approve of him, Colombo. Been voting Communist for years, and won't have anything to do with me. Very sharp businessman I'm told, and he has plans to turn this place into an hotel for German tourists. I'll probably end up in England. It's the one place left for characters like me. These days I'm told it's full of crooks with titles, and they all so very nicely thank you. That little house I told you about in the Cotswolds, Moreton, my friends bought it for me.'

I nodded but my thoughts were far away.

'And what about you, Avicenna?' I inquired.

'I shall be accompanying His Highness, naturally. Italy could be uncomfortable for me. And you?'

'Perhaps I'll take you up on that rich widow you suggested and stay in Rome. Possibly Colombo would offer me a job as I can't imagine I've much future in insurance any more.'

'Employ you, Signor Conte? Never. You are too gullible and prone to accidents. I'm afraid England is the place for you as well.'

We laughed at that, but I realised that what he said was true, and while the others went on talking, I sat and watched the fireflies and understood how much I would miss Diana. Perhaps it was the drink, but I felt I had never seen so many fireflies before. They were all across the terrace and the valley, flashing like moving stars between the trees, but I noticed that one was stationary and seemed brighter than the rest. I watched it, and its light appeared to grow like the tip of Avicenna's big cigar. Then in my slightly fuddled state I realised that it was not a firefly at all, but a far-off point of light on the hillside opposite. It went on growing rapidly, and finally I interrupted the Prince to ask him what it was. He frowned and peered across the valley.

'Dear God, another fire! With the dry weather we've been having the countryside's like tinder. It looks as if it's just below that farmhouse Colombo was telling us about. One of our terrorist friends must have left a cigarette or something, careless bugger. With any luck it could burn out.'

But it didn't and we watched it growing like a living thing, nourished by the nighttime breeze.

'Shouldn't we telephone the fire-brigade?' Colombo asked.

'Pointless, I'm afraid. They'd take an hour to get here, and there'd be precious little they could do.'

'But what about the house?'

'Looks as if it could be just as well I didn't bother to restore it.'

We watched in silence then as the fire went spreading out across the centre of the hill like an army preparing to advance. This happened swiftly for there were a lot of old neglected olive trees which must have ignited instantly from the burning undergrowth. Soon the whole hillside was on fire and we could even hear the distant crackling as sheets of orange flame flared up into the night. The flames were brighter than the moonlight and despite the distance I could see the house clearly now, a low-roofed, single-storeyed farmhouse half hidden by a line of trees.

The blaze was quite spectacular and in its way it made a grand finale to the evening, like a bonfire specially put on for our release. Soon the breeze was bringing the scent of burning olive wood across to us. The Prince poured us more of his delicious brandy, and we sat and watched in silence, like guests of honour at a Guy Fawkes party.

'You're going to lose that farmhouse,' said Colombo, but the Prince said nothing, merely smiling and raising his hands as if

237

it didn't really matter. But Colombo was right, for by now the fire had reached the oine of trees and the house was clearly silhouetted by a wall of fire. For a while it looked as if it might survive with its thick stone walls, but the flames grew fiercer. Soon it was engulfed in fire. Then with a sudden whoosh of flame and crackling the roof fell in. The place burned furiously, then gradually the flames subsided and the walls remained.

The hillside burned out swiftly too, and now that the fire had claimed its victim, it went as quickly as it came. Soon there were only odd red patches where the undergrowth was smouldering, and a thick pall of smoke rose high and started drifting down the valley. It reached us and we started coughing and our eyes were watering.

'The show is over,' said the Prince and drained his glass.

I was feeling very strange by now. It must have been partially the drink, for my head was spinning, but something seemed to tell me that my private world had ended. I find this hard to explain, but possibly the fire had reawakened wartime memories of danger and destruction. At the same time I had a vivid sense that somehow the virus of my personal disaster had been burned away as well. It was as if the flames had cauterised my fate. I had lost everything but suddenly I felt that I was free.

I staggered to my feet.

'You look exhausted, Signor Moreton. Bedtime for all of us I think,' said Avicenna.

Colombo rose as well and nodded.

'Tomorrow morning I am driving down to Rome. Fairly early, Signor Conte, but if you'd like a lift I'll take you to Colonel Rossi. He'll want to see you.'

I hadn't thought of that, but thanked him and accepted. Then, somewhat less successfully, I thanked the Prince for dinner. He was still sitting at the table, finishing his cigar, unaffected by the smoke, and apparently amused at the state that I was in.

'My pleasure, Moreton. Glad you enjoyed it. Avicenna here

had better help you up to bed. My apologies for all the trouble we have caused you, but I think our little comedy is over.'

I didn't see the Prince again: he wasn't up next morning when we left for Rome, but Avicenna pottered out in a large white dressing gown to see us off. He was looking rather like I felt – sleepy and baggy-eyed, and considerably older than I remembered.

Colombo was already in the car, and for just a moment we stood and looked at one another. Our role in each others' lives was over and we knew it. He had started off the whole sequence of my personal disaster and played a crucial part in making it continue. But that was behind me now – and so was Dr Avicenna. Suddenly this saddened me, but I had the sense not to suggest we met again in England – nor for that matter did he ask me my address.

'Try and enjoy life, Signor Moreton. I think you have learned to see its funny side. And don't forget me.'

'No chance of that! And when you do make contact with your son, make sure that I'm informed about the child when it's born. I'd like to know about it.'

'But of course.'

I went to shake his hand, but he put his arms around me as Italians do and kissed me on the cheek. He had bad breath and such behaviour normally embarrasses me acutely, but for once it didn't. Quite what this proves about me I have no idea. It certainly amused Colombo as we drove away.

'Signor Conte – what a thing to happen to an Englishman! Why didn't I have a camera? But tell me one thing, Signor Conte. What was it about that monkey that you liked? Why did you put up with him?'

'I had no choice.'

'I think you did. He was trouble from the first day you saw him, and you could have refused to have anything to do with

239

him. Why the fatal fascination Signor Conte?'

I paused to think about this as the castle slid from view behind the cypresses. I could still see the blackened outline of the hillside opposite smouldering faintly after last night's fire.

'I've never known anybody like him.'

'That's no answer.'

'I suppose not. Perhaps I simply liked the way he made things happen.'

'But he was crazy and a crook.'

'Of course. That too was part of the attraction. Colombo, you and I are sane and reasonably honest, but sanity and honesty are limiting. Old Avicenna was the joker in the pack. He broke the rules and seemed to offer one the chance to do the same. Besides he was very human, and possessed his own brand of sincerity.'

'And just look where it got him. Look where it got you all.'

'True! I suppose he's ruined me, just as he did the Prince, but possibly we wanted to be ruined. There are times in life when human beings do, and that's when they're vulnerable as if to a disease. Avicenna carried the disaster virus. It's quite simple when you understand.'

Colombo gave a swift snort of impatience then, and paused to light a cigarette with the electric lighter on the dashboard of his car.

'Disaster virus? Signor Conte, please talk sense.'

So I did my best to explain the Moreton Theory of Disaster. He listened patiently enough, but was clearly unconvinced. Soon we were on the motorway.

'And you are now cured of this disaster virus, Signor Conte?'

'I only hope so.'

'So do I. I'm worried that it could be catching.'

'Not for somebody like you. You've seen so much disaster in your time I imagine that you've grown immune.'

That seemed to satisfy him, and for a while we drove in silence. My thoughts were on the last time I had made the journey up this same road with Avicenna in the old green van. It seemed an age ago, and I could have been a different person.

We were nearing Rome before Colombo spoke again.

'Signor Conte, before I leave you, there is something I must tell you. It is about your wife.'

'My ex-wife.'

'At the moment she is still your wife. I debate whether I should tell you this, but I believe I should. At the moment there is nothing to be done, but for the future – well, you never know, and it is best you understand the truth.'

'You know, you sound just like Avicenna. He was always promising the truth.'

'Well, that can't be helped. But the fact is that I brought the Signora to the castle as you know and was with her on the journey. She was desperately worried about you and I think she blamed herself for what had happened.'

'I'm sure she did, and now if you please we'll change the subject.'

But Colombo shook his head.

'Not until I've had my say. I don't believe she told the truth about the baby, Signor Conte. I think she said that it was Petinacci's simply because she thought that it would save your life.' He spoke with some embarrassment, for he must have known the effect his words would have on me.

'You've no proof,' was all I could think of saying in reply.

'Of course I haven't. How can you prove such things, but I'm sure I'm right. She spoke very fondly of you, and was still looking forward to returning to London with you. She said so several times.'

The conversation was becoming painful – and I told him so, but he wasn't to be put off.

'Signor Conte, you forget that in matters of this sort I am a professional. I tend to know when women tell the truth about such things and when they lie. I'm sure she lied to Petinacci.'

'For God's sake why?'

241

'I ask myself the same damned question. Just before we all met Petinacci, Avicenna had quite a talk with her. Alone.'

'So what?'

'I am convinced that bastard made her change her mind. I think he told her that for everybody's sake she had to go off with Petinacci and tell him that the child was his. I think —'

'Think!' I shouted. 'It's too late to think. She's gone. It's over. Why can't you keep your thinking to yourself?'

'Calm down now, Signor Conte. Nothing's over. If what I say is true, she went with him to save your life. But if the child is yours, she'll have to let you know. She'll be in touch. If you are sensible, you can still get her back. It's hope, Signor Conte. And you should not think badly of her.'

I was too shaken by all this to answer him coherently, but he seemed to understand, and we continued into Rome in silence. He dropped me at the Carabinieri Headquarters where I was due to meet Colonel Rossi, and as we said goodbye he suddenly remembered something.

'Oh, Signor Conte, just as your wife went down the tunnel with that Petinacci character, she gave me this, and asked me to see you got it. She said she sent it with her love.'

He felt for his wallet, and handed me an unmarked envelope. Inside I found a photograph, and realised it must have been that snapshot Bunjy Ripley took of us on the beach that night, and which Diana said she had destroyed. It was not very good of me; few photographs ever are, but my wife was exactly as I liked to remember her, my own Diana, not the hunting goddess who had betrayed me in the end.

I saw that she had scribbled something on the back.

Elly darling, Trust me, and one day we'll be like this again.
All my love,
D.

I had a long wait for the Colonel, but his assistant – a bull-necked, moustachioed young sergeant – insisted that he had to see me, and would not be long. Something had delayed him on the case that he was handling.

I thought this sounded faintly ominous, but my mind was full of what Colombo had just told me. Was it possible? Could she still come back? How could I get in touch with her? And was she in any danger?

Once again everything had changed, and I would have to think my next move out extremely carefully. I still had to know the truth, but first I wanted to get back to London. As long as the Colonel didn't take too long, I would have ample time to catch the evening plane.

It was one o'clock when the sergeant summoned me and led me down the long corridor I recognised to the Colonel's office. Even then I had to wait a few more minutes, and when the Colonel came he was profuse with his apologies.

'Ah, Signor Moreton. You must excuse me, but I was kept longer than I intended up at Mariella. We've found Petinacci.'

'Found him? Where?'

'I am afraid that he is dead. Some of my men discovered his body, what was left of it, completely *carbonizzato* in a burned out farmhouse near the castle where he held you prisoner. I had to go there to identify him. Luckily we had his dental records.'

Horror gripped me, but he seemed oblivious of this, and smiled amiably at me as he continued.

'Not pleasant, but one gets used to such things in the course of duty. His hands had been tied, and the fire had been started deliberately. We're working on the theory that it was a sort of execution by some other members of the MPM in revenge for what occurred with you and the Prince.'

He paused and I sat in silence, dreading to ask the question that I knew I must.

'Was anybody with him when they found him?'

The Colonel laughed.

'Now why should you ask that? As it happens there was, but it's something of a mystery. We found some remains, but they were so badly charred that they've not been identified. I doubt they ever will be. I've a hunch they're female. Probably some wretched girlfriend he was mixed up with. It could be that red-head who was his mistress on and off for years. He had her back when your wife returned to you. Poor silly bitch, I'll have to check.'

'I'd not bother,' I said bleakly.

'Not bother, Mr Moreton? Oh, but we have to. We police-men have to tie up every detail in a case like this. It's what we're there for.'

He positively twinkled with goodwill.

'Talking of which now, Mr Moreton, there are just one or two formalities I must trouble you with before you leave for London to rejoin your lovely wife. How is she, incidentally?'

'Quite fine,' I said.